Incident at Lahore Basin

Clive Radford

ISBN: 978-1-62420-564-4

Credits
Cover Artist: Designs by Ms G
Editor: Amanda ArmstrongContents

CONTENTS

Chapter 1: Tempest

Flameout! Pilot Wing Commander Dale Latham's Tornado zoomed groundward. As the aircraft stalled, rolled and flipped over into a spiral dive, its altimeter decremented at an astonishing rate.

He had to act fast. Initiating the engines start-up procedure, he managed to engage one RB199. Singing into life the turbofan generated thrust, allowing Latham to push the stick forward making the aircraft nose down, then increase throttle setting to full power. Miraculously, the Tornado settled, enabling him to apply back pressure to the stick levelling the wings, the aeroplane regaining steady-state flight, Latham recovering altitude as he tried to ignite the second RB199.

Approaching RAF Lossiemouth, backtracking from a combined RAF-Luftwaffe sortie over the Rhineland, navigator-weapons officer, Flight Lieutenant Harry Beaumont, warned of severe hailstorm conditions ahead. As the Tornado slowed from supersonic speed and descended from 30,000 feet over the Moray Firth channel, she hit the inclement weather. Far worse than expected, a freak set of climatic conditions had conspired to generate the mother of all storm clouds, cumulonimbus building a trail blazer of epic proportions.

As the Tornado passed beneath 15,000 feet, she encountered heavy rain and tennis-ball- sized hailstones, the contaminants ingested into the engine's inlet ducts leading to dual-turbofan flameout.

Whilst Latham struggled to re-start the second RB199, Beaumont contacted Lossiemouth Air Traffic Control, advising their predicament. Asked if the Tornado wanted to register a Mayday call, Beaumont answered in the negative. Confident of Latham's flying skills, he knew the pilot would be reluctant to pull the ejector seat handle, releasing the canopy and sending both aircrew into space, abandoning the Tornado to crash into the Moray Firth.

Latham had never lost an aircraft. He certainly did not intend to let the £14m fighter-bomber end up in the drink. Albeit, the second engine refused to spark into life, further ingestion of the life-threatening hale defeating his attempts. Though capable of flight on a single engine, prudence dictated under the tempest onslaught, having both turbofans operational equated with minimising further danger. Gaining height, the Tornado rose above the cumulonimbus wrecker, permitting the second engine inlet duct to clear of ice debris. Sustaining the re-start protocol, at last the stagnant RB199 burst into life, the gained extra thrust making the aeroplane nose-up. Deciding not to risk landing at Lossiemouth through the storm, Latham called RAF Leuchars, requesting permission for an emergency landing.

South of Lossiemouth by 90 miles, Leuchars allowed the Tornado to land without any further troubles, her aircrew reporting the flameout incident, and staying until clement weather prevailed over the Moray Firth locale, allowing then to return to Lossiemouth.

Beaumont's assessment of Latham had been spot-on. Wholly aware that the UK taxpayer owned the platforms he carried out missions on, spanning his RAF flight career, Latham had made it his business to ensure any aircraft allocated to his charge remained in one piece from take-off to landing. A trait inherited from his father; a sense of responsibility in all matters came to dominate his life from an early age.

Sometimes the quality resulted in gladness and fulfilment, whereas on other occasions, it got him into hot water, his innate sentiment to duty subduing imperilment factors.

Chapter 2: Karachi Tumult

Aboard an Emirates Airlines flight en route from Dubai to Karachi, businessmen Dale Latham and Rendall Gilmour, defence system contractors for Armstrong-Eliot, gazed out of the cabin window at the Gulf of Oman, recent fond memories of success further firing their trading appetites.

"Well, if Pakistan is as productive as the Emirates, this trip will pay for itself ten times over," Latham extolled, pushing back his dark quiff flop from his forehead, his deep violet blue eyes still bright and alert after the successful conclusion of their United Arab Emirates Air Force transaction.

"Yes," Gilmour agreed, also brimming with zest from the splendid outcome. "It's *very* gratifying to see six months of meticulous negotiation produce a positive aftereffect."

"I suppose it's symptomatic of the 80-20 rule."

"For sure. But until Major-General Morcos put pen to paper, I was convinced we were in for the long haul, and the air force requirement could fall into the 80 per cent hard slog, no outcome category."

"Quite. From a supplier angle, it comes down to the benefit of executive clout without recourse." Producing a perceptive face, Latham lamented, "to achieve the same upshot at MoD takes at least half a dozen counter-signatures and, an interminable wait."

"Mmmm. Mind you, a few months ago, when the French and the Americans were sniffing around the Emirates market, it might have been an entirely different story. Those air force and ministry officials made no bones about playing contractors off against each other when it came to—

" Gilmour made a quotations-sign with his hands and fingers. "Management consultancy fees."

"Assuredly." Tapping his colleague's arm, Latham validated, "but for the air force technical evaluation confirming our systems are far more advanced compared to the equivalent offerings from Uncle Sam and the French, there could have been a bidding war, undoubtedly translating into a large dose of management consultancy fees outlay…possibly upfront."

"The company wouldn't wear that."

"No."

"Let's hope we can pull off the same trick in Pakistan."

"God willing and the creek don't rise." Hesitating, Latham shifted into a formal register. "By the way," he began, his preempting lead-in catching Gilmour's complete attention. "Changing the subject, Rendall, you've met Bill Kimble before, haven't you?"

"Yes, last spring in London, when we were going after the Pakistan Navy laser-guided munitions upgrade programme. I got to know him quite well while you were in Singapore chasing their air force requirement. Then, he acted as cultural attaché to the Karachi British Deputy High Commission." Chuckling, Gilmour denounced, "miraculously, overnight he acquired business credentials and is now the commercial attaché."

"What's he like?"

"Oh." Gilmour shimmied his head. "Standard model, old-school, diplomat material. Solid and reliable, but regrettably, entrepreneurially uninspiring. However, he's extremely personable and thorough, plus nimble on the up take, if you get my meaning. And, most essentially, he's seasoned. Done stints throughout Asia and Africa, so he knows his beans. He always comes across as highly accommodating, but there's a firm edge to his character he deploys when necessary. He's nobody's fool."

"Right. He sounds like just the type we need to pave the way for us with Pakistan Armed Forces." Settling back in his seat, Latham imparted a guarded aspect, as if about to confer a caution. "You've er, you've not flown into Jinnah before, have you?"

"No." Gilmour rendered him a curious gawp. "Why do you ask?"

"It should be fine once we've been processed into the hands of the British Deputy High Commission, meaning Bill Kimble."

Making an agitated face, Gilmour questioned, "how do you mean, Dale?"

"Only, the immigration M.O at Karachi's Jinnah International can be testing."

~ * ~

Presenting thorny challenges to unaccustomed travellers, Karachi's Jinnah International Airport had indeed gained a reputation as a notorious destination.

Foreseeing visions of Eastern delight, often inbound air passengers were shocked to find themselves greeted by sour faces and loaded guns. Though rarely culminating in violence, when the tinder box did ignite, those on the receiving end of threats and browbeating imagined they had spent their final day on God's green Earth.

European expectations regarding global human rights for non-Pakistani travellers were soon seen to be an illusion. Used to, at worst, neutral facial expressions from occidental country airport bureaucrats, their encounters with Karachi officialdom were frequently distinguished by sneers and glares. For those affronted by the bombast, their counter objections instantly ratcheted up the duress, enforcers taking the harassment to ever increasing levels of menace. If the unfortunate did not relent, they were frogmarched away by armed guards for further humiliation behind closed doors, the inquisitors' subsequent fulmination often taking the form of a tirade of insults and gibes. When those under the hammer lost their cool and reacted to the blatant intimidation, their provoked blast back diminished on realisation a germ-ridden, sweaty cell awaited, if they did not kowtow to the aggressors.

Having negotiated the airport minefield, sporadically worse followed when foreigners were distressed to find the sickening excesses of Sharia Law being enacted out before them in crowded Karachi suburbs, their protests met with derision and howls, not just by Islamic zealots, but remarkably, the authorities as well.

Touching down at the airport, the Armstrong-Eliot emissaries noticed a series of buses awaited to take the Emirates Airlines flight passengers to the terminal for customs clearance.

"Time to prepare for a stifling physical environment," Latham gibed.

Sure enough, disembarking into heat-energy soaked, lung-burning air, like other Western passengers, Latham and Gilmour took a few moments to acclimatise to the climate. Stepping down the mobile stairs, they immediately noted armed guards surrounding the aircraft. Not an unusual sight in the Middle East, the soldiers turgid body language and their near-to action stations bearing set the military welcome apart. Whereas earlier in the trade tour, the Armstrong-Eliot men felt quite comfortable during the same deplaning routine in Jordan and Syria, here they sensed tension.

"Not the friendliest of people, are they?" Gilmour remarked.

"No." Latham glanced left and right, half expecting to see a fracas in play, or someone being escorted to the terminal for interrogation. "I wonder if there's been some sort of security incident?"

"Possibly," he replied, a knock-on consequence then overtaking him. "*Oh*, I hope they don't keep us in customs and baggage reclaim for too long. I'd really like to get the formalities with Kimble over, pronto, so we can retire to the Avari Towers Hotel and rehearse our plans for tomorrow's meetings with Pakistan Armed Forces."

With the buses jam-packed by passengers, their very close proximity to each other causing unintentional body bumps and nose-to-nose brushes, the military gave the signal to depart for the terminal, half a mile away. As the motorcade neared, Latham and Gilmour fingered their inside jacket pockets for their passports and visas in preparation for immigration handling.

Whilst non-Pakistani passengers joined a lengthy line of foreign nationals awaiting their turn for processing, Pakistani nationals were briskly whisked through passport control. Above the disenchanted queue, ceiling-mounted fans squeaked away, their downdraft doing little to alleviate the suffocating heat. After what seemed like hours, the businessmen's passports and visas were stamped, and they made their way to the vast baggage reclaim hall, already teeming with hundreds of passengers, frantically trying to find their belongings on endlessly circulating carousels piled high with suitcases and trunks.

Again segmented into Pakistani nationals and foreigners' queues for the next stage, customs control, passengers trundled out of baggage collection, laden with their belongings. Several rows of fixed tables with customs officers and armed soldiers to their rear came into the travellers' eyeline. Extensive, and moving at a snail's pace, the queues resembled a vast chorus line, gyrating in exceedingly slow motion. To their front, Latham and Gilmour saw fiery exchanges between brusque civil servants and irritated travellers.

"Not like in the Emirates, is it?" Gilmour observed.

"No. Compared to my previous time here, they've ramped up the intimidation a few more notches," Latham informed.

Bored with queuing, the Armstrong-Eliot envoys became allured by the chipper conversations of a large group of buoyant Australians in a parallel queue, their antipodean twang betraying their country of origin. In the primary of a series of test matches, Pakistan was due to play the Aussies at the Karachi National Stadium the next day. Unlike European and American passengers, they seemed unaffected by the acute heat and high humidity conditions, their cricketing conversations distracting them from physical discomfort.

"Clearly, the Aussie supporters are in fine fettle," Latham drawled. "Wonderful looking personalities aren't they, with their distinctive clothing banners proclaiming support for the baggy greens?"

"Absolutely. One of life's sureties is, if Australia plays in any sports competition, they will always draw a strong following."

Nearing the limit of their patience, those queuing continued to move onwards at a glacial pace. Undergoing due practice, suitcases and hand luggage opened and rifled through by baggage inspectors caused much consternation to their owners, and further back, trepidation in traveller ranks. For most, it became their foremost experience of unanticipated tacitness, taken to a level well beyond thoroughness, the agencies' petty acts symptomatic of flagrant alienation, their mannerisms openly transmitting the unwelcome message.

Despite their exposure to the murkier shades of international business, nothing prepared Latham and Gilmour for the unforeseen occurrences they were about to encounter.

Converging on the baggage inspection desks, the two Englishmen discriminated for themselves that, without exception, inspectors opened every case, foraging through their contents without care, much to the bewilderment and annoyance of their owners. More galling, those executing the screening appeared to be enjoying their work, traveller cries to be careful met with smirks and grins. In the adjacent queue, the normally happy-go-lucky Australians were becoming increasingly resentful of the harsh treatment, the draconian imposition over the top and indefensible.

"There has to be a flap in play to warrant this degree of intrusion," Latham submitted.

"I don't think so, Dale." Gilmour nodded to a separate part of the customs inspection hall. "Take a gander over to your far left where the locals are being handled."

Turning in the given direction, sure enough Latham saw Pakistani nationals moving swiftly through the customs process, no bags opened and searched. "Hhmmm, this is not good," he bemoaned. "I've been subject to some rugged baggage examinations in the Middle-East, but this is off the scale by way of intrusiveness."

"If it's not a security alert causing it, what do you picture it is?"

"Could be anything." His kisser awash with perplexity, Latham hunched his shoulders. "Perhaps some international situation the Pakistanis have taken umbrage about, but I'm guessing."

"Well, I've got some personal mementos in my bag, and I don't relish the prospect of some uppity customs official pawing them."

"Just smile and stay cool, Rendall. It will all be over in a jiffy."

Edging forwards, the exporters clocked first-hand little subtlety existed in the probing method, the passenger preceding them seeing his bag constituents strewn over the checkup desk surface, many landing on the floor, their owner making noises about the encroachment but the attendants taking no notice during the procedure.

Stepping on, a customs officer barked at Latham, "passport and visa," his fashion blunt, his visage belligerent.

Narrowing his eyes at the discourtesy, albeit, Latham still meekly handed over the documentation.

"What is the purpose of your visit?"

His even temper waning, Latham replied, "the purpose has just been established in passport control."

Gaping menacingly at the aggravated traveller, the customs officer seethed, but said nothing. Instead, the gape mutated into an intense scowl.

Relenting, Latham advised, "business."

"With which organisation?"

"Pakistan Armed Forces."

Rattled by the unexpected reply, the aggressor backed off slightly.

"Did you pack your bags yourself?"

"Yes."

"Open all of the bags, your laptop case as well."

Latham went to work on the bags, the functionary gleefully emptying their contents onto the table. After rummaging through his clothing and his toiletry bag, he instructed Latham to replace the cargo. Applying the same invasive scrutiny to the lap top case, he then okayed Latham to proceed on.

Tapping his colleague on the shoulder, Gilmour quipped, "kept your cool, did you?"

"Your turn next," Latham curtly replied.

Gilmour's baptism resulted in a treasured framed photograph of his wife and children ending up on the floor, its glass cover smashing and indenting the photograph.

"Oh, for *goodness* sake," he complained. "Look what's *you've* done." Picking up the precious item, he frowned at the unconcerned tormenter. "I don't know whether the breakage is down to your carelessness, or inherent barbarism. Either way, I'll be making a claim against Jinnah International Airport for damages."

"Rendall," Latham discreetly chimed, attracting him. "Come on. We can deal with this…" About to say, 'at the Deputy British High Commission', he thought better of it. "…later."

Over in the Australian queue, after customs staff broke several items from his suitcases, one angered Aussie gave as good as he got.

"*Hey*, basket case" he shrieked, "I hope you are going to pay for this damage."

Grinning contemptuously at the outraged Aussie, the offending culprit muttered something in Urdu under his breath to another officer.

"What did you call me?" the Aussie hissed. "You little punkhawallah, you little *shithead*."

Snarling something indecipherable back, the bully swopped some words with his colleague, then called for an armed guard standing at the back of the inspection area to join them.

"Hey, Mister Jobsworth," the Aussie pressed, "I asked you what you called me?"

With the armed guard at their side, both of the baggage inspectors grinned insolently.

"You are not in Australia now," the principal official mocked. "Here, you are subject to our laws."

"Oh, yeah!" the Aussie blared, stomping ahead. "And how would it be, if we treated you lot like this at Sidney Kingsford Smith Airport, hey? You'd be screaming racism, wouldn't you, you *jumped-up*, little prick."

Hotfooting around the baggage inspection desk, the armed guard faced the Aussie, aiming his rifle at him.

"Gonna shoot me, are you?" he taunted in a gruff voice. "Come on then, stick your pea-shooter in my chest." Peeking back along the queue, he outstretched his arm and pointed. "The Australian press are down there, and I'm sure they're taking all this in." Advancing so the rifle nozzle pushed into his abdomen, he jeered, "come on, you little *bastard*, pull the trigger."

By now the dispute had caught the eye of everyone in the opposite queue, travellers gazing across the divide, riveted by the standoff, Latham and Gilmour included. Then they heard the click of the rifle safety catch being taken off.

"My god," Gilmour jabbered, "he's going to shoot him." Staring at Latham, wide-eyed and open-mouthed, the savvier businessman gestured back with a hand motion to stay calm.

"Come on," the Aussie chided, forcing his body further into the rifle nozzle. "What you waiting for…got *no* guts?"

Surrounding the antipodean, other army guards armed their weapons and directed them at him. Falling silent, the baggage inspection hall wrung with tension, all check-up stations ceasing activity, bystanders transfixed by the deadlock.

About to say something more, Gilmour glimpsed at Latham, then the reverberation of automatic security doors opening captured his full regard. A VIP contingent came into the customs hall, escorted by what materialized to be Pakistani government movers and shakers.

Noticing the standoff, the VIPs cast inquisitive gawks at their hosts, the guards concurrently lowering their rifles. Hastily moved through the customs hall by their hosts, some VIPs ogled back, sensing a disruption had taken place, but none stopped to query their escort relating to the source of the contretemps.

~ * ~

"What the hell sparked such a severe level of maltreatment from that customs rabble?" Gilmour growled, as he and Latham burst through the customs hall connecting doors and into the arrivals concourse.

"Whatever it was, just put it to the back of your mind. Let's concentrate on the commerce in hand."

Exasperated, Gilmour replied, "I suppose you're right, but it's infuriating."

"Is that Kimble holding up an Armstrong-Eliot notice, over by the water cooler?" Latham prompted, trying to keep his companion from further explosions.

Scrutinising in the given direction, Gilmour authenticated, "yes, that's him."

Sluggishly proceeding across the chock-full concourse, the representatives waved to Kimble.

"Gentlemen," he brightly greeted as they closed in on him, "welcome to Karachi."

"Hello, Bill," Gilmour replied, extending a hand, "good to see you again. I'd like to introduce Dale Latham to you."

Grasping his hand, Kimble said, "your reputation goes before you in business circles. How are you, Dale?"

"Fine. Good to meet you. Ben Finch held the commercial attaché position during my prior visit to Karachi."

"Moving up the promotion ladder, Ben has been reassigned to Dhaka. I've been in post since January. Before he left, he gave me a review of prominent executives selling their wares into Pakistan's military market. In particular, he rang your praises very highly."

"Hah, he's always one for exaggeration," Latham modestly replied.

"Erm, Bill," Gilmour began, his mien burdened with disquiet, "is there some kind of a flap on?"

Kimble raised his eyebrows, Latham espied almost dismissively, his cordial face unperturbed by the enquiry. "Why do you ask?"

"We've just been subjected to the most hostile customs inspection I've ever known. Some Australian chap in another queue objected to them poking roughly in his baggage, and they detained him at gunpoint. If not for a group of VIPs passing by the area, god knows what might have happened."

Kimble's pleasant attitude did not change. "I've got a car waiting outside to take us to the British Deputy High Commission."

"Well, thank you for the consideration, Bill, but what about answering my question?"

Surveying the immediate area, the diplomat counselled, "come on, it's not safe to talk here. You never know who's listening."

Not one to react in public, Kimble's civil service training had imbued him with a continuous sense of reserve. No matter what the circumstance or looming crisis, he could be relied upon by the Foreign Office to provide ambassadorial services with lightness of touch and surety of action, his old-school Establishment heritage and Winchester and Oxford education ensuring no diplomatic incident fazed him.

Stepping out of the cooler airport arrivals concourse onto an adjoining pavement crammed with people waiting for a lift or trying for a taxi, Latham and Gilmour were hit by a blast of moisture-filled heat. Unlike desert heat in the Emirates, soothed by fresh breezes coming off the Persian Gulf, the physical atmosphere encircling Jinnah International suffered from air pollution emanating from Karachi's industrial area and saturated roads, plus domestic smells thrown up by a tightly soaked urban conurbation. New to Pakistan, Gilmour glowered after inhaling his initial breath. Expecting nothing less, Latham took the fiery inhalation in his stride.

Inside the British Deputy High Commission's Daimler DS420, Gilmour resumed his offence. "On the basis this limousine is not bugged, Bill, can you now tell us what is going on?"

"Rest assured, the Daimler is clean," Kimble replied. "We regularly sweep all British High Commission buildings and vehicles."

"And?" Gilmour pressured.

"Ahh—" Clearly reticent to come clean unless compelled, he bared his teeth. "You want to know if what you sustained in customs inspection could be categorised as unusual or a regular event?"

"*Yes*," Gilmour asserted. "But more to the point, what caused it?"

"Well, all I can say is, since the Gulf War the Pakistan Government has been pulled between two opposing poles."

"The West and the extremist Muslim fellowship," Latham astutely stipulated.

"Quite. And in the lower levels of the public structure, unequivocally those dealing daily with Westerners, advocacy is coming down firmly on the side of what Dale calls the extremist Muslim fellowship. Remaining the central gateway into the country, Karachi appears to be in turmoil to foreigners. Though most Pakistanis are pleased Saddam Hussein's claws have been clipped, nonetheless, they esteem the Gulf War as Western interventionism striking at the very heart of the Islamic world. Operation Desert Shield leading to Operation Desert Storm restored commercial stability to Kuwait, and prevented the Iraqi invasion of Saudi, but it's not ended in the West being seen as the saviour doyens by most Muslims."

"Hence the ill treatment of Westerners at the airport?" Latham proposed.

"Yes. In the main, Pakistani Muslims are far more zealous than Arab Muslims. The Arab countries have been made immensely rich by means of oil, whereas a life of poverty awaits most Pakistanis."

"So they take their vengeance out on the Christian West," Latham postulated. "The perceived enemy of Islam."

"Quite. We know what's going on, but we need to keep the Pakistan Government onside."

"For both commercial and military reasons?" Latham posed.

"Much more military imperatives," Kimble confirmed. "Earlier this year, we got word from our intelligence services, they'd identified fragments of various Islamic fundamentalist groups had coalesced into a single entity in the early 1990s, largely in Afghanistan. It didn't have a name back then, but we knew along with the Mujahedeen, the band were instrumental in deposing the Afghan warlords. The name, Taliban, emerged when they captured Kandahar and began to impose Sharia Law on the Afghan population. They are ultra-Islamic fundamentalists, with ambitions to rid the Middle-East of all Western influence, and slaughter every Christian."

"*Good god*," Gilmour exclaimed. "Their agenda is well beyond the aspirations of Saddam Hussein."

"For sure. Saddam is a dictator with an appetite for empire building, whereas the Taliban are Muslim fanatics, unrestrained by any human rights code, and driven to make the entire globe an austere Islamic State. Terrorism is their byword, and they have a proven pedigree for fighting." Backing his head away, as if repulsed by the gravity of the Taliban's rise, he educated, "the movement traces its origins back to the Mujahedeen during the Soviet War in Afghanistan. They are renegades at present. Notwithstanding, we know they are backed by some very rich, high-potency Muslim families, and probably, Iran. The fear is, if their numbers and military capability continue to grow, they might topple the pro-West Afghanistan Government. Should it transpire, Pakistan could fall, leaving the path open to invade India, and a possible World War III, involving nuclear weapons."

"You're implying Pakistan will roll over under military threat from the Taliban," Latham put forward. "Surely her military supremacy is far in excess of anything the Taliban can muster?"

"Military hegemony is not the problem, Dale," Kimble disclosed. "Confidentially, we have intel suggesting some in the Pakistan military and the political structure could side with the Taliban, and promote a populist uprising. If such a seed change ensued, the threat to India will be unstoppable." Adventuring into a prescriptive viewpoint, he warned, "when you go up country to Rawalpindi, you're likely to pick up the anti-Western sentiment amongst the Pakistan Army, certainly in the ranks." Facing Gilmour, he designated, "you could find the same when you meet the Pakistan Navy at Port Qasim. Anyway—" Maturing a wry glint, he justified, "perhaps now you will begin to understand why we are turning a blind eye to abuses perpetrated by customs personnel at Jinnah International. To say the least, the locus is delicate. We find ourselves perpetually trying to balance diplomacy with assertiveness to maintain patronage from those in the Pakistan Government and the military supporting the West."

"I can see the dichotomy," Latham concurred, "but how does it square with the Pakistan Armed Forces wanting the latest target finding systems from Armstrong-Eliot?"

"Huh," Kimble groaned, shaking his head, Latham detecting an imminent clash of interests. "Therein lays the contradiction. Exports help with our balance of payments. Thus, HMG wants your company to supply the Pakistani requirement, and in principle, under the terms of NATO friendly nations agreements, Armstrong-Eliot will be allowed an export license, however—" He scowled. "If your equipment fell into the hands of the Taliban through furtive channels via sympathizers in the Pakistan military, it'd be a disaster."

"I'd surmise the Pakistan Government interpret not granting an export license to be tantamount to HMG saying, you're in collusion with terrorists?" Latham tested.

"Yes, and the political ramifications of them making incorrect conclusions are too horrendous to contemplate."

After paying their respects to British Deputy High Commissioner John Soames at the High Commission, and hearing his take on Pakistan's volatility, Kimble dropped Latham and Gilmour off at the Avari Towers Hotel.

"Get a good night's sleep," he fostered. "I'll pick you up at 08:30 tomorrow for our meeting with Pakistan Armed Forces."

"Aren't you joining us for dinner?" asked Gilmour.

"I'd love to, Rendall, but duty calls elsewhere this evening."

As the Daimler pulled away, Gilmour turned to his colleague with a jaundiced expression. "What do you make of Kimble's turndown, Dale? Usually, Foreign Office diplomats can't wait to dine out at a contractors' expense."

"Judging by Soames' guarded comments appertaining to the ambiguous state of play in Anglo-Pakistani political and commercial initiatives, there are more pressing matters on Kimble's mind."

Suddenly, a loud crack rang out in the far distance, the Englishmen instinctively ducking down in response.

"I think it came from the Jamshed Town industrial area," Latham speculated, peering to the north-east. "Doubtless a machine-powered manufacturing process has suffered catastrophic failure."

"Hhhmm. Measured more like a rifle shot to me."

"Oh, I doubt it, Rendall. If Pakistani militants were intent on creating carnage, there'd be much more than the report of a single bullet being fired. Besides, their favoured weapons of choice are the sword and the dagger."

"Maybe I'm being hyper." Opening his eyes wide in acknowledgement, he confided, "but Jinnah's oppressive reception is still grating on me."

"Relax. We're in-country now, soon to be surrounded by the Pakistani military. Believe me, Pakistan Armed Forces are well capable of quickly dispatching any terrorists or insurgents. Unlike Western armies, they are not in the habit of taking prisoners, or adhering to the

Geneva Convention. It's a puissant message for aggressors to digest before going up against them."

"You mean, it's a deterrent?"

"Yes."

"Nevertheless, if Kimble and Soames are right about elements of the military having Islamic fundamentalism sympathies, then who can we trust?"

"I suspect the numbers are not great, and those diplomats are being overly bleak to keep us on our mettle. Okay, there is always the possibility of a few disenfranchised officers turning rogue, but I'd discredit there are any of field rank, and without champions in the executive layer, I can't see any coup attempt being successful."

~ * ~

As the blast furnace environs gave way to more a temperate climate in the evening, Latham and Gilmour sat in the hotel's plush restaurant discussing the next day's meeting.

"I did some research on the senior players whilst back in Blighty," Latham told his colleague. "Brigadier Syed Cham is well connected in both the government and the army hierarchy by way of family connections. Before achieving head of procurement for sensor systems status, he served in the Frontier Corps and the Special Services Group, and currently sits on the Army Cantonment Board."

"What did you discover about Vice Admiral Mahmood?"

"Adnan Mahmood served in the Naval Strategic Forces Command Special Services Group, before transferring to the Directorate-General for Naval Technologies Complex. Both officers are reputedly very savvy about C4I2 and over-the-horizon target finding systems."

"So, assuming they are the key decision makers, the staff you meet at Rawalpindi and those I meet at Port Qasim will be the assessors?"

"Yes, I read it the same way. All we have to do tomorrow is qualify the requirement and position our offering."

Grimacing, Gilmour stated, "let's just hope they are regular officers, with no inclination to abuse their buying muscle and enter the payola corral."

Equivocal in his yellow endorsement, his associate uttered, "mmmm, some hope."

Over the preceding two years, Latham and Gilmour had qualified and sold a myriad of Armstrong-Eliot military systems into procurement organisations. Virtually an automatic operation under the buoyant market created post the Gulf War, they equated it to shelling peas. Likened to negotiating a maze or working out a solitaire solution, the buyer-side personalities often formed the only significant variable in the supplier-end user engagement. Buyers had the whip hand, part of the sellers' skill, to meld their approach according to pre-meeting intelligence, and most essentially, the mood of the buyer during meetings. Whether good or not so good, the sellers' background and domestic situations had to be shelved during the selling routine, a facade required to mask off both joy and heartache, the role requiring absolute professionalism in front of the buyer, free from any personal emotions.

Conversely, buying sway allowed those in charge of the purse strings to indulge in allowing their personal circumstances to colour their frame of mind, the task of the seller, to be sensitive and empathetic to the buyers' behaviour. Achieved more through an appreciation of the human condition, rather than the precepts of solution selling, often the sellers' ability to perfectly read buyer disposition built the difference between a victorious or failed involvement.

Whereas in the main, European and American buyers were less prone to indulging in temperament theatrics, in other parts of the world, knowing the universality of their exulted post, some buyers took immense pleasure in testing the sellers' patience to the limit, openly allowing whatever cheered or plagued them to impinge on the buying interchange.

Latham's experience of the Middle-East had thrown up the occasional self-indulgent buyer, his challenge, to keep their personal prospectus separate from the trade agenda. Often, it could be accomplished by playing a many-shades-of-pleasure card from his corporate amusements portfolio, it's range covering all human frailties and secret desires. Flesh pots, professional companions, alcohol, and even soft drugs could be brought into play, though officially, Armstrong-Eliot had no knowledge of such affliction-relieving or aspiration-filling enterprises. That clandestine and often sinister world played out the fruits of temptation in parallel to the main game, it's composition virtual in the context of the selling stratagem, but a necessary adjunct to smooth the sale, neither seller nor buyer acknowledging the diversion across the negotiating table.

Senior military officers with complex personal lives and various mortal weaknesses were prime candidates for out-on-the-rim corporate accommodated distractions, their buying roles infusing them with a sensation of entitlement, even a necessity they should play out the full gambit of their self-indulgence.

Armstrong-Eliot's Latham and Gilmour wondered if Brigadier Cham, Vice Admiral Mahmood, or other purse-strings empowered senior officers they interfaced with, fell into this category.

Aside of what commentators termed, 'extra-curricular activities', consultancy fees were also a contentious issue, requiring the exact reading of kinesics and perpendicular speech to precisely decode the expectation. Few on the buying side called outright for the oiling enabler of the contract award. On the contrary, hints were made utilising inference and subtle remarks, aimed at stimulating the seller to take the lead. Either way, it panned out as a line item in the contract, euphemistically entitled, 'management consultancy fee disbursements', an approved label enumerating supplementary costs, and essentially recognised on the supplier's balance sheet without objection by company auditors.

With bribery publicly against the law in most countries, the payment of such disbursements could be reliant on the same arcane delivery methods associated with national intelligence service agencies. During his military systems supplier career, Latham had delivered brown paper bags brimming with assorted currencies to numbered Swiss bank accounts in Geneva, the prosecution well-trodden by legions of business mediators over at least 100 years, Swiss bankers shrewd on the transaction to a level beyond secrecy and discretion. Privately sanctioned by the Swiss Government, and accepted by offshore governments worldwide, such deposits and withdrawals constituted a crucial part of their clientele covenants. Providing a convenient portal for all parties to make money; the bank, as an upshot to short-term interest gained from investing credits, governments enjoying increased corporate tax revenues sequent to industrial sales creating booming balance sheets, and the recipients of the management consultancy services payola, basking in their new-found wealth, the facility had cosmopolitan backing. Of course, if interfering journalists or a whistleblower exposed the scheme, the house came tumbling down, and heads rolled all round.

"Let's not leave anything to chance," Latham prescribed. "At some stage, Cham and Mahmood will hint contract award is contingent on management consultancy fees. When it occurs, I suggest we grasp the nettle and deal with it immediately."

"Yes," Gilmour concurred. "Best to get it out of the way to clear the path ahead of any bear traps." Curling his upper lip, he declared, "I never feel good about this part of our role, albeit a necessary adjunct to the sale."

"No—" Wrinkling his nose, Latham conceded, "but we all know, if we don't want to do it, then we have to step down from the business carousel."

Chapter 3: Quid Pro Quo

1992 saw a sharp rise in the worldwide market for smart-weapon technologies, the Gulf War providing an in-theatre shop window for prospective buyers to witness the omnipotence of precision-guided munitions and their delivery platforms, courtesy of CNN News and other television media. Used to less sophisticated weapons, it caught the imagination of the military worldwide, national defence procurement proxies briefed by their armed forces to acquire the Western technologies, export licenses permitting.

Building on the success of their microprocessor-based air, sea and ground systems, market-leading, military computer and avionics systems supplier Armstrong-Eliot had been in the vanguard of the smart technologies evolution. With a military heritage going back to the advent of electro-mechanical computers in the late 1940s, through the valve, transistor and solid-state LSI circuit blueprints following up to the mid-1970s, the company had gained a global reputation as a tried and trusted supplier to platform manufacturers, including BAE Systems, Northrop-Grumman, Lockheed and a host of other enterprise-scale suppliers of military aircraft, ships and land-based vehicles. Founded on their command, control, communications, computing, intelligence and information systems (C4I2) expertise, Armstrong-Eliot engineered sensor technologies designed to furnish theatre-battlefield commanders with a 'look-over-the-horizon' capability, without having to expose military and human resources to the enemy.

Gulf War TV footage did more to market the strategic gains and effects of such capabilities, than a whole army of incentivised-up-to-the-hilt, pinstripe-suited salesmen and streetwise, book-smart marketers could accomplish. Consequently, when Operation Desert Storm triumphantly ousted Iraqi invasion forces and stormin' Norman Schwarzkopf motored into Kuwait City, military procurement branches had telephone, telex and fax facilities running red hot in their pursuit of acquiring the miraculous technology.

Inundated with requests for information and ball-park pricing for their smart technologies from government intermediaries wanting to give a fresh lease of life to their aging military fleets, or invest in brand new weapon delivery platforms, Armstrong-Eliot readily responded to their enquiries. Customer facing managers like Latham and Gilmour found themselves occupied in a perpetual world tour, qualifying requirements and selling solutions, Pakistan the latest in a long line of interested parties.

Since leaving the Royal Air Force, wedge-shaped, tall, easy on the eye Dale Latham had been conducting transactions in the Middle East for over ten years, first with Dandridge Defence & Air Systems, before being head-hunted by Armstrong-Eliot. During his vendor tenure, he had learnt not to expect consistency with either customer organisations or government bureaucrats. If a sales technique worked on one trip, it did not necessarily produce the same sure corollary on a second. Likewise, airport officialdom's demeanour drifted in directions driven by national politics and local fervour, rather than traveller expected *de facto* courtesy standards, as he and Gilmour had endured at Jinnah International.

Distinguished by absolute stability, and behind the authorised Islamic mask a Western standpoint, both Saudi Arabia and the Emirates bore little difference to business undertakings in the West, the buy-sell protocol persisting pretty much in line with the universal status quo. Additionally, management consultancy fees, a euphemism for backhanders, never formally admitted to by either contractors or clients, or their respective governments, were an integral part of the Middle East business model.

When Europeans threw their hands up in horror, apropos what they perceived to be bribes, Dale Latham burst their high-minded, self-righteous bubble, citing consultancy fees or such-like monetary disbursements existed all over the world, as part of the sales treatment, even in Europe and the United States.

International business had been undertaken with inducements as an integral ingredient, since trading commenced way back in the mists of time, and long before 20th century morality merchants with politically loaded agendas crept out of the woodwork, crying foul. In their insular realm, everything maintained regulated and above-board status, a far cry from the actuality of real-world business. Latham often reminded the sanctimonious ilk, particularly those in the public domain, they too were not immune from participating in mutually beneficial trade, aiding their advancement up the political or civil service greasy pole. 'Wasn't that also a bribe?' He rarely received a counter retort in response.

In practice, those decrying payolas were often their principle recipients. Corrupt council employees accepted inducements from builders for granting construction on green field sites. Senior police officers received brown envelopes containing cash to peer the other way, allowing criminals to effectuate their sordid vocation. British politicians hid behind the Official Secrets Act to cover up their astronomical fiscal blunders, taxpayer money wasted tens of thousands of times over compared to the relatively low value disbursement consultancy fee given to a middleman. The hypocrisy and mendacity appalled Latham, edicts and judgments pontificated by the paragons of virtue not put into practice behind closed doors.

Nowhere as broad a Middle-East exposure compared to Latham's, before their present trip, Rendall Gilmour's know-how consisted of the odd interface with Arab clients back in Blighty, plus a previous visit to the Emirates and Saudi, neither producing any controversy, let alone conflict. Government mandarins and the company ambassadors he negotiated transactions with were painstaking but courteous, nothing untoward in any shape or form alarming him.

Joining Armstrong Eliot as an apprentice, he had risen the technical and project management ranks, before transferring into the company's business development department, working alongside Latham for the past three years, his customer territory centring mainly on Europe and the Americas. Differentiated by an adherence to international ethical and moral standards, at least portrayed by high-gloss, generated perception at the national level, those geographical sectors represented the bulk of the defence systems' supplier market.

Though Gilmour had dealt with some hairy moments in Central and South American airports, they were in Christian capitalist regimes, their national identities attuned to the precepts of international trade, independent of what warts grew internally, the demarcation blessing him with a sense of calm reassurance. But by no means immune from gratuity temptation, on occasion in the pueblo he had been propositioned by key decision makers to make provision for their eventual retirement or a holiday home in the Caribbean, in exchange for a large contract award.

~ * ~

Collecting the businessmen at the appointed time, by 09:00 hours Kimble and the Armstrong-Eliot troupe were ensconced in a large meeting room at Pakistan Armed Forces Regional HQ Karachi, with a team of senior officers led by Brigadier Cham and Vice Admiral Mahmood. After all round introductions, Latham and Gilmour tabled some elementary inquiries touching on operational requirement scope and drivers, then gave a top-down overview on the company, its market-leading target finding systems, and a suggested way forward, Kimble in observation mode during the session.

"So, Mister Latham," Brigadier Cham began at the briefing's conclusion, "if I understand you correctly, you are saying Armstrong-Eliot can set up a demonstration of your GF-486 target finding system, mounted onboard a British Army Lynx helicopter, on Salisbury Plain."

"Correct, Brigadier. Furthermore, we can also accommodate customer references with various armed forces in the Middle East, providing a more convenient forum for checking out the GF-486 in-service performance."

"Mmmm, I take your point." Turning to Mahmood, he whispered something in his ear.

"Mister Gilmour," Mahmood opened, "can you supply similar references for the NF-486 target finding system?"

"Of course we can, Vice Admiral. The NF-486 could be demonstrated onboard a Royal Navy frigate, or alternatively, with either Turkish Naval Forces or the Royal Saudi Navy."

"Good." Adopting a quizzical front, Mahmood delineated, "from what we have been able to gather from your sales literature, the NF-486 and the GF-486 are both based on a common set of electronic and mechanical modules."

"Quite correct, Vice Admiral."

"Can you outline the benefits and advantages of this design M.O?"

"Certainly. Along with the AF-486 variant aimed at airborne platforms, the NF-486 and GF-486 target finding systems are engineered on a universal set of interoperable modules. This revolutionary concept provides benefits in the form of inter-service interchangeability, commonality of product support equipment, and integrated logistics support, fruiting low life cycle costs."

"You mention a common set of interoperable modules across the three variants, Mister Gilmour. How much commonality is there?"

"80 per cent of the modules for a given solution are selected from a core library of hardware and embedded software. 20 percent of the modules are special-to-type, dependent on the platform the apparatus is to be installed in. The non-core modules cater for given military service operational requirements, meaning the in-service role, and the platform peculiarities housing the system."

"I see. Sounds like an excellent construct philosophy."

"You're right, Vice Admiral," Latham interjected. "It's why our target finding systems have been adopted by air forces, armies and navies throughout NATO, and beyond. Further, what it means in terms of operational costs, is a saving on maintenance support provided by improved meantime between failures and mean time to repair, and longer in-service times between scheduled maintenance compared to existing enemy platform identification systems. Moreover, commonality of supply to NATO armed forces and NATO allies, affords the facility for cross-nation battlefield support akin to spares and repairs, thereby satisfying the ability to fight in theatre without retreating."

"A valuable asset," Mahmood complimented, taking in his colleagues' approving carriages. "I'm sure we can all see the potential return on investment and operational flexibility your solutions offer."

"Maybe we can now take the opportunity to discuss specific Pakistan Armed Forces tri-service quantity requirements?" Latham suggested.

"Of course," Mahmood agreed. "Brigadier Cham, could you outline the army requirements?"

Obliging, Cham stated requisite numbers for various battle tank, light-armoured vehicle, and artillery configurations, as well as attack helicopters, both Armstrong-Eliot men noting the platform types and numbers. Mahmood then balanced the requirement with the Pakistani navy requirement covering surface vessels such as frigates and corvettes plus coastal patrol boats, Latham and Gilmour recording the inventory.

"Thank you for your indulgence, gentlemen," Latham eagerly accredited, cerebrating the deal progressed at the expected rate. "Completing the representation, on the basis the air force will also form part of the stockpile, can you outline their requirements?"

"They are still to be finalised, Mister Latham. As soon as the overall requirement is firmed up, we will let you know." Pausing, he adopted a rosy face. "By the way, can we presuppose as the number of systems required increases, the unit price lowers?"

"Yes, Brigadier."

"Right," Cham okayed, before facing Mahmood. "We have all we need for the time being." As Mahmood nodded his approval, Cham turned to address the Englishmen. "Your next stage is further requirement appraisal and technical approval. I understand you have meetings set up in Lahore and Qasim for this purpose."

"Yes, indeed we do, Brigadier," Latham validated. "This afternoon I fly to Lahore and Mister Gilmour will travel to Qasim."

"Maybe Mister Kimble, Mister Gilmour and you can join Vice Admiral Mahmood and myself for lunch?"

"Very gracious of you, I'm sure we—"

Before he could complete the sentence, Kimble cut in. "Excuse me, Brigadier Cham, unfortunately I have a prior commitment to fulfill.

Regrettably, I must excuse myself from your kind offer." Facing the Armstrong-Eliot men, he imparted, "I'll pick you up from HQ reception at one-thirty."

Pakistan Armed Forces had inherited their Karachi Regional HQ from the British Army. Created during the British Raj period, most of the Georgian and Victorian architecture buildings survived after the 1947 India-Pakistan partition, consecutive generations of field rank officers like Cham and Mahmood, bedazzled by their high-caliber ambience and sumptuousness. Crowning the dandy milieu, the dining room expressly wrung with the ghosts of a bygone age, when pomp and regal ceremony ruled daily routines. Replacement of British heads of state and noteworthy British Army officer portraits by Pakistani icons had not diminished its grandeur.

After some light banter during lunch, the Pakistanis moved onto issues about Armstrong-Eliot's history and go-to-market strategy, the Englishmen sensing the lead-in as a precursor to tabling the inevitable management consultancy fees issue.

"Tell me, gentlemen," Cham casually began, "how does your company register the requisite disbursements associated with major government purchases?"

Clearing his throat, as if indicating his thought processes were in line with the crux of the matter, Latham replied, "we are aware there are, shall we call them, hidden costs commensurate with a high-value acquisition. Such costs are catered for as management consultancy fees on the company balance sheet."

"I see." Glancing expectantly at Mahmood, the naval officer responded with a single nod. "Can we be guaranteed, if Armstrong-Eliot are given a clear field to supply our requirements, consultancy fees will er—" Initially vacillating, as if undecided about the solidity of his grounds, with conviction he established firmness. "Be attributed to those paving the way for such a competitive tender-free acquisition?"

"I'm sure you will appreciate we cannot strictly commit to such an arrangement, but should a contract be awarded to Armstrong-Eliot on the basis of unique selling points not available from other suppliers, then I am sure the company will be generous in the figure of consultancy fees."

Cham and Mahmood exchanged satisfied beams.

"Very well, gentleman," Cham resumed. "Of course, this arrangement is wholly conditional on Armstrong-Eliot's equipments passing technical assessment muster, and satisfactory references being rendered."

"By all means," Latham coolly sanctioned.

~ * ~

"Did you really have another appointment over the lunch period?" Gilmour questioned Kimble, as the threesome departed the Pakistan Armed Forces Karachi HQ.

"I discerned Brigadier Cham and Vice Admiral Mahmood had something of a private nature to discuss with you and Dale."

Latham grinned. "Very sapient, Bill."

"If it's not authentic over-the-counter business—" Leering accusingly at the commercial lieutenants, Kimble then glanced away. "I, and the Foreign Office, do not want to know about any undercover, *quid pro quo* deal you've struck."

"Quite."

Chapter 4: JSHQ Rawalpindi

Having completed their opening business gambit with Pakistan Armed Forces, Kimble deposited Latham at Jinnah International Airport, before taking Gilmour onto a requirement surveyor level meeting with the Pakistani Navy at Port Qasim.

Whilst walking across the domestic departures' concourse, Latham speculated if non-Pakistani inbound international passengers were still getting heat from customs officials. Though Kimble's explanation of the affray he and Gilmour underwent rang utterly plausible, something still nagged at him, substantiated by its intensity. He wondered just how far the standoff with the irritated Aussie might have gone, but for the fortunate distraction of VIPs passing by the customs hall. Accepting anything could have happened, encompassing incarceration or worse for the Aussie, he decided to put the occurrence to the back of his mind and concentrate on the commerce in hand.

Now part-factored on the net from the Cham-Mahmood meeting, during the Pakistani Airlines flight to Islamabad, he verified the business objectives he had set himself for the Pakistan Army valuators' meetings at Joint Staff Headquarters Rawalpindi.

Though acting as a facilitator to the sales mechanism, until they had reviewed their ruminations internally, contractors rarely discussed their premier meeting imprints of client emissaries with British High Commission staff like Kimble. Latham made a mental note to call Gilmour from Rawalpindi, enabling the pair to reciprocate on items resultant from the Karachi meeting, and determine any carry over actions before re-engaging with Kimble. After gaining the thumbs up from the appraisement teams, he knew, downline, Cham and Mahmood expected one-on-one meetings to round off the sales verdict. Though neither had given anything away regarding inducements in front of their staff, he assumed extra to the notion of the management consultancy fees they debated in private, possibly paid to dependable third-party recipients to help ensure anonymity, both expected the corporate entertainment card to be played.

Rather than drugs aboard a plush motor cruiser moored in the *Cote d'Azur* or grandstand trips to sporting events such as Formula 1, often powerful Muslim men hankered for illicit encounters with courtesans. Like all defence sector business development and sales directors, Latham's adjunct job title was chief entertainments officer, responsible for laying on whatever key decision makers wanted, under the guise of pleasure congress. During his stint at Dandridge and then Armstrong-Eliot, auxiliary to the usual fleshpot cravings, he had catered for the most unpredicted desires, incorporating setting up dates for men with actress doppelgangers via high-class dating agencies, and arranging for weekend visits to 5-star hotels in tropical paradises such as Tahiti and Curacao, with hot and cold running local girls.

As Latham's Mercedes taxi traveled along crowded streets en route to the Pearl-Continental Hotel Rawalpindi, he picked up on tension in the atmosphere. Almost palpable, local people appeared to be charged-up, even hostile. Much to his dismay, he saw two men being attacked by a far larger group, vicious blows reducing their victims to battered bodies and bloody faces. Further into the trek, he grimaced as a woman cowered before a man striking her with a cane, his beating dealt out with malice and no mercy. Then, nearing the Millat Colony locale, the sight of a man being stoned by a mob caused him to wrench. Glancing at the taxi driver reflected in the car's rearview mirror, Latham noticed he lasted totally unconcerned about the atrocity, maybe even silently applauded the grisly undertaking. Absorbed with Bill Kimble's patter during road journeys in Karachi, he had not taken in the behaviour of urban dwellers. Similar scenes had plausibly occurred, but he persisted transparent to them.

Largely outlawed by the Pakistan Government, Latham knew Sharia Law had little authorised support, but behind the statute, a blind eye allowed Muslim devotees to inflict the austere and uncompromising

Islamic ordinance, as they saw fit. In a zealous, witch-hunter-like frenzy, many fanatical Muslims interpreted Sharia Law as a means to enforce their will on others, the slightest transgression of the ordained code, originating in acts of barbarism as punishment. Additional to crimes such as theft, it applied to sexual deviants, pre-marriage chastity for women, dietary and presentation habits, the absolute piety of marriage, and most of all, a hatred of all non-Muslims.

When Latham conducted dealings in Pakistan on behalf of Dandridge in the mid-1980s, even staunch Pakistani Muslims saw the West as a valued ally because of the Soviet-Afghan war, fearing if the Soviets prevailed in Afghanistan, they'd surge into Pakistan. Similarly, if Iraqi forces overran Iran in the Iraq-Iran war, Pakistan was destined to be next on Saddam Hussein's hit list. Consequently, a Westerners' presence in Pakistan, especially one aiding their military defence became welcomed. At the time, Sharia Law had not been manipulated at the partisan-political level by Muslim extremists as a vehicle to subjugate fellow believers, and sow the seeds of discontent and intolerance. Notwithstanding, the Gulf War changed everything.

In the eyes of the fanatics, Muslims fighting communists, and Muslims doing battle with Muslims in accordance with tribal differences going back centuries, attracted endorsed permission. Though the Iraqis had brutally invaded Kuwait, kicking off the Gulf War, the broader Muslim world did not sanction American and British interventionism. Intrinsically involving the Christian West killing the followers of Allah, Muslim zealots condemned it as a throwback to the early middle-ages, when European Christendom united as a Crusader army under King Richard I, expelling invading Muslims from the Holy Land.

Westerners had warred against each other and non-Christian empires and caliphates for millennia, but when the conflict finished, and an armistice negotiated and signed by both victor and vanquished, resentment died away within a few decades, old combatants often uniting as allies. No such forgive and forget doctrine existed in the Muslim world. Saladin and the Muslim hordes were defeated and sent into retreat by the triumphant Crusaders, the humiliation never forgotten by Muslim clerics over the following centuries. Perpetuating the story, fanatics seized on the ignominy, rallying impressionable followers to wage jihad against the West, the carnage and wholesale slaughter of Christians enacted by the Ottoman Empire's invasion of Southern Europe conveniently set aside as a bi-product of Muslim conquest, the clerics insisting all Muslims should support the installation of an Islamic worldwide state as a matter of duty, and their forebearers were merely doing this in the drive to eradicate all non-Muslim doctrines and religions.

In the aftermath of the Gulf War, Latham rationalised Western precepts of compassion and kindness to a defeated enemy were not shared by Muslims, their agenda differing widely from caprices of Western ethics, such as atonement and reconciliation. In much the same way as Hitler and the Nazis tarried adamant and defiant in their beliefs without accord, clearly, a huge multitude of Muslims worldwide trusted in the absoluteness of Islam, without compromise or contradiction. Amongst the Muslim masses, when the fanatics called them to protest or take part in terrorist campaigns, it speedily surged from just beneath the emotional level into a menacing, banshee-like rage.

Explicitly, the West had seen it occur in Iran when Khomeini deposed the Shah, but most government observers categorised it as a national revolution, never perceiving the possibility of Muslim fundamentalism going viral. Whether ignited by wishful thinking, tainted liberal ideals, or sheer stupidity, howbeit, those failing to anticipate the domino effect were under no illusions post the Gulf War, Western leaders forced to credit Muslim terrorism gained pace by means of participating numbers and capabilities at a geometric rate. Quickly overwhelmed by an ever-increasing proliferation of Muslim terrorist organisations and an army of suspects, operating not just in the Middle East but worldwide, notably in the West's own backyard sequent to unrestrained immigration, Western intelligence services trailed behind in the counterintelligence game, their resources insufficient to suppress the enemy. Dogged military containment and behind the certified smokescreen negotiation were never going to quell multi-serpent headed Muslim terrorism. As fast as the West neutralised or turned one devotee, hundreds more sprung up, the epidemic beyond lenient conceptions of inclusion in Western society and religious tolerance, Muslims seeing such liberal idealism as weakness to be exploited.

Latham had seen the odd episode of Sharia Law retribution enacted in the past, but the regularity of the nauseating penalties he witnessed during the taxi journey made him realise there had been a sharp ramping up of chastisement to those accused of breaking the code. Maybe he had been blind to similar public brutalities during the previous part of the business tour in Saudi and the Emirates? Categorically, they were not immune from such barbaric deeds. With the holy city of Mecca, birthplace of Mohammed and site of his first revelation of the Quran in Saudi Arabia's hinterland, the Saudi administration were obliged to set an example and uphold Sharia Law for Muslims at large. For years, Latham had been hearing abhorrent tales of wholesale public executions, hands being lopped off for petty theft, and transgressors flogged, but like all streetwise, foreign exporters, he had kept his concentration on the business mission, and not indulged in reprimand and censure.

However, one high profile horror provided the source material for ATV's screening of the drama-documentary, *Death of a Princess*, adapted from the true story of young Saudi Arabian Princess Misha-al and her lover, both publicly executed for adultery, the cruelty resulting in worldwide condemnation, Latham amongst the hundreds of millions shocked by the inhuman act. Reacting to the telecast tit-for-tat, the Saudis banned the British Airways Concorde from its air space, making flights between London and Singapore unprofitable. Restrictions were placed on issuing visas to British businessmen, and the Saudis cancelled several British defense export programmes worth billions of pounds, the impasse only resolved by British Foreign Secretary Lord Carrington groveling to the Saudis, and in 1985, the British Aerospace led Al-Yamamah arms deal in exchange for 600,000 barrels of crude oil per day to the UK Government. Pragmatically, the knock-on economic downside of incurring Saudi wrath doused British exporters with a stolid, non-confrontational stance when it came to future Saudi domestic affairs, a blind eye and deaf ear attitude applied.

Dandridge were involved in the Al-Yamamah initiative, Latham inducted into the blind, deaf and dumb fraternity when he joined the company. Similarly, when he left for Armstrong-Eliot, the principle became reinforced, his new employers still smarting from the downturn in Saudi exports in the early 1980s. As a cardinal sequel to the donnybrook, he had disciplined himself to steer clear of controversy, and turn away when he chanced upon Sharia Law castigation being applied in public.

Now, he catechized if the adoption had masked off the growth of outrages to his sensibilities. Worse, might the incidence of public vengeance against transgressors increase in Islamic ruled countries, and demands made by Muslims living in the West for Sharia Law to be enshrined in government statutes be applied wholesale!?

~ * ~

Acting as the hub centre for Pakistan Armed Forces, JSHQ Rawalpindi dispensed policy plus strategic and tactical rulings for principally the army, the navy and the air force. In regard of the equipment procurement executive function, most service technical assessors and operational unit liaison officers were tasked with identifying fighting equipment requirements resided at JSHQ.

Kimble had identified Lieutenant Colonel Ghulam Bishara, Head of Battlefield Surveillance Systems Directorate, Pakistan Army, as the key officer responsible for analysis, and thereby a key influencer in the procurement of target finding systems. When a contractor landed on the horizon, Bishara marshalled a team of relevant arbiters and liaison officers to discuss army needs and gauge their wares against them.

Latham had originally met Bishara in Pakistan during his tenure with Dandridge, in those days Bishara holding the rank of major with the Pakistan Army Aviation Wing at AVN Base Multan. With common aviation and cricket dynamics binding their relationship, the two men got on well, a fast-emerging meeting of minds lubricating the wheels of the business transaction. When Bishara visited Dandridge in West London, June 1987, Latham took him to Lords to see England play Pakistan in the second test match of the series. A memorable occurrence, it eternally stayed with the Aviation Wing man.

"My dear Dale," Bishara opened, grasping Latham's hand as he entered his office, "how good it is to see you again."

"Hello, Ghulam. How are you?"

Thumping his chest with both hands and smiling gregariously, he bragged, "as fit as ever, though retiring from active air service for a desk-bound job five years ago has seen me put on a little weight. I used to work-out every day when flying, but now—" After pulling a downcast face then chuckling, he maintained his lightheartedness. "I rarely have the time to go to the gym. How about you? Does your injured left arm still give you trouble?"

"Some, but I've learned to live with it."

"Good." His gleam booming, he graciously offered, "come, let's sit down and barter a few words, before I take you along to our formal meeting."

"It'd be a pleasure."

Relaxing in comfortable easy chairs, they beamed at each other, their friendship distilled from a professional affiliation bringing about mutual warmth and cordiality. Latham had nurtured similar bonds with other client representatives, but Bishara hit the pinnacle, reciprocal likes and cravings allied to undiluted probity making him singular.

"So, you moved on from Dandridge?"

"Yes, headhunted by Armstrong-Eliot March 1989 into the role of sales director, airborne systems."

"I suppose there were financial incentives to make the move?"

"Dandridge were good payers, but the improved Armstrong-Eliot package became irresistible, and they are the market leader in battlefield target sensor systems, so I foresaw a bright future."

"Quite. Well I'm very pleased for you, Dale."

Continuing to chat about their professions and shared experiences, Bishara in particular taking great delight in reprising their visit to Lords with gusto, the pair rekindled their association before his aid knocked on his office door, telling him the rating team were ready for the Armstrong-Eliot meeting.

Following a score of introductions to Latham, Bishara felt predisposed to lay the foundation for his old friend. "By the way, gentlemen, don't go imagining Mister Latham is just another salesman. He has outstanding credentials for addressing fellow aviators. In another life, ex-RAF Wing Commander Dale Latham graduated from Royal Air Force College Cranwell, May 1970, and during the next 12 years, went on to accumulate over 10,000 flight hours, piloting Harrier, Jaguar and Tornado aircraft." Turning to grin at Latham, his eulogy then took on a more enumerated tribute. "I'm going to embarrass him further, by telling you he won the USAF Red Flag competition on two occasions at Nellis Air Force Base, flying a RAF Tornado GR1 defeating F-16s from the 64th Aggressor Squadron and F-15s from the 65th Aggressor Squadron, to take the much vaunted winners' trophy back to Blighty for Her Majesty Queen Elizabeth II to inspect." Dwelling, he scanned his colleagues with an affirmative face. "So, gentlemen, I'd advise all of you to treat the ex-Wing Commander with due diligence and respect."

Recovering from his shining RAF acclaim, Latham went to work, briefing the assembled team on Armstrong-Eliot's tri-service battlefield target sensor systems, and tabling precise points relating to the AF-486 variant for airborne platforms. During the subsequent Q&A, several of the operational unit liaison officers expressed an interest in AF-486 installations on the Bell AH-1S Cobra attack helicopter.

"We have Cobra in-service installations with the US Army, the Japanese Army and the Royal Jordanian Air Force," Latham informed them. "As mentioned to Brigadier Cham and Vice Admiral Mahmood during our meeting yesterday at Pakistan Armed Forces Regional HQ Karachi, we can furnish customer references for installations, for example, the Royal Jordanian Air Force."

Some internal discussion took place before Captain Bishen Hakimi of the Army Aviation Wing drew the Englishman's attention. "Mister Latham, we have a flight of army Cobras on detachment to IV Corps at Pakistan Air Force Base Lahore for a combined army-air force operation. I'd like to propose you come down to Lahore this afternoon to give us some idea of where the AF-486 system fits on the Cobra."

"Before you get carried away, Captain," Bishara interposed, "I have plans for Mister Latham this evening. He will be free for a trip to

Lahore tomorrow." Facing the Englishman with an affable disposition, he solicited, "if that's alright with you, Mister Latham?"

"Fine with me, Lieutenant Colonel, but to give the captain a heads up to his enquiry, the signals processor unit fits into the helicopter's avionics bay, and the infrared and low-level light sensors, plus the high-resolution cameras, are housed on pods mounted either side of the cockpit roof."

"And presumably," Hakimi posed, "the recognised battlefield picture is shown on a cockpit mounted display?"

"There are two choices," Latham listed. "We can either supply a dedicated display unit, or the feeds from the signals processor unit can be integrated into a head-up display over a MIL-STD 1553 serial data bus, as part of a combined target recognition and armament fire control system. And just to cap the sketch, the signals processor is engineered on the MIL-STD 1750A 16-bit instruction set architecture, and the operation program is written in MIL-STD 1589C JOVIAL high-level computer programming language."

"If we were to adopt your dedicated display unit, can the AF-486 target finding system outputs for target lock still be integrated into an existing armament fire control system?"

"Absolutely, Captain Hakimi. There are no system contention issues with such an operational in-service configuration."

"Right. I'll fix up some air transport for take-off at 06:00 tomorrow."

"Captain, I applaud your enthusiasm," Bishara broke in, "but may I suggest a more civilized departure time for our guest is 08:00 hours?" Smirking genially at Latham, he begged, "I haven't seen this fellow since 1987, and we have a lot to catch up on this evening. It could go on into the early hours."

"Yes, sir. My apologies. 08:00 will be fine."

Latham answered more queries pertaining to the AF-486 technical specification and performance before the assembly broke for lunch. Centred on logistics support, training, and contractual terms, comprising UK Government ECGD sales clearance sanctioned via export licenses and end user certificates, the afternoon session slid by, Latham confident the auditors were buying into the Armstrong-Eliot offerings. Finally, Bishara drew the meeting to a conclusion as the sun cast a tremendous collage of vibrant colours on the horizon, then escorted Latham to the officers' mess.

~ * ~

"You know, Dale," Bishara began as the pair strolled across the parade ground, "I've often deliberated about applying for a place on the RAF officer interchange programme."

"Oh."

"Yes, I'm a bit of an anglophile on the quiet, and even my narrow exposure to England and English people fueled the desire, but—" Smirking, his natural capacity for irony surfaced. "It is far too late to fulfill the want. I should have done it while still an active aviator. Dang it—" He shook his head. "Paradoxically, the scheme also applies to what you English call, desk-based-Johnnies, such as me."

"Tell me, Ghulam, why didn't you make the application when you were flying?"

"Ohh—" Holding up his hands in a resigned gesture, he divulged, "contrary dividends, some real, some fanciful, but mainly those associated with domesticity and family aspects. It's not so easy to fly the coup to a distant land. Senior family members frown on such ventures."

"But why?"

"Hah, my dear Dale, there is a world of difference between Western liberal attitudes and the calls made on a Muslim family man, above all, when the man's family is required to set an example in the community."

"I never took you for being staunchly religious."

"Oh, don't get me wrong, I'm not. For me, it has always been an obligation, neutrally celebrated without passion. My goal is being seen to do what is compulsory to placate my wife, the family elders, and set an example to our children, but behind the endorsed stance, I am secular in my beliefs."

"Might explain in part why your career has flourished."

"True. Neither the armed forces officer corps executive, nor the ranks of the political elite, rests in the hands of the Muslim zealots."

"Yes, over the years I've been doing trade in the Middle-East, I've identified my opposite numbers invariably have, shall we say, an earthbound standpoint."

"By nature, both politics and the armed forces are businesses. There is no scope in business for doctrinaire and inflexible philosophies, only reason and rationale, un-coloured by credo and dogma."

"True. But all the same, you should have made an application." Radiating a sympathetic comportment, Latham ascribed, "I can discern from your voice tone, you deeply regret it."

"For sure."

"I too have not always fulfilled my yearnings and ambitions, family commitments limiting my drive," Latham confessed. "But participating in an officer-interchange programme would not have posed a significant problem for me. May I ask, why do your family elders see such a project as counterproductive to the welfare of your family?"

"You are being diplomatic, Dale. I am sure you have worked it out already, but all the same, I will outline the objections they'd submit." Plunging into defensive modality, he vouched, "a married Pakistani officer on secondment to a liberal Western country, allowing all kinds of non-committal freedoms, if you take the gist of my meaning…." He advanced Latham a cautionary air. "….is considered to be too much temptation to ignore. Though I see cheating on my wife is extremely bad form, and I'd never commit such a heinous act, even so, the family elders are not prone to allowing temptation to be put my way."

"And your wife is of this opinion?"

"I have never voiced the topic with my wife, and I've gleaned the elders' probable reaction, brokered on their sanctity of marriage credo. No—" Letting out a brief laugh of fatalism, his metaphorical shackles apparent to Latham, he attested, "when still a young officer and single, I should have applied for the officer interchange programme."

"*C'est la vie*, as the French say, Ghulam. I'm sure you have had other compensations."

"True, but all the same, not applying is an eternally lost opportunity."

Negotiating the curved stairway leading to the officers' mess entrance, the pair stepped into an air-conditioned environment, Latham thankful for the respite from the intense outside heat.

Relaxing into deep pile, leather bound, lounge chairs, whilst nursing very large gin and tonics, the old friends continued their dialogue.

"It might be fantasy," Latham conceded, "but since arriving in Pakistan, I've fingered a distinct undercurrent of hostility towards foreigners and intolerance of Koran transgressors."

"Your antenna is not deceiving you," Bishara remarked. "The Muslim fanatics have been at work, sowing the seeds of disenchantment, and lighting contentious fires to stimulate unrest amongst the masses."

Latham went on to recount the Jinnah International Airport rumpus, and the barbarous tumults he had noted during his taxi ride to the Pearl-Continental Hotel.

"It doesn't surprise me," Bishara testified. "Some parts of the public sector, markedly those processing foreigners, have been infiltrated by religious militants. And yes, those portraying an austere Islamic nature, have taken it upon themselves to penalise others accused of breaking Sharia Law." Ashamed of some of his countrymen's actions, he squinted at Latham then rubbed his chin as if trying to foretell truth. "In my reckoning, Dale, it will get a lot worse before it gets better, and though the majority of the officer corps reside free from the excesses of the Islamic faith, I have heard there are a few extremist sympathizers." John Soames' conviction substantiated, he clocked Latham's eyes stretch wide open at the declaration. "Oh, they don't come out into the open, press for an end to free and democratic elections, and the installation of a dictatorial Islamic state. No, these are fifth columnists, their outward faces loyal to the elected government, but behind the cosmetic front, they work surreptitiously with Muslim extremist factions and even terrorists to bring the establishment down from within."

"Have you met such men?"

Bishara took a long pull on his drink. "No, but I am aware of their existence." Dithering, as if uncomfortable with the admission, he shifted around in his seat uneasily. "I shouldn't be telling you this, Dale, but be careful who you deal with. I don't mean in the armed forces procurement side. I can safely say, there are no bad apples within our ranks. It's in the lower to middle civil servant level, and in the civilian authorities where the contagion has mainly taken root."

"Hence the Jinnah International Airport fracas?"

His exasperation boiling over, Bishara thumped his glass down. "Precisely."

Chapter 5: Ground Attack

True to his word, Captain Hakimi laid on an Aérospatiale SA 330 Puma transport helicopter to ferry Latham, himself, five operational unit liaison officers, and three technical evaluators to Lahore.

As the helicopter climbed towards the hovering position over JSHQ Rawalpindi, from his passenger cabin window seat, Latham saw a crowd of people surging towards Barkat Plaza from Bank Street and Kashmir Road.

"What's going on down there?" he asked Hakimi.

Leaning to see through the porthole, Hakimi replied, "oh, it's nothing, Mister Latham. Just a gathering of the devotee hotheads, going to hear one of the mullahs' latest ravings. It's evolved into a daily ritual of late."

"Are the mullahs trying to incite sedition against the State?"

"*Huh*!" Hakimi cringed with rebuke. "They've been inciting sedition since the creation of Pakistan in 1947. Withal, after the Gulf War, their follower numbers have multiplied, resulting in what you see going on down there. The police keep an eye on them, and Federal Investigation Agency civil intelligence agents mingle amongst them, monitoring what is said. In the main, it's hot air, mullahs advocating the precepts of fundamentalism, and zealots clamouring for absolute Sharia Law to be instituted."

"I see. So, the Government is treating them seriously?" Latham tested, keen to ascertain if Hakimi's constructs coincided with those of Ghulam Bishara.

"It's a wait and see passive exercise, nothing bellicose or controversial. It's not even containment at present. Those in power are hoping the uproar burns itself out, without the police and the army having to bang heads and jail malcontents, leaving the mullahs to largely preach among themselves again."

Nosing-down slightly as she picked up horizontal speed when the pilot changed the pitch of the rotor blades from collective to cyclic, the Puma turned in a south-south-east direction towards Lahore, Latham straining to see events unfolding below. *More proof of a burgeoning meltdown*, he mused.

During the flight, Hakimi preoccupied Latham into replaying his RAF career.

"I must say, Mister Latham, to use your English phrase, you are a most unusual bird. I've never met an ex-RAF officer who has reinvented himself as a businessman."

"Good lord." Latham winced at the compliment. "I can assure you, Captain Hakimi, it's not in the mould of choice, but necessity."

Surprising him with his frankness, Hakimi moved, "if it's not an imposition, perhaps you'd care to enlighten me as to the drivers behind your vocation change?"

Smiling at the inquisitive officer, Latham then glanced out of the window, momentarily reliving in his mind the misadventure changing his working life.

Turning to Hakimi he proclaimed, "sometimes, notwithstanding meticulous planning and caution, a bolt hits you unexpectedly without warning. Heeding the rules of air safety, apart from a Tornado IDS flameout, I never came near to an air accident during my 12 years in the RAF. The same I cannot say for road safety, though the chapter originating in me leaving the RAF was not my fault."

"What happened, Mister Latham?"

"One fine spring day in 1982, during driving from RAF Marham to King's Lynn, an on-coming juggernaut lost control and side-swiped my car. In the ensuing tangle, my left arm ligaments were injured on the tendon. It inhibited the ability to fully extend my left arm." Pushing out his left arm, he demonstrated the restriction. "Declared medically unfit for air duty by an RAF medical board, it left me sidelined from flying. They decreed, without full mobility in my left arm, I ran the risk of not being able to pilot an aircraft correctly, especially under battlefield conditions."

"So you were given no alternative but to leave the RAF?"

"Oh, the service tendered a desk job, but er—" He grinned. "I demurred, thinking being continuously sat behind a desk with the thunder and whoosh of Tornados taking off and landing in the backdrop equated with purgatory. I'd known nothing else but operational flying since graduating from Cranwell. I knew I'd not be able to take watching others do something I loved, so I tested the temperature of the water about joining the aerospace industry as an aviation consultant. Dandridge offered me a very good remuneration package, so I took the job, rationalising at least I'd be involved with aircraft, quintessentially, doing something in the field working with military personnel, as opposed to being desk bound. After a year of acting as a consultant and gaining commerce skills and wisdom, Dandridge made me sales and marketing manager for airborne systems."

"Then you moved on to Armstrong-Eliot?"

"They head-hunted me March 1989 into the sales director role for target-finding sensor systems."

Aggrieved a fellow aviator had been grounded by no fault of his own, Hakimi postulated, "I'd guess it's stupid to ask if you miss flying?"

"Oh, don't worry," Latham convinced. "That cross to bear has been batted to and fro many times, and of course the answer is, yes. Fortunately, I have learnt to discipline my visceral stirrings. As the years went by, the loss of facility diminished, but—" He produced a wry expression. "When I'm close by military aircraft as part of my business role, the memories of flying come flooding back." Nodding his head from side to side, he admitted, "thus the torment is reignited."

Responsive to Latham's heartache, Hakimi changed the conversation point to a more positive theme. "I must say, Lieutenant Colonel Bishara's anecdote about your Red Flag successes fascinated me."

"Ohh—" Latham beamed. "The Lieutenant Colonel and I are old friends. He is very sensitive to my predicament and goes out of his way to promote my few achievements. He did much the same thing when I visited the Pakistan Army Aviation Wing at AVN Base Multan, as a Dandridge envoy. I dined with him the evening before an official meeting, and he tabled much the same probes. The following day, when he introduced me to the Aviation Wing meeting attendees, he bolstered my ego by pulling out highlights from my RAF C.V, Red Flag amongst them, just like he did yesterday. Blimey—" Conveying a sensation of disbelief, he illuminated, "remarkably, I became the first non-American to win the Red Flag trophy."

"How did it come about?"

"Up until 1980, the RAF had entered Buccaneer and Jaguar aircraft to fly against the F-15 then the F-16, both superior to the British entrants in terms of speed and maneuverability. When the Tornado GR1 came into service, we knew in theory she could outperform the American jets. Red Flag 1980 provided robust competition to test her out, going head-to-head in a plethora of aerial war games against the F-15 and the F-16." Lingering for more callback, he then elucidated, "the purpose of Red Flag is to train pilots and other flight crew members from the US and NATO countries for real air combat situations. It includes the use of enemy hardware, meaning Migs, and live ammunition for bombing exercises at the Nevada Test & Training Range, adjacent to Nellis AFB. The mission of the 414th Combat Training Squadron, meaning Red Flag, is to maximise the combat readiness and survivability of participants, by providing a realistic flight environment, and a pre-flight and post-flight training forum encouraging a free exchange of ideas."

"How does it work? I mean the simulated combat missions."

"The Red Flag exercise comprises friendly Blue Forces against hostile Red Forces. RAF entrants are part of Blue Forces, and as Lieutenant Colonel Bishara outlined, Red Forces comprise F-16s from the 64th Aggressor Squadron and F-15s from the 65th Aggressor Squadron, augmented by supplementary aircraft from the USAF, USN and the US Marine Corps."

"I see. So, you took the trophy in 1980 flying a Tornado GR1?"

"Yes, the feat repeated in Red Flag 1981. I'd er..." Restlessly blowing out, Hakimi sensed a downside corollary in the making. "...have been going for a hat-trick of wins in 1982, but for an out-of-control juggernaut ploughing into me."

"*Ohh*," Hakimi replied, his temperament oozing diffidence. "Now I feel very bad about asking you about your background, Mister Latham. It is a heart-rending tale for a fellow aviator to hear."

"Please, don't let it upset you, Captain Hakimi. I learnt to live with it long ago."

Not entirely true, Latham's chronicle purposely gilded the lily, so as not to totally depress Hakimi. He had adopted kid gloves on previous occasions, when queried about the road accident leading to him being grounded.

Ironically, just prior to the metamorphic hit, promotion to group captain beckoned for Latham. Interviewed by the RAF promotions board, consisting of air commodores and more senior officer ranks, he had been appraised to lead the Tornado IDS group, composing two operational wings, each with three squadrons, and headquartered at RAF Coningsby.

In pole position for the appointment, the promotions board waited for the outcome of Latham's medical board review before making a terminal adjudication. When the ruling came, his star went into decline, Latham told in no uncertain terms, without 100 percent fitness operational duty rating, the group captain post had to be withdrawn and his flight worthiness certificate retired. Shocked by the medical report, all the same, the promotions board decisions came as no jolt to Latham. He had seen injured pilots taken off the flight list in the course of his time with the RAF, never envisioning it could happen to him.

In the immediate aftermath of the downturn, he spent his days at RAF Marham watching Tornados take-off, their twin Turbo-Union RB199 jet engines making the ground shudder when the pilot engaged full thrust with afterburners at the start of rolling. A glorious cacophony of high-energy reverb and rumble; it rammed home the reminder that he would never again feel its effect from the aircraft's pilot seat.

Consoling words from fellow Tornado aircrew failed to tranquilize the blow. Though never bitter about his plight, he did indulge in copious amounts of high-octane liquor to anesthetize the misery, or took his frustration out on inanimate objects, kicking over waste baskets or slamming a fist hard down on a desktop, his insides a mass of jagged edges and biting spikes constantly gnawing at him. Apart from not making the journey, he knew he couldn't have done anything to avoid the road collision, fate and kismet responsible for his date with destiny. Just tens of seconds either side of the crash time, and he'd still be flying, and most ostensibly, as a group captain.

No longer deemed fit to fly, when he attended the promotions board, they assessed his acquired operational sagacity qualified him for strategic planning and operational requirements capture. In practice, it meant transfer to a desk job at Strike Command's Operation Centre in the nuclear bunker at RAF High Wycombe, or secondment to MoD's Procurement Executive at Main Building, Whitehall. Neither appealed to Latham. A few weeks later, he initiated his aviation consultant drive. When Dandridge Defence & Air Systems came calling, he resigned his RAF commission.

~ * ~

Approaching Lahore, the Puma slowed and from his cabin window Latham saw the Pakistan Air Force Base situated in the middle of the city. Turning the aircraft into wind, the pilot hovered the Puma 300 feet above the helicopter landing pad below, preparing to make a steady descent and landing.

Out of the corner of his right eye, Latham saw a white, red and yellow flash emanate from the ground, about a mile from the air force base perimeter. Instants later, a surface-to-air missile struck the Puma, smashing into her underbelly and exploding. Something crashed into his head producing a sharp, poleaxing pain and he blacked out.

Sometime thereafter, he started to recover consciousness, clocking the sky above and faces staring down at him. He could not quite work out where he was, his mind limited by mental inertia, and still to upshift into information retrieval. Then the flash came to mind. Moping at the recollection, the facial motion caused him agony. His nerve ends kicked in, and he moaned loudly with acute distress, his entire body signaling it had been battered as if by assailants using baseball bats.

Sensing a needle enter his right arm, he then thought he saw a familiar angel rise into the air before he sank into deep sleep.

Chapter 6: Recovery

On the next juncture Latham awoke, instead of sky he saw a white ceiling and a different set of faces gazing down at him. Muffled voices percolated into his hearing, and he detected his arm being held. Widening his drowsy eyes, the faces came into focus.

"Hello, Mister Latham, I'm Doctor Kassis. How are you feeling?"

Partially transitioning into a *compos mentis* condition, he begged, "where am I?"

"You're in the Combined Military Hospital, Lahore."

Winking repeatedly, he tried for memory recall, then his eyes stayed open. "The Puma…what happened?"

"We can talk about it later. I'm just taking your pulse. Right now, it's more important you tell us how you feel."

Shifting his weight slightly, Latham experienced a stabbing pang on his left side below his ribcage, and his neck seemed to be immobile, as if something restrained it. "My side hurts, and I can't lift my head."

Kassis faced two other medical staff. "Mmmm, it's definitely side whiplash to his neck." Refacing the patient, he warned, "you're going to feel sore for a while. Your left side above the hip is badly cut, and you've lost quite a lot of blood. Until you make it up, you are going to feel weak, and you're feeling the stitches we had to apply to secure the wound. You also had a gash on the left side of your head also needing stitches. Your neck muscles have been wrenched, and you will need to lie still for a few days to allow them to relax and recover, before your neck brace is removed."

"What about the rest of me?"

"Some minor cuts and bruising to your chest, but the rest of you is fine as far as we can see." Peering down the bed towards Latham's feet, he asked, "can you wiggle your toes and flex your ankles?"

Latham accommodated the doctor.

"Good, the movement indicates your legs are fine, but when you have recovered from your injuries they will feel like putty until you start walking again. Changing the subject—" His deportment modulated into an authoritative regime. "On the personal front, Pakistan Armed Forces informed the British Deputy High Commission at Karachi about your hospitalisation. In turn, they have contacted your next of kin and your employer."

Deliberating on the news, the patient then requested, "I'd like to talk to some people back home. Can you arrange a phone call?"

"We can, but I'd recommend you wait at least 48 hours, until your neck muscles begin to recover."

Affected by his neck aching with piercing irritation, he reconsidered. "Okay."

During the doctor's diagnosis, Latham's mind had harked back to the air strike.

"Doctor Kassis." Licking his lips to find moisture, he figured the worst. "What about the rest of the people aboard the Puma?"

"As I said, we'll talk about it later."

"Doctor," he pressed, "I *have* to know."

Sucking in breath, Kassis replied, "you'd better prepare yourself for bad news. Out of the 10 passengers and three crew, additional to yourself only four others have survived."

Latham scrunched up his eyes. "Is Captain Hakimi amongst the survivors?"

"I'm afraid not."

Distressed, the irrevocability of Kassis's narration made him cringe with deep regret. Though he had only been acquainted with Hakimi briefly, he had formed a considerate appreciation of the Army Aviation Wing officer, appraising him to be a very likeable person.

Further into the day, the nursing staff brought telephone messages to Latham from Bill Kimble at the Karachi British Deputy High

Commission and Rendall Gilmour in England. After completing his meetings with the Pakistan Navy at Port Qasim, Gilmour had returned to Blighty on the day of the Puma tragedy. The messages expressed the sender's best wishes for the patient's speedy recovery moreover, Kimble saying he'd soon be visiting Latham.

Laid-up and bored, the patient's mind drifted into overdrive about what had occurred. During his RAF tenure, he had never been involved in an air accident, or had to eject from a stricken aircraft. A keen believer in the maxim that there are old pilots and there are bold pilots, but there are no old bold pilots, he had always applied a careful and studious style to flying, managing to avoid mid-air collisions, and when required, successfully recovering jet aircraft from engine flameout, as he had achieved over the Moray Firth . Reluctantly, he appreciated even if he had been piloting the Puma, the cataclysm would still have happened, ground attacks on sitting duck hovering helicopters unavoidable due to the very short time between munition launch and target contact.

Undeniably, he knew both RAF and NATO ally aircrew who had lost their lives in flying accidents, but the Puma scrap represented his baptism in coming close to meeting his maker. He supposed the risk of ending up as an air catastrophe casualty had been left behind when he retired from the RAF. True, commercial flights were not immune from disaster, but the probability of life loss via an air accident is less than a million to one, whereas loss of life incurred by dent of road accidents metered out at a few tens of thousands to one. The cause behind the Puma mishap plagued him more than anything else. He had his own meditations on the matter, and intended to table them at the appropriate juncture.

~ * ~

Cascading into a listless malaise the next afternoon, Latham's sensitivity reenlisted when he received an unannounced visitor.

"Mister Latham."

Hearing his name being spoken, he raised his eyelids from dozing.

"Hello, Mister Latham. I'm Chanda Govinda." She beamed at him, as if willing his eyes to remain open. "I'm a member of the hospital patient support staff."

Studying the woman standing a few feet away from his bed, dressed in a full-length sari hugging her slim waist and emphasising her above average height, he gauged her to be in her late twenties. Slight of build and with a bronze complexion, she emitted warmth and compassion, ideal prerequisites for her occupation. Set in an angelic face, her large, deep-mocha eyes, small nose and generous mouth, coupled with her straight, black hair falling halfway down her back and curved around her forehead slightly over her left eye, combined to give her the blissful aura associated with many subcontinent women.

"Hello." Resting to make eye contact, his interpersonal skills kicked-in. "Miss Govinda is it?"

"Indeed it is." She moved nearer. "How are you?"

"Oh, just about coping is the best phrase to describe it."

"Good. Best to retain a positive state of mind when recovering from an injury." Perched over him, she reminded Latham of Parvarti, the Hindu goddess of love and devotion and consort to the god Shiva. Years earlier, during a Dandridge marketing visit to New Delhi, his hosts had taken him to some Hindu temples, one containing a large statue of Parvarti. "To give you some idea of my role, I'm tasked with seeing to any family and social issues on behalf of patients."

"I see." Yielding a vigilant face, with kid gloves he investigated, "have you been told about how I came to be in hospital?"

"Merely that you were involved in an accident. The precise pretexts are immaterial. My only concern is seeing to your welfare." Peeking down at a suitcase she had brought with her; she then went into vocation mode. "Apparently, your personal items, including your suitcase did not survive the accident. The nursing staff supplied hospital patient support with your physical dimensions, and we put together some clothing and shoe-wear for you." Gaping down again, she specified, "they're in this suitcase. It's a bit battered, but you can have the case as well."

"Many thanks. Did my passport and wallet survive the accident? They were in the inside pocket of the suit jacket I had on."

"Yes. Both are a bit charred, and feasibly you will need to get the passport replaced back in England, but it should do to get you through passport control. Both are in the suitcase with other burnt at the edges personal items, travel documents and air tickets."

Ogling blankly at her, as if unsure what to say next, his normal congenial frame of mind nulled by a combination of recent events and strong pain killers prevented further dialogue.

Appreciating his dilemma, she took the initiative. "Do you have family?"

"Erm…yes," he hesitantly replied. "Two daughters, Nicol and Penny."

"And your wife?"

Latham's head fell to one side, the stir rekindling his neck discomfort. "My wife is no longer with us. She died some time ago."

"Ohh…" Realising she had committed an unintentional *faux pas*, her mouth dropped open. "I'm very sorry, Mister Latham. Nobody told me about your loss. If I had known, I'd have been more sensitive."

"It's quite alright, Miss Govinda. Nobody at the hospital has delved into my domestic status, apart from asking for the name of my next of kin. In my drowsy state, I must have told them Amelia Latham, neglecting to use her married surname, Ferraby. She is my elder sister, but they must have presumed she is my wife. Whilst I'm out of Blighty on business, Amelia and her husband Clement take care of Nicol and Penny."

"Nevertheless, I feel very bad about asking."

Empathetic to her embarrassment, Latham updated the conversation trajectory. "So, what services can you perform on my behalf?"

"Oh, communication with your family and employer. Tending to your recreational needs, and providing company when you need it."

"It all sounds very comprehensive."

"We do our best to assist our patients," she gaily replied, her sense of affinity sticking to Latham.

"Will you take a seat beside me?"

"Thank you."

She drew up the chair adjacent to Latham's bed. Whilst assuming the sitting position, momentarily her face came close to his, the bouquet of her perfume drifting into his nostrils manufacturing a pleasant sensation.

"May I ask you something?" he posed.

"Go ahead."

"You're not Pakistani, are you?"

She lowered her head, Latham immediately computing he had been indiscrete.

"My heritage is Indian."

"Yes, your name rather gives your ethnic identity away." Indecisive as to whether to pursue the line of inquiry, he dithered. Adopting a subtler tack, he then canvassed, "how do you come to be working in a Pakistani hospital?"

"Goodness me." She gulped. "The answer is very long and complicated."

~ * ~

Despite Churchill predicting a bloodbath of epic proportions, the partition of India into the sovereign states of the Dominion of Pakistan and the Union of India, later the Republic of India, began 15th August 1947, taking over ten years to complete. Riots preceding partition in the Punjab province resulted in over 2million people being killed in executes of retributive genocide by Muslim, Sikh and Hindu followers, the great stateman's portent proved right. Over 14 million people were displaced during the partition, forming the greatest mass movement in human history, Muslims fleeing to East and West Pakistan, Sikhs and Hindus heading for India. Partition lasted as the cause of much tension between Pakistan and India, their mutual nuclear arsenals facing off against each other, military skirmishes, standoffs and posturing, frequently taking place along the demarcation border lines.

In 1886, Chanda Govinda's great, great grandparents on her father's side had established a small farm at Shahdara on the outskirts of Lahore in Punjab. Over the succeeding decades and family generations, the farm had grown, the Govinda extended lineage enjoying an above average lifestyle on its' proceeds. Customarily a Hindu family, Chanda's grandparents had converted to Christianity in 1925, all their children baptised as Christians but given traditional Indian names. Chanda's father, Prasad, had married Lalita Joshi, an Indian Christian woman, their union producing five Christian offspring, also given conventional Indian names, counting the youngest daughter, Chanda, born in 1966.

Partition had fundamentally affected the Govindas when the Indians and the Pakistanis divided old Punjab into West Punjab in Pakistan, and Punjab, later East Punjab in India, Lahore in West Punjab. Though they knew Muslims deemed Hindus, Sikhs and Christians as infidels, not to be tolerated, howbeit, the Govinda clan refused to move to the newly created Union of India, and by default, forfeit their estate to Pakistan. Many of their family, interconnected by way of marriage and living in India, appealed to Prasad's father Dinesh not to be stubborn. Bolstered by Prasad and his other children, Dinesh did not relent. Despite the wholesale genocide between Pakistanis and Indians, they elected to stay on their farm and tough it out.

As the Dominion of Pakistan took root, intolerance of remaining native Indians and the tiny Christian community in the new state intensified, especially after Pakistan stationed itself an Islamic Republic in 1956. Many Hindu and Sikh Indians were killed by Muslims, or under intense pressure, fled to the Union of India.

Not immune from the carnage, in summer 1959 the Govindas came in for cruel treatment, Dinesh and four other family members murdered in an unprovoked attack whilst they worked the farm fields. Though Prasad recounted the barbarities to the Lahore police, little remedy eventuated, the culprits never apprehended. The atrocity and subsequent lack of police cognizance appalled Prasad, Lalita, their children, and Prasad's brothers and sisters and their families.

When Chanda came into the world, some of the Govinda family had finally relented, moving to the Republic of India after further family members had been murdered. Prasad, Lalita and their children endured. Then in 1972, Prasad went missing whilst in Lahore, in the long run, his mutilated body unearthed in a ditch.

~ * ~

Giving a potted reply to Latham, Chanda covered her family history, and how her current circumstances came about.

"After my father's death, my elder brothers and sisters joined a civil rights group. They campaigned for the human rights of ethnic and religious minorities in Pakistan, the authorities viewing the group at best with suspicion, and at worst with notions of sedition."

"How are your family nowadays?"

"Mahendra and Radjit, my two eldest brothers were jailed in 1979 on charges of sedition. When they were released in 1982, their families insisted on moving to India. My mother Lalita died the same year. Since, other family members embodying my two elder sisters and their families have fled to India."

"But you have stayed?"

"Yes," she validated, her manner resolute. "I am stubborn. When I turned 18, I joined the civil rights movement."

"What about your family farm?"

Shaking her head disconsolately, she acquainted, "as part of the penance apportioned to Mahendra and Radjit, the Pakistani administration confiscated our farm, handing ownership to a Muslim family."

"Did you receive any compensation?"

"Not a single rupee."

"I see," he accepted, fostering an attentive visage. "Where do you live now?"

"When they took the farm, the intermediaries allowed my family members to work the land for wages from the gifted owners, enabling us to rent a house in Lahore. But as others progressively left for India, I couldn't manage the rent with my limited earnings, so I moved to a small furnished apartment, not far from this hospital."

Frowning at the memoir and subconsciously jerking his head back, the pulled neck and facial muscles exertion inflamed his neck aggravation. "My god, what a bleak tale," he garbled, trying not to let his soreness effect his speech. "I'm very sorry about your problems and the tragedies hitting your family, Miss Govinda." Adopting a suitably grim carriage, he enquired, "how do you earn your income now?"

"At age five, my family sent me back to India for my formal education. My high school leaving certificate has enabled me to do some bookkeeping work for small firms and merchandising companies in Lahore. I also get a tiny payment from the Combined Military Hospital for my work as a patient support officer."

"I'm amazed an ethnic Indian is allowed to work here."

"Under the footing of partition, the Pakistani superintendency is obligated to endow hospital facilities for non-Muslims, incorporating Hindus and Christians. It is for these groups I am tasked with providing patient assistance. You being a Christian, is the key to why I've been assigned to you."

"The hospital admin presumed I'm a practicing Christian?"

"Yes."

"Aahh." Rolling his eyes upwards and to one side, Chanda anticipated sadness in the making. "Though my parents had me baptized by the Church of England, services never held any fascination for me," he explained, "whereas my wife, Fiona, practiced the precepts of Christianity daily. She saw the good in everybody. Only when I lost her, did I truly realise how special she had become to me. I loved her so much..." Opening his mouth involuntary, he exhaled sharply, his aura sinking into a tender palate. "...still do. Since the day she died, I've never entertained the whimsey of another liaison, let alone re-marriage. She left an impossible gap to fill. Oh—" He half-smiled. "Occasionally, I meet someone who might turn the tide, but invariably the fancy turns out to be a pipedream. In the cold light of day, I distinguish I can neither give my full love to another, nor impose a sham alliance on them."

"I'm sure your wife brought you immense joy."

"She did," he humbly replied, articulation of Fiona's demise making sentiment well up inside of him. Rarely did Latham mention his late wife in conversation, let alone share his agonies with a third party.

Regaining self-control, he identified, "you are the first Christian I've met in Pakistan. Is it true, behind the scenes, Christians are persecuted, victimised, and treated harshly?"

Chanda lowered her head again. "Yes. Like Hindus and Sikhs, Christians are marked for verbal and physical abuse by Muslims. If the police see it, they often turn a blind eye. Because Iraq has mainly been defeated by Christian forces, the persecution of Christians has worsened since the Gulf War."

"How do you cope with it?"

"Well, unsurprisingly—" She pressed her lips together, her despair obvious to Latham. "Unlike in England, there are no race relations laws to protect minorities from Muslim abuse in Pakistan. We have to grin and bear it."

~ * ~

When Chanda left, Latham mentally revisited what she had told him, before recapping on his own experiences in Muslim countries. Apart from a few open-minded and enlightened people like Ghulam Bishara, and he reckoned most of the officer corps, moderates were far and few between. Many people he had met in the civil public sphere had at best been brusque and condescending. Others he found to be vicious and totally intolerant of the non-Muslim world. Some in authority had even set about their own kind.

Reevaluating an altercation from his Dandridge days, when he visited Pakistan AFB Samungli near Quetta, before going on to meet Bishara at AVN Base Multan, the mull over made him shiver. Wanting to discuss avionics upgrades to their Dassault Mirage III reconnaissance and Mirage Five attack aircraft fleets, Group Captain Babar Nazari, his PAF contact at Samungli, fitted the intolerant bracket. As the pair walked from the base security entrance to join other air force officers in the meetings block, Latham caught sight of a warrant officer laying into a stood-to-attention aircraftman with a cane.

Stopping abruptly, he had barked, 'Is that absolutely necessary, Group Captain Nazari?' 'Mister Latham,' Nazari inflexibly retorted, 'you are here to tell us about how your company can improve the operational effectiveness of our Mirage fleet with an avionics upgrade, not interfere with how we deal with underperforming aircraftmen.' Latham boiled internally, but ever the diplomat and focused company appointee, refrained from contradicting Nazari's austere attitude to disciplining. Further exposure to Nazari over the course of the next two days confirmed him to be a sadistic character, charged with venom and capable of authorising or personally carrying out savage retaliation on airmen failing to meet his expectations.

Replaying what he had witnessed to Branden Godfrey, the then British High Commissioner at Islamabad, Godfrey reacted in general terms, indicating what happened in the Pakistan military not to be HMG's business, and Latham shouldn't discuss what he had seen with others. Appalled by the reproach, Latham objected, but ultimately obeyed the prescribed course of, make no waves.

On another instance in Karachi, he saw a crowd stone a woman for committing adultery, the ghastly spectacle sickening him to the point of retching. Savvy to the fact it'd be futile, he did not bother to inform the British Deputy High Commission.

Considering again what Chanda Govinda had told him about her family's tragic history at the hands of Muslims, on reflection, it should not have surprised him.

~ * ~

By the weekend, Latham sat up in bed during the day, the neck brace removed but his neck still buttressed by a collar. Surplus hurt from his body injuries had largely ceased, though much of his chest and left side tarried bruised. He made phone calls to Armstrong-Eliot Airborne Systems Group Managing Director, Matthew Chapman, and Amelia, telling them his health had improved and he'd be back in Blighty soon after receiving discharge from hospital.

Never one for idleness, he rapidly surrendered to boredom with reading material and watching the odd television broadcast in English. With a measure of mobility answering his cognitive commands, he gingerly attempted a few steps before a nurse reprimanded him, insisting he reverted to bed until Doctor Kassis said otherwise.

Champing at the bit, the next week brought a visit from the military police and the Punjab provincial police service. Kassis had kept them at bay until Latham travelled the road to physical recovery, and the dismay of hearing about the air crash fatalities and its immediate impact had waned.

As they sauntered into his room, Latham instantly twigged a discordance in the making.

"Mister Latham?"

"Yes."

"I'm Colonel Sharif with the Pakistan Army Corps Military Police." Twisting to face the officer by his side, he introduced, "and this is Chief Inspector Aman of the Lahore Police. We are investigating the air crash you were involved in."

Intrigued by the obvious impatience of the pair, Latham did a quick survey of his inquisitors. The tall, elegant, clean shaven Sharif had an academic way about him, more like a British air crash investigator than an archetypal, hard-nosed, military policeman. Inversely, Aman radiated austere Islamic red tape, his beard, piggy eyes set in an intransigent, bulbous face and stout build, giving the impression of absolute dedication to enforcing the law with extreme prejudice.

Of the same ilk as Ghulam Bishara, along the lines of being a family man with no strong religious convictions, after graduating from the University of Karachi with a degree in mechanical engineering in 1961, Danyal Sharif joined the Pakistan Army Corps of Engineers as an officer entrant. Initially responsible for dams, canals and flood protection when formed in 1947, at the entreatment of the military's top brass, an appended science and technology command to the Corps' remit enabled a means of lessening Pakistan's dependence on Western expertise, Sharif a contributing player to the cause.

After playing major roles in the Military Engineering Service and the Frontier Works Organisation, Sharif was assigned to the science and technology command, with special responsibility for airframe advancement. Seeking a new challenge, after 25 years of service, encompassing action in both the 1965 and 1971 Indo-Pakistani Wars, he transferred to the Pakistan Army Corps Military Police.

An altogether different beast, Khurshid Aman, the youngest of four offspring was born into a devout Islamic family with a Persian heritage, his father, Sardar, a staunch fundamentalist adhering to Sharia Law and instilling the doctrine into his brood. When Persian Prime Minister Mohammed Mosaddegh fell out of favour, becoming deposed in the 1953 *coup d'état*, Shah Mohammed Pahlavi increasingly employed an autocratic mode, sidelining Islamism in favour of further instituting the principles of a secular state. Appalled, Sardar moved his family to Lahore, Pakistan the same year, Khurshid born in 1954. Brought up on a diet of Islamic fundamentalism, a hatred of both the Shah and all non-believers, Khurshid adhered to his father's doctrine without exception. By his early teens, he had thoroughly immersed himself in the teachings of the Koran, his father befriending him with mullah zealots, intensifying the process. Khurshid wanted to be a cleric but the mullahs persuaded him he could better serve the Islamic cause by entering public service and working the establishment from within to help bring about a fundamentalist state. Age 16, he joined the police. A staunch bastion of Pakistani government law, his career briskly gained traction, enabling him to make his way up the ranks.

When radical Muslim cleric Ruhollah Khomeini came to power in 1979, instituting an Islamic Republic after Persia's Islamic Revolution, the Shah and his family fled to exile in Egypt. A grand day for the Aman family, Khurshid erected a large photograph of Khomeini in the family's house, hoping one day for a similar champion to rise in Pakistan, forcing the country in the same direction.

"The air crash," Latham reiterated. Wincing at the woeful remembrance, he squinted. "Perhaps, Colonel Sharif, we can start by you telling me what actually befell."

"Yes, certainly, but to begin with, can you tell us what you remember?"

Reluctance consuming him, Latham closed his eyes. "We were coming in for landing, the Puma hovering above the helicopter landing pad. Whilst talking to Captain Hakimi, sitting in the aisle-seat next to me, out of the corner of my right eye, I saw a flash from the ground. Then a thunderous resonance filled the passenger cabin, and something heavy hit me on the side of my head, knocking me out. The next thing I knew entailed staring at the sky and clocking some faces from the ground. So—" Opening his eyes, he peered at Sharif expectantly. "Can you fill in the missing detail?"

"Yes…," he uneasily responded, sensitive that putting Latham through an ordeal so soon after the blight might impact his recovery from the injuries he had sustained. "Emergency services resources were on the scene very speedily. After dowsing the smoldering wreckage with Halon, along with other survivors, they pulled you from the wreckage. It must have been their faces you saw."

"That flash," Latham interrupted, "it was a Stinger, wasn't it?"

"Possibly."

"But it didn't hit the fuel tank, did it?"

"No." Sharif balked at the grisly thought. "If it had, there'd have been no survivors. From witness statements' we have to-date, and the initial air accident investigation report substantiated on the wreckage, a surface-to-air missile hit the underside of the Puma and exploded, causing complete engine failure and partial loss of control. As you know, stored kinetic energy in the rotating rotor blades allows for a dead man's curve landing. Witnesses saw the pilot desperately trying to make a controlled landing from the hovering maneuver, but the stored energy soon exhausted, the aircraft crashing to the land, tail first, partially cushioning ground impact of the cabin and flight deck. It's the overriding fortuity why you and a few others survived. Those killed, died from collision impact breaking their necks, or from shrapnel when the surface-to-air missile exploded."

Sucking in breath at the severe conclusiveness of the statement, Latham adjudged, "so, I'm very lucky to be alive?"

"Indeed you are, Mister Latham," Sharif confirmed, venturing nearer to his bed. "It's very important for us to establish who fired the missile."

"I understand there is a fresh terrorist threat recently come to light called the Taliban. Could they have been the fountainhead of the attack?"

"Maybe, but there are other possibilities."

Stunned by the unforeseen assertion, Latham blurted, "you astonish me."

Coming into the fore of the debate, Aman steadfastly spelt out, "Mister Latham, you are in a part of the country heavily blighted by widespread violence in the partition of Pakistan and India, 47 years ago."

"The Punjab."

"Yes. Geographically speaking, we are in West Punjab. On the other side of the Pakistan-Indian border, less than 20 miles from Lahore, it is East Punjab. A legacy from partition, some Indians have refused to move to East Punjab." Stepping closer to the Englishman, Latham became mesmerised by Aman's doll-like, near-to black eyes, sensing immense vitriol existed behind his counterfeit cordial facade. "Some of the residual and their descendants are political activists in the drive for all of the Punjab to be Indian territory."

Dubious about the claim, Latham imparted a wary face in response.

Noting his skeptical decorum, Aman proclaimed, "we are aware of an underground crusade in East Punjab, dedicated to unifying all of Punjab under the Indian flag. Understood to be the Indian Punjab Reunification Movement, it has been in operation for at least 30 years and has agents and sympathisers here in West Punjab."

Electrified further by the assertion, Latham queried, "are you intimating, this so-called Indian Punjab Reunification Movement might have been responsible for bringing down the Pakistan Army Aviation Wing helicopter?"

"Until our research is concluded," Sharif neutrally circumscribed, "we are not ruling out any prospect."

"I am cognizant with the resentment on both sides of the Pakistan-India border, particularly in the Punjab," Latham propounded, "but I find it taxing to credit Indian reunification confederates in West Punjab were responsible for the attack on the Puma."

"We have it on good authority from the Intelligence Bureau, the Federal Investigation Agency, and undercover officers in the Punjab Police," Aman uncompromisingly stipulated, "elements from the PRM could have fired the surface-to-air missile."

Still unconvinced, Latham's problematic countenance expanded. "Mmmm, if I had to make a wager, I'd back the Taliban, or some other disenfranchised Muslim band of terrorists."

"Why?" Sharif asked.

"Because it is common gossip, such groups are funded by rich Muslims, many in Saudi, and dare I say it, the Iranian Government." He noticed Aman burn at the allegation, his eyes opening wide with acrid censure.

"True," Sharif certified, also drawing the evil eye from Aman, "but conversely, it is possible the PRM could be similarly funded by rich Indians, or the Indian Government."

"If it were so, your security agencies combining the Intelligence Bureau would have established the link long ago and threatened to expose the Indian Government to the UN." Fleetingly halting to collect more constructs, he then continued. "With respect, Colonel Sharif, you are making a futile attempt to cast blame on a very unlikely originator. I don't doubt there's an indigenous fringe element in the West Punjab Indian community, wanting to see the whole of Punjab under Indian control, but I can't see the level of such a campaign rising above local politics, protesting and minor civil disobedience. I've positively never heard of an act of terrorism enacted by the PRM."

"There is a first time for everything, Mister Latham," Aman resolutely upheld, "and rich Indians outside of the subcontinent might fund para-military sorties in West Punjab."

"I will admit, it is a possibility."

"Good. I'm glad to see you remain open-minded on this matter." His persistence increasing to cut to the chase, Aman took on a more presumptuous demeanour. "Tell me, did you inform anybody about the flight from Rawalpindi to Lahore?"

Unsure as to the context of the issue being put forward, Latham pursed his lips. "The evening before the flight, during a telecom, I did mention it to a colleague staying at the Avari Towers Hotel in Karachi."

"Did you use your mobile phone for the call?"

"No. Lieutenant Colonel Bishara, Head of Battlefield Surveillance Systems Directorate in Rawalpindi, advised me to use the landline from the JSHQ officers mess."

"I see. And what did you discuss with your colleague?"

Taking in the query's barely hidden syntax, Latham recoiled his head back. "Rendall Gilmour and I critiqued a meeting we had with senior army and navy officers at Pakistan Armed Forces Regional HQ Karachi, earlier in the day. You can't possibly think—"

Sharif cut him off. "No," he assured. "We checked out Mister Gilmour's landline calls from the Avari Towers Hotel where he stayed in Karachi, and his mobile calls. None were suspicious."

"So, huh…I can't believe I'm posing this. Are you theorising, the landlines into JSHQ are tapped?"

"Well, there is evidence to promote the notion." Sharif hunched his shoulders, as if accepting the practice without reservation. "Terrorists do listen for a convenience to enact carnage."

"Alternatively," Latham countered, "whoever fired the surface-to-air missile, might have been seeking a random opportunity to bring down a Pakistan Armed Forces helicopter."

"Granted. We also derived the same contingency."

Estimating his visitors had more on their minds than just examining him on the Puma destruction, Latham seeped into a tentative comportment. "Colonel Sharif, where is this line of examination leading?"

"Let me answer," Aman aggressively piped up. "Regardless of our attempts to limit exposure of the episode, the helicopter calamity has made international news. Unless we track down and deal with the culprits hotfoot, other anti-Pakistan elements might surmise there is a chink in our intelligence armour and exploit the imagined shortcoming to commit further terrorist crimes. We cannot allow such a circumstance to arise. It's paramount we demonstrate to the world that we're capable of catching terrorists, bringing them to trial, and executing the letter of the law as punishment."

After taking in the ambitious plan, Latham rationally advocated, "I don't see what else I can do to serve you in your quest."

"You are our only lead," Aman specified. "You are the out-of-the-ordinary conduit at both ends of that doomed flight."

"But there are other survivors from the attack. Why not interrogate them?"

"They are all military functionaries and have been thoroughly vetted. Though random by way of take-off times, the Rawalpindi to Lahore flight you were on, took place quite regularly." Unable to confine his xenophobia, he sneered. "But this is the foremost occasion the flight included a foreign civilian as a passenger."

"Sorry—" Inundated with ambiguity, Latham let out a slight chortle. "I'm not understanding this. What exactly are you driving at, Chief Inspector?"

"It is recognised, terrorist agents watch for foreign nationals at airports. Those collected by embassy cars are easily spotted and followed. You and Mister Gilmour could have been trailed and spied on while you were both at the Avari Towers Hotel, before your visit to Pakistan Armed Forces Regional HQ Karachi."

Flabbergasted by Aman's learning of his schedule, he gabbled, "it seems you've discovered everything about Mister Gilmour and me."

"We have, by validating your activities with Pakistan Armed Forces Regional HQ Karachi." Brooding, he hit Latham with a stern regard before continuing. "The terrorist web could then have monitored your passage all the way to Rawalpindi. They could even have seen you climb aboard the helicopter, shrewdly guessing its probable destination and contacting other terrorists in Lahore." Closing in on the patient, he leant over him. "From the prognostication, I'm sure you can work out the chain of following events."

Latham's incredulity heightened. "You are suggesting I constituted the target?"

"A Pakistani aircraft being downed with Pakistani military servicemen onboard is one thing. If the aircraft also contains a foreign national, clearly involved in military supplies, it is another."

"You mean—"

"I mean," Aman belligerently asserted, "it'd make good propaganda for any terrorist organisation to tell the world media they were responsible for the act of terrorism, fueled by a commitment to send a message to the West—" He lent further over the patient. "Don't sell arms to the Pakistani Government, or your military supplier representatives might end up as toast."

"It's a formidable message, Mister Latham," Sharif augmented, "and one we do not wish to see aired."

"But you said just a few moments ago, the helicopter drama has made international news."

"It has, but with no reference to a possible terrorist attack. And, the endorsed news announced by a Pakistan Government spokesman made no mention of you."

"You must surely have gathered both the British Deputy High Commission at Karachi and Armstrong-Eliot knew I travelled aboard the Puma?"

"Yes, but MI6 has requested them to stay quiet about it."

Aghast at the declaration, the mere mention of MI6 confounding him, Latham mumbled, "I see. So, you have all the angles covered to contain this thing?"

"Apart from the perpetrators access to the media," Sharif itemised. "However, let us assume they do not know your name, or managed to photograph you. If they do make a public statement before we apprehend them, both the Pakistan Government and the UK MoD will deny a British military contractor was aboard the aircraft. In an attempt to create fear, terrorist groups are always claiming one thing or another. If they do make a public statement, the world at large will see it as groundless pie in the sky."

Restoring his standing posture, Aman projected in an apparently unconcerned manner, "such an impasse then leads to the potentiality of your abduction by the terrorist group."

"To parade me in front of a camcorder," Latham jabbered, "and have me make a statement authenticating I journeyed aboard the Puma?"

"Precisely," Aman confirmed, completely ignoring the facetious sarcasm. "They'd send the tape to a friendly television news agency for broadcast."

Floored by Aman's fanciful perspicacity, Latham quivered his brow. "Accepting the terrorists' *modus operandi*, Chief Inspector, nonetheless, this all appears to be excessively far-fetched. You are building up the helicopter attack into a major security issue."

"It is speculation, Mister Latham," he credited, "but should you suddenly disappear from this hospital, and by the grace of Allah, we were to meet again, I'd hate to say, I told you so."

Aman's retort left Latham speechless, until his private room door opened, and Chanda Govinda stepped inside, diverting his gaze.

"Oh," she murmured, "I'm so sorry, I..." Her jaw dropped.

Sharif and Aman faced her.

Her wits returned. "Excuse me."

As the door slid shut against its closing spring, Aman voiced, "can you identify that woman, Mister Latham?"

"She's a member of hospital patient support staff."

Aman and Sharif exchanged sombre features.

Refacing Latham, Aman admonished, "she is also a suspected member of the Indian Punjab Reunification Movement." Conjuring up a vilifying face, he remarked, "she is not suitable company for you."

~ * ~

The following day, Bill Kimble took the early morning flight from Karachi to Lahore to visit Latham, on his arrival the patient relaying on his conversation with Colonel Sharif and Chief Inspector Aman.

"Sharif looms impartial and non-partisan," Latham gauged at the finish of his narration, "his military skillset imbuing him with a facility for coherent appraisal, but Aman definitely has an axe to grind. Founded on his bordering-on-aggressive stance, I got the overwhelming hunch he wants to nail a non-Pakistani for the terrorist offense."

"Yes, I must agree," Kimble grimly concurred, his mind kicking into the plausible reasons behind the full-frontal offence. "And the bold inference you could be abducted, does add weight to your suspicion." Dwelling, his bearing drooped into a prudent domain before he carefully chose his next words. "It's virtually tantamount to a threat."

"What do you make of it, Bill? Are they just trying to scare me, or is there some credence to the danger, and an as yet still to be identified bunch of terrorists will be coming for me?"

"Hhmmm. Westerner kidnapping in this part of the world is not unfamiliar," he articulated, his tenor academic leaving Latham dazed by the cold-blooded, near-to accepting reply. "You might recall, while trying to negotiate the release of among others, Brian Keenan and John McCarthy, Terry Waite got taken captive by the Islamic Jihad Organisation in 1987, and not liberated until 1991."

"Yes, I recollect the TV news feeds of his release." Latham grimaced, struck by the awakening of submitting to terrorist captivity for many a year. Irritably putting the vision to the back of his mind, he snapped, "what about the claim of a news blackout, regarding me being aboard the stricken Puma?"

"Oh it's perfectly true," Kimble established, his tone now back to measured. "The Pakistanis contacted British High Commissioner Augustus Dawson in Islamabad within an hour of the shoot-down. From there, the Foreign Office and MI6 got involved. They ensured the news from a Pakistan Government source, not mentioning a UK national boarding the helicopter, acted as the official press release. No television pictures or photographs of the crash site were published, just a verbal commentary on television, and only text in the newspapers."

"What about this perception categorising the PRM could be responsible for the Puma attack?"

"Highly unlikely, but we can't dismiss it until the actual violators are captured. HMG is still of the opinion the Taliban were responsible."

"Why are they so sure?" Latham shot back.

Kimble's review gathered pace. "The Taliban do not recognise secular and non-Islamic governments. Even pseudo-democratic Muslim states with Western connections are deemed to be unacceptable. For instance, Pakistan, and of course over 1,000 miles of north Pakistan borders with Afghanistan. Pivotal on the austere terrain, it is largely undefended. Many Taliban members are Pakistani Muslim extremists. There is much intelligence to suggest, even corroborate, the Taliban has clandestinely crossed into Pakistan, with the objective of creating mayhem and carnage."

"Leading to a popular Islamic fundamentalist uprising and deposing the government of President Khan and Prime Minister Bhutto."

"Quite. So you'll fathom the Taliban were the most likely generator of the surface-to-air attack."

"Mmmm, substantiates what I put forward to Sharif and Aman." Pondering for a few seconds, he confided, "I can only speculate as to what extent the PRM is a thorn in the side of the Pakistani authorities, but incontestably, Chief Inspector Aman is searching for an excuse to come down hard on Indians living in Pakistan. Indian Hindus, Sikhs and Christians only form about 2 per cent of the population, but in light of current unrest resultant from Operation Desert Storm, I get the distinct portent the Pakistanis prefer their number to be zero."

"Well, if the Taliban ever did prevail, those poor devils would not be long for this Earth."

"Again, I might be wrong, Bill—" He hesitated. "But over the years I've been doing transactions in Pakistan and India, there has been no forgive and forget attitude from the Pakistanis apropos partition, whereas Indians have come to terms with the carve up of the old India."

"Yes, you might be right. Currently, over 14 percent of India's population are Muslims, and on the whole, they are tolerated by the majority Hindus."

"I suppose it's down to the difference between the two religions. Hindus and Sikhs are passive, with no record of antagonism, let alone invasion and imposing their will on others in the shape of force and coercion, whereas Muslims have a long history of continuous aggression, barbarous works, and empire building."

"Yes, absolutely accurate. It could account for why Muslims have been accepted in India, and why Hindus and Christians are persecuted in Pakistan."

"Of course at the commercial level, I've detected the people I face off against are the same the world over, whether it's Europe, the Americas or Asia. There are physical differences, and a wide variety of accents and clothing attire, but they all speak English, and the business-to-business protocol etiquette remains universal. We rarely see their wider societies and populace characteristics."

"Your observation holds water. Anyway—" Wanting to keep concentration on the principle essence, Kimble adopted a pragmatic stance. "Enough philosophising, the matter lingers, what are we going to do about you?"

"How do you mean?"

"Well, Deputy High Commissioner Soames wants to get you back to Blighty *tout de suite*."

"You mean, he's concerned for my safety?"

"Partially, but it is more motivated by the need to show the Pakistanis a clean pair of heels in respect of yourself."

"I'm a political embarrassment?"

"I'd not go quite so far as that. It's more a matter of not leaving anything to chance. If there is the remotest potential you are in danger from whatever terrorist faction, HMG wants you out of the interdictor zone pronto. We don't want another hostage crisis arising."

"Kind of you to be stimulated by the right motivations," Latham mockingly retorted.

"Now don't go getting all precious, Dale. With your military credentials, embedding involvement in Foreign Office diplomacy, I'm sure you will savor we are both pawns in this scheme."

"Yes, you're quite right." Blowing out, he released pent up frustration. "Okay, I'll play the game."

Over the course of the next few days, Latham's recovery continued to progress, Doctor Kassis allowing him to take a few steps within his room, and later, up and down the corridor.

"If you continue to recover at this rate, Mister Latham, we can remove your stitches Monday next week, and after a few days convalescence, you should be fit enough to travel."

"*Ohh*…superb news, Doctor," Latham replied. "I started to go doolally being holed up in this room, but now I can see an end date to the recovery process, it puts me in the right frame of mind to endure the remainder."

Never one to hinder testing his limits, as soon as the stitches were removed, Latham began regaining motive action. Setting himself the goal of walking further session by session, four times a day, at the outset, he negotiated the matrix of corridors leading away from his room and the main wards, before venturing into the forecourt. As his wounds repaired and his leg muscles became used to working again, the odd twinges of pain sequent from the exercise decreased.

In his mind, he'd soon be back in Blighty.

Chapter 7: Confession

When Chanda Govinda next came to check on the patient, Latham perceived a change in her persona, the open body language she exuded on their previous meeting replaced by a withdrawn veneer.

"I'm so glad to see you again, Miss Govinda," he greeted in an up-tempo voice, attempting to stimulate her lighter shades.

"And I, you, Mister Latham," she echoed as best she could.

"Forgive me saying so, but you seem more than a little shaky today."

She put a finger to her mouth, denoting for Latham to remain quiet. Closing the door, she then went about the room, probing behind curtains, under the bed, and in the wardrobe and chest of drawers.

Standing by his bedside, she proclaimed, "it's okay, we have privacy."

"You were hunting for listening devices?"

"Yes." Still distrustful, she stared towards the door, as if half expecting unwelcome visitors. "You can't be too careful. The police and the Intelligence Bureau have spies and listening devices everywhere."

Staring towards his room window, a ghostly patina consumed her physiognomy. "I received a visit from the policeman questioning you the other week, when I excused myself."

"You mean, Chief Inspector Aman?"

"Yes. He wanted to know why I visited you. I told him my duties encompass attending to the needs of Christian patients." Facing him, she shared, "he has come to see me in a legitimate capacity before."

"Oh, I see," Latham mindfully drawled, not taken aback by the admission, her heritage making her a victim for Aman's evident dislike of Indians.

"The police keep a watch on people involved in civil rights. He interviewed me with reference to my position on the topic, reminding me my brothers had been jailed for acts of sedition against the State." Abjectly hunching her shoulders, she muttered, "I didn't argue the fact. As you English say, the agencies hold all the cards. They determine what is truth, as they see it."

"What else did he say to you?"

"Aman told me the police are investigating the air force base air crash. He intimated the administration suspect the PRM might be responsible for the incident, and the police visualise I am a member. He said my association in civil rights for ethnic Indians and Christians is a cover for working for the organisation." Her melancholia increasing, her face hung of her cheekbones like a contorted mask. "He confiscated my passport and I am virtually under house arrest. I'm only allowed out to perform my bookkeeping work and my patient support labours, and I'm banned from meeting with other Indian Christians and Hindus."

"But why, Chanda?" Faltering, he appreciated the over familiarity. "I can call you Chanda, can't I?"

"Of course. As I say, it's down to my family history of protesting about Indian maltreatment, and my affiliation with the civil rights group."

"Does this mean, you *are* a member of the PRM?"

"It is true to say, I have had some dealings with them, but I'm not a member." Ceasing, she fixed him earnestly, clearly about to declare a decisive observation. "I've put two and two together. You were involved in the air base crash, weren't you? That's how you came to be a patient at this hospital."

"Aren't you the clever girl." Deliberating, he goggled away. "Well, I fancy there's no profit in denying it."

"Can you tell me what happened?"

"Well—" He shillyshallied. "I assume, officially, it still remains classified."

"I promise, it will go no further."

"Okay. I travelled from Rawalpindi into the air force base at Lahore onboard a Pakistan Army Aviation Wing Puma. As it hovered above the designated landing site, a surface-to-air missile hit the helicopter. Out of the 10 passengers and three crew, only four others and I survived the attack." Wavering, his deportment fell into a dreamy condition. "You might not believe this, but when they pulled me from that stricken helicopter and injected pain killer into me, for the briefest of moments, I saw Fiona in the guise of an angel, looking down on me and smiling before she vanished, and I passed out. It was almost if she had been watching over me, pulled me from the burning wreck, made sure I was going to live, then ascended back to heaven." Re-consumed in the ethereal phantasm, he vacillated. "What do you think of that?"

"Oh I believe you. Since *time immemorial,* such near-to death symbiosis with religious lost love ones have been known to happen to those on the earthbound side of the equation. Count it as a blessing."

"I do. It's just…the visitation was so unexpected. I'm still trying to put the episode into perspective. Was it all in my flooded-with-emotional-images mind, brought on by latent stress, or did it really happen?"

"Best not to dwell on the matter and over-diagnose. Just accept it as a gift from heaven."

"Yes, I'm sure you're right. Anyway—" He gyrated his head. "Enough other-worldly whimsey…segueing into the now, you think Chief Inspector Aman detects the PRM are responsible?"

"He didn't say outrightly, but his line of review demonstrated he hoped the PRM were responsible, though he admitted his brief is to work in tandem with the Pakistan Army Corps Military Police to track down the actual culprits."

"Yes, I gathered the same understanding from Aman and Colonel Sharif of the Pakistan Army Corps Military Police, when they interviewed me about the tragedy."

"If it were true, and I contest it is, attributing the air disaster to the PRM contributes to the ammunition needed to round up all Indians for no telling what fate."

"You might be right. Conversely, the British reckon an evolving band of Islamic fundamentalists called the Taliban are more likely to be responsible. I also subscribe to this view. One of their ambitions is to create mayhem in Pakistan, leading to an overthrow of the Government."

"I have heard of the Taliban. They are brutal to both non-conforming Muslims and non-believers inclusive of Christians in Afghanistan." Reflecting on the budding threat, Chanda then revealed, "independent of what the joint investigation reveals, I have a horrible feeling Aman will see to it we are blamed."

"Well—" Fanning out his hands, he indicated commonality of notion. "Over the past week, I've been brooding if the Taliban were the perpetrators, they chose Lahore Pakistan AFB, calculating the PRM might be blamed. There are many Pakistan Armed Forces bases in the north of the country not far from the Afghanistan border, allowing an attacking force a fast getaway. Why heighten the risk of being caught by selecting a base nearly 300 miles from the border, unless, they had an ulterior incentive?"

"Yes, I see what you're driving at."

Hitting her with penetrating features, Latham petitioned, "so Chanda, what are you going to do about Chief Inspector Aman's focus on you?"

"It's what has got me so down." Puckering her lips, her perplexity took an upwards stride. "I just can't be certain."

~ * ~

Several days came and went, Latham's recuperation continual, his strength restoring. After his stitches were removed, Doctor Kassis allowed him free passage throughout the entire hospital and its grounds, to foster revitalisation of his walking motion. On returning to his room, primarily he experienced wobbliness consequent from the extended workout, but his body soon came to terms with the load and he remastered normal walking.

Neither Colonel Sharif nor Chief Inspector Aman revisited him, though he did get the odd sign of being watched while he walked in and out the hospital grounds. Dismissing Aman's conjecture regarding terrorists could abduct him as a tilt at trying to frighten him, he rounded out if anyone watched him, it'd be an undercover policeman.

Finally, Kassis pronounced him fit to travel and arrangements were made for Kimble to come up to Lahore again to escort him back to Karachi. So as not to over exert himself, Kassis suggested he rested up for one day at the Avari Towers Hotel, before Kimble put him on a British Airways flight to Blighty.

A few days prior to the commercial attaché's scheduled arrival in Lahore, Chanda Govinda came to see him again, Latham at once noticing she projected an even more distraught phiz than on the previous instance she had visited him.

Sensitive to her predicament, he softly implored, "whatever is the matter, Chanda?"

Ruffled and forlorn, her head slumped down. "Chief Inspector Aman came to my apartment again. He made it very succinct, he wanted the names and addresses of PRM members from me." Her voice tottering, she lingered gaping at him. "I have 48 hours to give him what he wants, or steps will be taken to detain me for further inquisition…and you know what that means."

"Yes, I do."

"Dale, I've been strong for such a long time, but I'm not sure how I'd stand up to intense interrogation." She sat on the side of his bed, her poise near to frantic. "After the atrocities perpetrated against my family, my father and my brothers in particular, I couldn't live with myself if I betrayed fellow Indians, many of them Christian. But—" Her face amassed in turmoil, she assigned, "since Aman took my passport away, I can't cross the border legally."

"I see," he acknowledged. "So what do you have in mind?"

"Regrettably, I have no choice but to leave for East Punjab. I have a cousin on my mother's side of the family living at Amritsar, about 15 miles due east of the Pakistan-India border at Wagha." Her distress worsening, fretfulness overtook her. She knew she had to take a chance with him. "I appreciate we only met a few days ago," she uttered, "and it's a lot to ask, but I need your help to get me across the border?"

Swinging his legs of his bed, Latham walked to the ground floor room's window, browsing the hospital courtyard and grounds, as if caught in the throes of a major turning point in his life. Since Fiona's death, he had promised himself, in honour of her Christian beliefs, he'd favour anyone needing his assistance. The right circumstances to fulfil the pledge had never come about, but now, an unexpected juncture presented itself to deliver on the commitment.

Facing Chanda, he solicited, "can you get a map of the area?"

"There are maps in the hospital library." Catching on, her mood up-shifted into buoyant. "Give me five minutes and I'll be back."

In her absence, Latham meditated about his intended exploit again. He had no wish to orphan Nicol and Penny, but the more he crunched it, the more he wanted to help Chanda, thereby fulfilling his self-made pledge. Such an opportunity might never arise again.

When Chanda backtracked with the map, Latham noted glumness had overtaken her again. "What is it now?"

"On my way to the library, your daughters came into my mind. Suddenly, I strongly comprehended I will be putting you at risk."

"You must be clairvoyant. They percolated into my abstraction whilst you were away." Smiling at her, he encouraged, "let's take a gander at the map before we weigh up the risk angle."

Heartened by his positivism, Chanda spread an ordnance survey map of Lahore and the surrounding area for up to 50 miles on the bed.

"The official border crossing place is at Wagha, about 15 miles from the outskirts of Lahore."

"I see." Pouring over the map north and south of Wagha, Latham queried, "are you *au fait* with the areas either side of Wagha?"

"Yes. The whole zone is known as the Lahore Basin, comprising of small villages, farms and scrubland."

"What about the fence line?"

"Two 15-feet high, barbwire fences, about 8 feet apart, with concrete stanchions set in concrete bases, and coiled barbwire in the central reservation between the two fence lines. Floodlights are on both sides of the border."

"Are the fences electrified?"

"No."

"How far apart are the floodlights?"

She dwelt. "If memory serves, one about every 100 yards, on both sides of the border, mounted immediately next to the fence."

"Are there any blind spots on the fence line, where floodlight beams do not brighten the entire fence?"

"I'm afraid not."

"Any surveillance cameras?"

"No."

"Good. Thank God for that blessing. What about guard towers?"

"There are none, but armed mobile units patrol both sides of the border in light-armoured vehicles."

"Mmmm…might offer an escape option." He perused the map again. "How often does the Pakistani border unit patrol the fence line on the south side of Wagha?"

"Once an hour, 24 by seven. Same as for the north side."

"And I take it the Indians also patrol the fence at the same frequency?"

"They do, but not at the same start time. It's staggered by about 5 minutes."

Frowning, he remarked, "you're very well-read about the border security arrangements."

Her mouth opened slightly, her awkwardness patent. "In my heart of hearts, I could see this situation arising long ago."

"Why?"

"Contingent on my family's history, the authorities will not be satisfied until all the Govindas have been removed from Pakistani society. It's why Aman is so hot on my tail, chasing for any excuse to imprison me. Accordingly, I made it my purpose to familiarize myself with the border security in the Lahore Basin."

Latham scanned the map. "I'm seeking somewhere quiet, where the adjacent road is at least a quarter mile from the fence line, and the fence is well away from residences and farmhouses, and preferably with a tree line next to the fence line."

Chanda signified a locale about 8 miles south of Wagha. "Here at Jattanwali there is open country and a tree line, but it runs parallel with the road on its west side, so a passing Pakistani patrol vehicle can still see the fence line with binoculars."

"Presumably, the patrol vehicles are based at the Wagha border crossing?"

"Yes."

Cogitating, he performed a nimble mental calculation. "Assuming an average speed of 40 mph, a patrol will take 12 minutes to reach Jattanwali, aggregating a there and back total of 24 minutes, and leaving 36 minutes for the remainder of the patrol, computed on an hourly rate. Mmmm." Pensively he advised, "we had better belt and brace it, to ensure precisely how much time we have. We'd need to time how long the patrol takes from Jattanwali heading south, to when it passes Jattanwali heading back north to Wagha. The interval will determine how much time we have to complete the caper, without being discovered by either the Pakistani or Indian patrols."

Standing to his full height and narrowing his eyes, he ruminated on the objective. "Regarding the crossover itself, there isn't sufficient time to dig under the fence line and going over the top is too complex. Cutting the fence is our only practical alternative. Do you have any industrial strength wire cutters?"

"Phew!" Her intonation surged into upbeat. "I have *many* tools left over from the farm, wire cutters with 30-inch long handles amongst them."

"They will do nicely. I'll also need some workman's gloves. Having twigged you have probably escaped, I don't want to give the police a head-start with fingerprints when they eventually rummage your apartment."

"I also have workman's gloves in the farm tool bag."

"Good." After making inward consideration again, he submitted, "we'll have to launch the escape late in the evening under cover of darkness, and when the area is quiet. Pakistan Army ground forces don't have night-vision infrared goggles as yet, so we'd be safe from them sensing our body heat signatures. Moreover, we'd need to find an out-of-

Clive Radford

direct, line of sight place to hide, not far from the fence, should the need arise."

Studying the Jattanwali area again, he denoted a potential escape spot. "The road is parallel to the fence and about a quarter mile from the fence line here." Pausing, imaginable conflict gripped him. "Do the patrol vehicles ever go cross-country?"

"Only when they see someone by the fence."

"Good. Do you have some binoculars and a car?"

"Yes. The binoculars are from the 1950s and belonged to my father. I also have a 22-years-old Hillman Avenger. It acted as the family car."

"Is it still serviceable?"

"Oh yes, I use it occasionally."

"Right. Here's what we're going to do. This evening, when the hospital night staff come on, I'll climb out of my room window and walk to your apartment. Where is it by the way?"

"Not far, just two blocks away at 2 Imtiaz Shaheed Road."

"We'll take your car and drive to Jattanwali. I'll cut the fence wires, and you can escape into East Punjab."

"Ohh—" She beamed and grasped his hand. "Absolutely fine, Dale. I will walk to Bharopal and wait in the bus station for the bus service to Amritsar to start the next morning."

"You won't be able to take much with you, just a suitcase."

"I've been taking family possessions across the border at Wagha to my cousin Vasanta's house in Amritsar for years. After the farm confiscation, I didn't take any chances with the remaining family possessions. All I have in my apartment are my clothes and a few personal items. They will fit into one suitcase."

"Okay, the subterfuge needs to be persisted for as long as possible. Now—" As he pondered further, he tapped his bedside table with a finger as if it increased his absorption. "You don't come to the hospital every day, do you?"

"No. Just a few times a week, when my bookkeeping permits."

"So you will not be missed tomorrow?"

"No. My next scheduled visit to the hospital is the day after."

"Right, it gives a promising 48-hour window before anybody realises you are missing. From my angle, someone from the Karachi British Deputy High Commission is coming to collect me tomorrow for onwards journey back to England, so I will be long gone from Lahore before Chief Inspector Aman starts his inquest into your disappearance." Ruminating on the plan, he analysed the pros and cons. "To double the guarantee of the deception, when I come back to Lahore from Jattanwali, I will park your car wherever it is now, then go inside your apartment to return the car keys."

"Okay," she replied, excitement written into her features. "I'll leave the door on the latch when we go, but I'll take the house key with me."

"Good. So if anyone subsequently enters your apartment, they will find the car keys, and with the car outside, deduce you are out doing your bookkeeping work."

"Yes, sounds plausible." Her positivity grew. "Oh, do you *really* think we can pull it off, Dale?" she crooned.

"If we get the right breaks, yes."

"I do hope so."

"Right, Chanda," Latham assertively began, wanting to demonstrate leadership and instil belief in her, "put the map back where you found it and expect a knock on your apartment door at ten pm."

Chapter 8: Jattanwali

Like clockwork, the hospital staff made their final visit to Latham's room at 09:30 pm. He let a few moments go by, then dressed, climbed out of the window, and crept along the side of the hospital block building towards the open courtyard area he walked during the day.

Perusing left and right, he made sure no one else loitered about, then made his way around the courtyard periphery to the exit leading to Abdul Rehman Road. Converging on the road, he picked up on Lahore nightlife clamour; people chatting as they made their way up and down busy streets to restaurants and meeting venues, the rumble of motorised traffic mixed in with the clanking of donkey-driven carts, and the background hum of transitory vehicles on the Canal Bank Road dual-carriageway, Lahore's main crosstown traffic highway.

Proceeding east, he soon saw an Imtiaz Shaheed Road street sign affixed to the wall of an apartment block. Turning north, he logged number 2 as the starting apartment block on the left-hand side. To its front, a long line of parked cars evanesced away into the distance, counting a bronze Hillman Avenger with a black vinyl roof, no more than 20 yards from the apartment block. Cautiously edging on, he rang the bell to the ground floor apartment, Chanda opening its front door within seconds and ushering him inside.

Distinctly disturbed about something, she bored into Latham's eyes.

"What is it?"

"In my push to escape Aman's clutches, I didn't consider how dangerous this could be for you, and...your daughters have crept back into my mind." Standing very close to him and staring up into his eyes, she canvassed, "Dale, why are you doing this? You hardly know me."

"Let's just call it Christian charity."

"But—" Her woeful dial changed to perplexed before relaxing. "Oh, your wife."

"After Fiona's demise, I've always promised myself if the opportunity arose, in her honour I'd lend a hand to a Christian in distress, distinguishing she'd have done the same thing." Not wanting his charge to be downhearted during the escape escapade, impairing her determination to succeed, in a methodical manner he asked, "have you got the wire cutters and the rest of the gear?"

"Yes." She reached down to her already packed suitcase, picking up the wire cutters along with the binoculars and workman's gloves off the top of it.

"Good. I'd better put on the workman's gloves now." Delivering an emphatic dial, he beckoned, "come on, let's go. I'll drive, you direct."

As they moved to depart, Chanda stopped abruptly and turned back drawing his concentration. "It has just struck me. This will be the last time I ever see this place. It's a strange vibe, marking the end of my life in Pakistan."

Latham placed a comforting hand on her shoulder. "Be optimistic. A new life awaits you in India, free from being spied upon and hounded by Chief Inspector Aman."

"Yes, of course."

He smiled at her. "Come on."

~ * ~

Joining traffic heading to the east of central Lahore, the Avenger seamlessly melded into a procession of vehicles, before ultimately heading down Barki Road, leading southeast out of the city, and into the Lahore Basin. At Durgpura, Chanda directed Latham to turn left for the outlying villages of Padri and Manhala, before going on to Jattanwali. By 11:30 pm, Latham had parked the Avenger on the east side of Jattanwali, not far from the road running parallel to the fence.

Scrutinizing the area between the Avenger and the fence line through the binoculars, the formidable immensity of the construction dazzled him. Sure enough, as Chanda had outlined, stand-mounted arc lights on the Pakistani side, adjusted to face down, lit up the fence line. In-between, the scrubland and farm fields resembled a near to flat orientation, with only the odd overgrown bush offering a limited degree of hiding cover.

"Right," he began, "with little obvious cover, we'll have to oversee timings for the patrols on both sides of the border very precisely, before going forward to the fence line."

"It's much flatter than I remember," Chanda volunteered, "the scrubland had more bushes on the prior occasion I visited this area."

"Landscapes change over the seasons. Never mind. It makes little difference anyway. Time to get invisible."

Driving the Avenger behind a farm building, he ensured they still had a good panorama of the road in both directions. Fortunately, the pair did not have to wait long until the distant racket of a heavy vehicle rumbling along the road from the north, attracted their hearing. An instant afterwards, a Pakistan Armed Forces light-armoured vehicle slid by, heading south. Latham's watch read 11:46 pm.

After five minutes of vigilance, they then saw an Indian army light-armoured vehicle heading south on the other side of the fence line. At 00:22 am, the Pakistani vehicle reappeared, heading back north to Wagha, the Indian vehicle reemerging five minutes later.

"Evidently, my calculation works out correct. We have about 36 minutes to cut the fences, get you to the Indian side, and me to reach the car, before the Pakistani patrol arrives back in this area. As soon as the next patrol passes heading south, we'll make for the fence."

A tension-filled interval elapsed before the southbound Pakistan Armed Forces vehicle next passed the concealed Avenger. Latham peeked left and right to ensure the immediate area tarried clear, then checked his watch. It read 00:47 am. "Okay, let's get on with it," he instructed.

Rushing to the fence line, Latham with the wire cutters and binoculars, Chanda carrying her suitcase, the pair tried to keep a low profile, so as not to unnecessarily advertise their presence, should anyone be watching from nearby farm buildings.

"Ye *gods*, I felt that," Latham disclosed as they crouched down midway between two concrete stanchions. "It's the first time I've run since beginning my recuperation."

"Are you okay?"

"Just a little stiff, but it will pass."

He went to work on the Pakistani fence line, cutting a gateway hinged at the side, and large enough for him to slither through. Edging into the central reservation, he cut the coiled barbed wire, pushing it aside in both directions. Crawling onto the Indian side, he cut the fence, again hinging it at the side. Signaling to Chanda, she jostled her suitcase into the passage he had created, Latham furthering the action, by pushing it through the hole on the Indian side. Lastly, Chanda wriggled into the opening, joining Latham in the central reservation.

"I owe you my life, Dale."

"Just drop me a line, care of Armstrong-Eliot, when you are safe with your cousin."

She threw her arms around his neck and hugged him, Latham reciprocating the gesture.

"Thank you, so much," she whispered, her eyes blooming with both gratitude and nervousness.

"You're welcome, Chanda. Try to keep your head down as you scoot for cover. When you are sure you have the area to yourself, make for Bharopal, and don't look back."

"Goodbye, Dale."

"Good luck."

Crouching further down, Chanda crossed into the Indian side of the fence line, picked up her suitcase and quickly scurried to some bushes a short distance away, Latham watching her movement. Peering over the frontier, she made sure no one dawdled about, waved back to her saviour, then dissolved out of his line of sight.

Breathing a sigh of relief, Latham lashed up the fence on the Indian side as best he could, pulled the coiled barbed wire together to give the impression it remained unbroken, then after clambering back to the

Pakistani side, made good the fence. His watch read 01:13 am. He had 10 minutes to cross the scrubland and the road before reaching the Avenger and driving off, before the Pakistani patrol resurfaced heading back north.

Spying in both directions to make sure the road remained clear, he grabbed the wire cutters and the binoculars, before assuming a semi-crouched down position, and hurrying back towards the road. He had made it halfway across when he saw a man walking along the road heading south. Throwing himself flat, he monitored the man with the binoculars. *Likely a farm worker,* Latham thought, *going home after perhaps visiting relatives in Jattanwali.* Humming to himself, apparently altogether consumed in his own world, the man did not bother to glance to his left at the fence line.

When he had totally evaporated, Latham started to move again, only to hear the rattle and clang of a vehicle coming up the road from the south. It had to be the Pakistan Armed Forces patrol! Estimating it to be a quarter mile away, he reckoned he had insufficient time to make it back to the Avenger before the vehicle's headlights illuminated him. To his left, a small mound materialised. He decided to take refuge behind it, let the patrol pass, then proceed on. Pressing his body shape into the mound, he saw the vehicle's headlights revealing the area between the fence line and road. Wedging himself further into the hiding retreat, he hoped he had made the cut fences and coiled barbwire refurbishment sufficiently secure, so as not to draw the patrol's attention. Continuing to approach, its engine noise remained constant, evincing it did not decelerate. As the vehicle came level with Latham's concealment point, the noise volume attained maximum amplitude, then decayed as it headed north for Wagha.

Keeping an eye on the fading vehicle, he got up and ran. Much to his surprise, just before reaching the road, the farm worker he had seen only minutes earlier, came out from along a tiny pathway not far from the Avenger, instantly clocking him.

Coming to a shuddering halt the man gawked at him, elevated his right arm and motioned accusingly, before shouting something in Urdu. Running up the road after the patrol vehicle, he gesticulated and yelled again. Latham rushed on, jumped into the Avenger, and executed an agile three-point turn, aiming the car back along the lane he and Chanda had used earlier to reach their checkpoint. In his rearview mirror, he saw the Pakistani patrol vehicle reversing back up the road, the farm worker jumping up and down encouraging it to hurry.

Chapter 9: The Chase

Flooring the Avenger's accelerator pedal, Latham headed for Manhala, the narrow lanes connecting outlying villages in the Lahore Basin proving difficult to negotiate at speed in a car with soft suspension and slender tyres. In his rearview mirror, he glimpsed headlights about a mile behind. As the lane veered to the left, before he near-to flew over a small canal bridge and picked up Manhala Road, he lost sight of the following headlights. Passing through Manhala at speed, a few people by the side of the road were lured by the howl of the Avenger hurtling by, then trained on its diminishing exhaust drone as it melted into the distance. He wondered if they had noted the car's registration number, and consequently the pursuing patrol stopping to ask about the identification. Worse, had the farm worker recorded the number!? Either enabled tracking of its owner's address, culminating in the patrol calling ahead to the Lahore Police, and a reception committee awaiting him back at Chanda's apartment.

To obviate the possibility, on the north-west side of Manhala, Latham accelerated to 85 mph, the Avenger straining under his demand. Keeping an eye on his rearview mirror, hearteningly, no impending headlights came into view. Passing a road sign annunciating, Central Lahore 7 miles, he knew to return the way they came, he should turn left of Manhala Road into a maze of lanes and hamlets to come out onto Barki Road at Durgpura. With his heart thumping like a hammer and sweat dripping of his face, he calculated under the stress of evading his followers, he might crash the Avenger, or lose his way. Neglecting the inverse course downside, he carried on, hoping further Central Lahore signs were posted along the route.

On the north side of Wara Sitar, Manhala Road became Jallo Road at the Bedian Canal. Taking another peep in his rearview mirror, under the dingy night sky in the far distance, he saw headlights on full beam reflecting off small buildings back in Wara Sitar. Pressing on, he reduced speed at Jallo, allowing him to take in the Lahore road signs directing him north. Ditching the reciprocal return route, instead he turned left onto Canal Bank Road, leading into central Lahore. In-line with other vehicles, he raised the Avenger's speed to 70mph. Further along the main trunk road, he avalanched into a perturbed state when traffic buildup reduced speed to 40 mph at the Lahore Ring Road, supposing the following vehicle continuing at high speed, its lights flashing to clear a path.

His rearview mirror had been filled with vehicle headlights since joining the trunk road. He figured if the patrol still pursued him, red and blue warning lights would be flashing on the vehicle, but apart from white lights he saw nothing else. Had he lost them in Jallo? Nearing the junction of Shalimar Link Road, he saw a road sign for the Combined Military Hospital, and turned due south onto the link road, the hubbub of the trunk road traffic waning behind him. Heading south at reduced speed in a local sleeping residential area, he turned right onto Abdul Rehman Road, familiarity with the location easing his anxiety.

Gradually edging the Avenger to the junction with Imtiaz Shaheed Road, he spied about for police cars, but all endured quiet. Maybe he had been over-cautious about the car number plate being taken by the farm worker and Manhala residents, and thereafter the Pakistani Army border patrol vehicle liaising with the Lahore police to apprehend him on his return to Chanda's apartment?

Little by little, he drove slowly past 2 Imtiaz Shaheed Road searching for signs of anyone hiding in the vicinity. Fortunately, it appeared to be clear. Parking the Avenger in an open spot, he turned off the engine, opened the driver door, and listened. Immediately, he heard chirping bush crickets and backdrop traffic noises in the distance, but nothing else. He licked his lips trying to find moisture, but his mouth had long dried resultant from intense stress generated during the white-knuckle ride journey. Surveying in all directions again, he made sure of his isolation, grabbed the wire cutters and the binoculars, eased himself out of the driving seat, gently closed the car door and locked the vehicle. Maintaining vigilance, he walked to Chanda's apartment, the front door still on its latch.

Inside, he placed the car keys where Chanda kept them and removed the workman's gloves. Using his handkerchief to avoid fingerprints, he put the wire cutters, binoculars and gloves in the tool bag, stuffed it in a cupboard, took a definitive inspection to make sure no proof of him being there lingered, then left the apartment after releasing the latch with his handkerchief-covered hand.

Auditing his wrist watch, the hands indicated 02:42 am. Still plenty of time to meander to his hospital room, well before the nursing day shift came on at 06:00 am.

Sustaining caution, he edged along deserted Abdul Rehman Road, and into the grounds of the Combined Military Hospital, keeping a watch out for hospital night staff. On reaching the window to his room, he heard the wailing of a siren advancing into the area. Rapidly climbing back through the window and listening, the siren reached maximum pitch as it passed the hospital before declining, then ceased completely.

Taking off his day clothes, he hung them in the wardrobe, showered in the room en suite, put on his night robe, and got into bed, his mind racing about the siren screech arresting further down Abdul Rehman Road, about opposite Imtiaz Shaheed Road. Had he been right about the patrol contacting the Lahore Police after all, and they were breaking into Chanda's apartment?

~ * ~

Managing to drop off after a while via a combination of exhaustion from the escape caper and taking a couple of sleeping pills, he descended into a dream state, headlights following his every move, his fleeing from their unremitting glare getting ever closer, the spectre seeming to engulf him as he tried in vain to evade its grasp. Sometime down the line, he drifted out of the chimera hallucination, his awake sensations signalling someone pushed his shoulder. Squinting his eyes open momentarily, Chief Inspector Aman accompanied by three other police officers took form.

"Wake up, Mister Latham. We need to ask you some questions."

As his eyesight blossomed firmly open, Latham registered electric light illumination, howbeit darkness still reigned outside visible through a gap in the window curtains. Scanning further into the depth of the room, he saw a night nurse standing in the doorway with a hand across her face trying to hide her flowering trepidation.

Grimacing, he asked, "what is it?"

"Please lever yourself up into the sitting position," Aman requested.

As he did so, he tried to comprehensively engage his thought processes to combat what he knew to be coming next. At once, he sussed the plan he'd made with Chanda, including a 48-hour window for him to travel to Blighty before the police raided her apartment was fatally flawed.

"Mister Latham," Aman pressured, "did you leave your room yesterday evening?"

Realising he had to play it fast and loose to avoid the police chief catching him out, he calmly answered, "I've been here since the hospital night staff came on at nine-thirty."

"I see." Pulling at his beard with his right hand, whilst resting his right elbow in his left hand, Aman moved nearer. "A few hours ago, an incident took place at the border." Eyeing Latham intensely, the Englishman abided expressionless, his RAF anti-interrogation preparation coming to the fore.

~ * ~

Aircrew always stood the chance of being shot down over hostile territory. If they survived the ordeal, capture by enemy forces blossomed as almost inevitable. A treasured resource for learning about in-theatre RAF deployments, numbers strength, and order of battle intentions, captured airmen were seen by the enemy as fair game for protracted grilling to the foreshadow of death.

Holding out against physical and mental torture had been part of Latham's RAF training, an aspect never logging in his mind when the notion arose to join the service.

Born 26th September 1950, young Dale grew up with his elder sister Amelia at Cheadle Hulme, their parents detached house and its large back garden providing an Aladdin's Cave adventure playground for them to fashion and fly paper airplanes. The grounding led to Dale constructing a few radio-controlled model aircraft, his father and himself flying them at Bruntwood Park. His fascination with flight burgeoned further after his parents took their children to the 1964 Farnborough Air Show. Leaving Dale breathless, the magnificent sights and high-tech sounds of airborne aircraft, noticeably the RAF English Electric Lightning supersonic interceptor, stayed in the forefront of his mind. Back at Cheadle Hulme, he told his family after schooling he wanted to join the Royal Air Force, the unequivocal resolution in his ambition amazing them.

Educated at Manchester Grammar School, he left with six O Levels and three A Levels, joining the RAF, 1st September 1969 as a flying officer candidate. Graduating from Royal Air Force College Cranwell, May 1970, Pilot Officer Dale Latham was assigned to 4 Squadron RAF Wittering, piloting Harrier GR1s before the squadron moved to Widenrath, West Germany. Promoted to Flying Officer, December 1970, Flight Lieutenant, February 1972, and Squadron Leader in August 1974, he looked set for an exceptional flying career. Assigned to 41 Squadron RAF Coltishall, September 1975, he took charge of a Jaguar squadron, advancement to Wing Commander in the coming July 1979. April 1980 saw Latham assigned to 2 Squadron RAF Marham, commanding a Tornado GR1 wing, before the wing became based at RAF Lossiemouth.

During his stint with the RAF, he had been subject to anti-interrogation drilling on multiple occasions. One extremely daunting experience occurred out of the blue at Widenrath. Off-duty, he had gone into Monchengladbach with fellow air crew to relax in a bierkeller frequented by many British Armed Forces personnel on secondment in West Germany.

Going outside to take a breath of fresh air, three men dressed in long coats and wearing face masks seized him, bundled him into the back of a car at gunpoint, and blindfolded him. Picking up on his sleeve being rolled up and a needle plunging into his arm, he then blacked out. When he regained consciousness, he found himself tied to a chair in a room without windows, and two high-intensity lights trained on his face. Still donning masks, his assailants proceeded to pump him about 4 Squadron, and the Harrier GR1 jump-jet, a unique flight platform. Their Eastern European accents suggested he had been abducted by Warsaw Pact agents and resided on the other side of the Iron Curtain. Roughing him up and slapping him around, his instruction came into play, Latham stubbornly refusing to cooperate with his examiners. Blanking his mind of the intelligence they sought, instead, he conjured up a brick wall to focus his concentration on. Infuriated by his stubbornness, their persecution resulted in multiple facial cuts and bruises, but still he remained tightlipped.

The third degree worsened, Latham subordinated to simulated drowning by covering his face with a towel and pouring water over it. Still non-responsive to his inquisitors' probing, in reply, he only gave his name, rank and serial number. Relentlessly going on for two days, Latham held out, refusing to provide details of squadron operational sorties and the secrets of the Harrier. In the end, the dominant assailant pointed a gun at his head, telling him if he still refused to cooperate, he'd be executed. Shaking his head and closing his eyes, he concurrently heard the gun's trigger mechanism cocking, and firing, the closeness of the volley's crack ringing in his ears.

When he opened his eyes, the antagonists had taken off their masks. A door opened and a smiling RAF officer breezed in. The whole thing had been a staged simulation. He had never left Monchengladbach. Though he passed the test with flying colours, it left an everlasting mark on him. He hoped he'd never have to cope with such a dehumanising challenge again.

~ * ~

"We understand from the Pakistan Army Frontier Force Regiment," Aman continued, "one of their border patrols confronted a violation in the Lahore Basin adjacent to the border fence line at Jattanwali, during the early hours of today. A local farm worker saw a white man running away from the fence line, just after a patrol unit went by. When he shouted for the patrol to stop, the white man drove away in an unidentified car. The patrol raced after the car but lost it on the outskirts of East Lahore." Pausing the bulletin, he ogled Latham again, the Englishman nourishing his poker face. "When the patrol returned to Jattanwali, they inspected the fence line opposite to where the white man had been seen. It had been cut on both sides of the border. The central reservation coiled barbwire had also been cut." Edging towards the window, he drew back the curtain slightly then replaced it, as if verifying some channel with which to confront the suspect. Refacing Latham, an accusing sulk blazing in his physiognomy, he strode purposely towards him. "Whoever did it had been careful to conceal the cuts by splicing together both the barbwire and the two fence lines. It is transparent to us, someone, or a number of people, escaped from the Pakistan side of the border into India, and the white man aided their escape."

"This is all very fascinating, Chief Inspector Aman, but I fail to see what it has got to do with me."

"Let me finish the story, Mister Latham." Grinning menacingly, his posture bombastic, Aman delineated, "we have been keeping tabs on a certain woman of your acquaintance. Before coming here, we vetted this woman's apartment and discovered her to be missing. One of my officers touched the bonnet of her car, finding it to be warm, signifying the car had recently been used. We also located wire cutters in a bag concealed in a cupboard in her apartment." Coming forward, his inflated temper heightened. "Can you guess who I am talking about, Mister Latham?"

"No." Persuasively, he folded his arms. "I can't."

Aman bore at him, his displeasure plain. "The woman under review is Chanda Govinda, the same woman who briefly came into this very room, when Colonel Sharif and I were interviewing you about the downed Puma at Lahore Pakistan AFB."

"And so?" he parried, persisting his stonewall stance.

"Mister Latham, I warned you about this woman, saying she's not suitable company for you. Obviously, my warning has gone unheeded. I divine you mellowed a friendship with her and aided her escape to India."

Maintaining his artificial *laissez-faire* attitude, he queried, "why should I help her?"

"I'll give you three reasons. One, you were very dubious about the PRM being responsible for launching a surface-to-air missile at the Puma, preferring to credit the Taliban are responsible. Two, she is a Christian, and you are also a Christian. And three, you are the only white man she has come into contact with for many years. Put all those facts together, and it is prudent to deduce you are the white man seen by the farm worker at the fence line."

"Convenient speculative suppositions, Chief Inspector Aman."

Beginning to fume, Aman went to the window again, throwing open the curtains in a manifestly simulated act of exposing the suspect's method. "You had the motive and the means. I think as soon as the hospital day staff had made their final check on you, minutes after, you climbed out of this window, and made your way to Chanda Govinda's apartment in Imtiaz Shaheed Road. You then used her Hillman Avenger to take Miss Govinda to Jattanwali, where you cut the fence lines." Marking the Englishman with an outstretched finger, he pronounced, "I intend to prove your involvement, Mister Latham, and when I do, you will be put on trial as an enemy of the State."

Chapter 10: Arrest

Bill Kimble arrived at the Combined Military Hospital late in the morning with a large carrier bag housing new clothing for Latham, his intent a quick turnaround to take him back to Karachi looking business-like. Strolling into the civilian patients' building, he became astounded to find an armed guard outside Latham's room.

"Excuse me," he begged, his display expectant. "May I go into Mister Latham's room?"

"Just a moment, sir."

Going inside, instants later he resurfaced with Chief Inspector Aman, and closed the door behind them.

"Good morning," Kimble judiciously greeted, sensing all not to be well. "I'm Bill Kimble with the Karachi British Deputy High Commission."

"Good morning, Mister Kimble. I am Chief Inspector Aman with the Lahore Police."

Kimble gasped. "Has something happened to Mister Latham?"

"We are quizzing him about his possible tie in the escape of a terrorist suspect."

"*What?*" Kimble's mouth dropped open, involuntarily paralyzing his normal immaculate deportment. "What do you mean?"

Aman narrated the events of the previous evening and early morning hours, outlining his suspicions about Latham's role in Chanda Govinda's escape to India.

"Your conjecture is preposterous," he retorted. "It's just guesswork. You don't have any solid and irrevocable verification of

Mister Latham's complicity." Hurling Aman a caustic blaze, he commanded, "let me inside, I need to speak to Mister Latham."

Casting a disparaging face at the British diplomat, Aman lethargically opened the door. Entering, Kimble saw Latham propped up in bed with an armed guard either side of him.

Twisting about, he gloomed at Aman. "Is this really necessary, Chief Inspector?"

Aman nodded, and the two-armed guards joined their comrade outside of Latham's room, while he entered with Kimble.

"Hello, Dale," Kimble coolly expressed, his connotation aiming to make light of the matter. "I understand you are in a spot of bother."

"Yes, patently the Chief Inspector weighs I am some sort of Scarlet Pimpernel messiah, who whisks away undesirables over the border."

Turning to Aman, Kimble's face lit up in a pastiche of diplomatic poise. "Can I please talk to Mister Latham in private, Chief Inspector?"

Albeit his reluctance plain, he replied, "of course, but first, can I enquire what is in your carrier bag?"

"Just a fresh set of business clothing for Mister Latham."

"May I examine the carrier bag?"

Kimble held out the item, Aman breaching its folded top to reveal shoes, socks, a two-piece suit, shirt, tie and underwear. "That is fine, Mister Kimble."

"Glad you approve," Kimble wryly remarked, taking the bag.

As the room door shut, Kimble walked swiftly to Latham's bedside.

"*Dale*," he admonished, "what on Earth have you got yourself involved in?"

"As I said, Aman presumes I spirit the disenfranchised into India."

Not sure if the British national acted facetiously, Kimble recoiled. Reappraising his position, he resolved to preserve a serious tack. "This Chanda Govinda person?"

"Yes."

"Are you acquainted with her?"

"She's with the hospital patient support team."

Dropping into a provident mood, Kimble went to the window, staring at people milling here and there in the forecourt, whilst collecting his machinations. Refacing Latham, his mode betokening a vexed man, he voiced, "whether you are involved or not, is not the germane issue. My only concern is, can the Lahore Police prove your alleged collusion?"

"I can assure—"

"No," Kimble interrupted, "don't tell me anything. It will only serve to implicate the British Deputy High Commission and by association, the Foreign Office." Advancing the cross-examination, he grilled, "is there any proof of your connivance?"

"No."

"Right then," he positively asserted. "Let's get you out of here."

Opening the room door, he ushered Aman inside, two armed guards following him.

"Chief Inspector Aman, in the face of the fact you have no hard testimony pertaining to Mister Latham's cooperation in this escape, I will be taking him to Karachi for onwards journey back to England."

"No, Mister Kimble, we will be detaining Mister Latham for further scrutiny."

Stepping forth commandingly, his manner now intransigent, the diplomat blared, "Chief Inspector Aman, may I *remind* you, Mister Latham is a British citizen. Unless you can yield substantiated data proving he has been involved in assisting someone to illegally cross over the border into India, then I am duty bound to inform you, Her Majesties Government will not tolerate any further restriction on his movements."

Turning to the guard on his left, Aman whispered something in Urdu. The guard left the room.

"Mister Kimble," Aman began, his pronunciation placid but deliberate. "I'm sure you will appreciate we have procedures to complete before anyone suspected of collaboration in aiding a terrorist can be released."

"We will be leaving this hospital for Allama Iqbal International Airport at 3:00 pm to board the PIA 16:20 flight to Karachi..." He checked his watch. "...leaving you four hours to stage your evidence, Chief Inspector."

Aman glowered at the affirmation. "I will need to speak to my superiors before I can confirm your adjudication is acceptable."

After charging the armed guards to stay at their posts outside Latham's room, he left, proceeding to Lahore Police HQ.

"Now," Kimble began in an agitated tone, "tell me exactly what has occurred here during the last 24-hours."

Latham recounted how he had been awakened in the early morning by Aman, and accused of aiding the escape of a suspected terrorist across the border, Kimble's attitude remaining neutral and non-judgmental throughout the tale.

At its conclusion, Latham examined, "have you ever faced anything like this before, Bill?"

"Yes." Frowning, his disconcertion evolved as all too evident to Latham. "In Dhaka."

"What happened?"

"Ohh." Slumping into an ambivalent state, not clear-cut he should recite the wrongdoing, Kimble uttered, "it er…it involved a British national accused of drug smuggling by the Bangladeshis."

"Had this person smuggled drugs?"

"By matter of degree, yes and no. The accused, a young woman, indeed confessed to taking in heroin, but the Bangladeshis insisted she had been pushing the stuff." Shimmying his head as if the memory still caused him grief, he relayed on, "they produced 10 kilograms of high-quality heroin, telling the British High Commission she had all the hallmarks of an international drug dealer. We had already liaised with the UK police, and yes, she did have a record for using, but not for dealing."

"So, it transpired as a set up?"

"Clearly. 10kg of pure heroin has a street value in the millions. It is also a considerable physical size. You'd need a large suitcase to store it, and of course, like in Pakistan, Bangladeshi airport customs open all baggage, so there's no way she could have brought it into the country undiscovered." Wrinkling his nose, the retelling of the eventual outcome clearly still plagued his sense of injustice. "They were hunting for a scapegoat to cover up a big-time drug dealer, who, shall we say, had, and probably still has, enormous influence with the Bangladeshi authorities."

"A Bangladeshi national?"

"Yes, and one who ran in Bangladeshi government circles. Of course, it was all hushed up at the government to government level, the Bangladeshis telling HMG, it'd not be in their interests to uncover the real culprit."

"You mean, HMG let this woman take the wrap and swing in the wind?"

"Yes. We knew her to be innocent, and, we knew the name of the real perpetrator, but by all that's holy—" Sneering, he regretted, "sometimes diplomacy does not come down on the side of the innocent. Sometimes knock-on issues come into the reckoning, and the bigger picture purview prevails, the minnow sacrificed to save the greater shoal."

"And her sentence?"

"10 years, but she'd be out in five. Howbeit, five years in a Bangladeshi hell hole is a lifetime, and the victim was neither physically nor mentally strong."

"When did all this occur?"

"Her imprisonment got under way in 1989."

"So, she'll be out this year?"

Contorting his face into a lour, Kimble projected a mournfulness. "What remains of her, yes. Not the Foreign Office's finest hour, those involved, consisting yours truly, continue to bear a heavy burden of remorse and regret."

Breathing out uneasily, for the premier time in the Chanda Govinda affair, Latham began to realise his fate could be determined by political drivers, Chief Inspector Aman candidly having those at his disposal. "Couldn't you have got her transferred to a UK prison?"

"My friend, what we are talking about here is not crime and punishment, and in her case, uncorroborated crime. It came down to international bartering to protect the guilty, and not make waves potentially further exposing and embarrassing affected parties. In Bangladeshi eyes, she had been let off lightly, resulting in status quo conservation between them and HMG."

"And the guilty party is still dealing?"

"He is, but he never steps outside Bangladesh, and a watertight insurance policy encircles him, courtesy of the Bangladeshi Government."

"So the dealer is part of the Bangladeshi government structure?"

"Yes."

"Oh, *Lord*." Latham's head fell to one side. "The corollary is depressing and dispiriting."

"During my time in the Foreign Office, I have heard about many similar cases in places like Jakarta, Lagos and Harare, where Westerners have been set up to carry the can for local bigwigs that either have government credentials, or government protection for their illegal enterprises."

Attracted by his palpable downheartedness, Kimble noticed Latham's complexion had paled, and he stared into space, as if consumed by recent episodes. "See here, Dale," he began, "under the circumstances, I'm not sure I should be discussing these cases with you."

"Mmmm. I'm beginning to wish I hadn't slated the matter."

~ * ~

As leaving time neared, Latham changed into the clothing Kimble had brought him, packed the suitcase Chanda had given him, and gathered up his personal items and travel documents surviving the Puma downing, including his charred passport.

Keen to stay ahead of Aman in the cat and mouse game, Kimble urged, "come on, Dale, let's take the initiative, and make for the airport."

Opening the door, he became confronted by the commanding guard. "I'm sorry, sir, but we can't let you go until we have authorisation from Chief Inspector Aman."

His walkie-talkie RT crackled with background noise, enticing Kimble's attention. "I'd be grateful if you could please contact the Chief Inspector."

Obliging, the guard handed Kimble the RT, the communication already open to Police HQ.

"Chief Inspector Aman, this is Bill Kimble. Can you please stand down your guards and allow Mister Latham and myself to take a taxi to the airport?"

Kimble heard some muffled voices over the RT speaking in Urdu before Aman asked him to hand the RT back to the lead guard.

After a short conversation again in Urdu, the lead guard set the RT on standby and notified, "we will escort you."

Uneasy about the offer, Kimble recognised he had no choice. "Very well."

"What exactly went on there?" Latham snapped, when Kimble reentered his room.

"Oh, I'm not sure, but with the little Urdu I do understand, I gathered our trip to the airport might not be user friendly."

Pensively, the two Englishmen got into the back seats of a Lahore Police Land Rover Discovery, one guard driving, and the lead guard in the passenger seat. As they set off, another Land Rover Discovery, fully laden with armed guards, followed.

"I just hope we're being taken to the airport and not police headquarters," Kimble whispered to Latham.

"Yes, the same brainwave crossed my mind as well."

Buzzing with traffic and commerce, the streets peripheral to the hospital resembled a backwater Persian bizarre; people going about their daily trade under very hot and humid conditions, either negotiating deals or shopping for food stuffs and trinkets. When the lead Discovery pulled up at a busy T-junction, Latham became drawn to the abhorrent exhibition of a woman being thrashed by two men, while a mullah and a small crowd leered approvingly. Tugging at Kimble's cuff and indicating, the British diplomat gaped at the spectacle and resignedly shook his head. The woman began to scream.

"Aren't you going to *stop* that?" Latham emphatically appealed to the commanding guard.

Gawking forrad, he sat impassively, as if the repugnant occurrence had washed over him and he had no concerns.

"*Hey*, I'm speaking to you."

Twisting to face Latham, he exhorted, "you are in enough trouble. Do not make your fix even worse."

Latham rendered Kimble a fractious stamp, the diplomat opening his hands in response, denoting the gibe to be cosmetic.

A gap in the traffic allowed the Discovery motorcade to turn right onto Aziz Bhatti Road.

"I say, "Kimble blurted, "you're going the wrong way. Allama Iqbal Airport is in the opposite direction."

Turning about again, the commanding guard stipulated, "we are taking you to Chatterjee Road Police HQ. Chief Inspector Aman wants to ask Mister Latham some more questions."

Glancing at his watch, then at Latham, Kimble griped, "just as I dreaded. We'll miss our flight if he keeps us long."

"There are plenty of other flights to Karachi," the commanding guard reminded him.

Fuming internally, Kimble glared but did not argue the assertion. Noticing his charge's ashen veneer, he prompted, "it's okay, Dale. Just let's tackle the Chief Inspector's shenanigans, and we'll catch a later flight."

Emanating indetermination, nevertheless, Latham replied in the affirmative. "Right."

~ * ~

A legacy from when the Indian subcontinent resided as a British colony, Chatterjee Road Police HQ retained a colonial ambience, its décor reflecting a time when the British Raj administered the region, its ornate ceilings and walls stained with spent tobacco smoke, its sparse wooden furniture set up in administration and interview rooms polished by thousands of police staff uniforms and impregnated by a multitude of suspects' sweat.

Commensurate with recent above normal levels of political unrest and agitation in the Muslim world, it had been supplemented with the necessary interrogation instruments to act as an inquisition centre for the Intelligence Bureau and the Federal Investigation Agency, as well as undercover officers in the Punjab Police. In so doing, the interior had been subjected to a further downward leap into one-sided autocracy with the introduction of target monitoring apparatus.

Taking in the grim surroundings, Latham's heart plunged into his stomach, his imagination accelerating into overdrive. Categorically, he had been in tight spots before, particularly during his RAF spell, but he had never been escorted into a police station under armed guard, the savage visions he spawned delirious with the stuff of nightmares.

"Wait here," the commanding guard dictated, leaving the Englishmen in the foyer with the armed guards.

"Just stay calm, Dale," Kimble encouraged. "I'm sure the Pakistanis don't want this to mushroom into an international diplomatic incident."

"Maybe, but indisputably, Aman has a divergent agenda. My best guess is, he is a fanatic, who enjoys persecuting non-Muslims."

"Well—" Pressing his lips together, he then brusquely rebutted, "just let's see. I have another card to play."

"Oh, what?"

"Bear with me."

A while thereafter, Aman arrived, taking the two Englishman into an interview room, leaving the armed escort on standby.

"Before we begin, Chief Inspector Aman," Kimble stated, "I'd like to make a call to British Deputy High Commissioner, John Soames, in Karachi."

"For what purpose, Mister Kimble?"

"Under the covenant of the Geneva Convention, if a foreign national is detained by the police, that national's embassy should be informed."

"Very well. You are welcome to use the landline. Do you need privacy?"

"No. I want you to hear what I am saying, and the Deputy High Commissioner's response."

Kimble made the call.

"John, it's Bill Kimble. I'm with Dale Latham and Chief Inspector Aman at the Lahore Police HQ. We've run into a quandary I'd like to discuss with you."

His diplomatic schooling prompting his sensibilities, Soames instantaneously latched onto the politic nature of the call. "Go ahead, Bill."

"I'm putting the telephone receiver on speaker-phone option at my end, allowing the Chief Inspector and Mister Latham to overhear our conversation."

Attuned to playing the game, Soames coolly backed, "fine, best to keep everything out in the open."

Outlining chapter and verse regarding Latham's jam, and impressing on Soames the Lahore Police had no proof *vis-a-vis* his confederacy in the clandestine escape of a supposed Indian woman terrorist across the border, Soames responded, saying there was no case to answer, and after Aman had verbalised his issues, Latham should be free to continue his journey to Karachi. During the interchange, as if bored by the staged protocol, Aman sat impassively, nonchalantly rotating his thumbs.

Finishing the call, Kimble felt upbeat Latham's position persisted watertight, and soon they'd be on their way to the airport.

"Mister Kimble, may I now review what Mister Latham told us when we cross-examined him in the early hours of this morning?" Aman requisitioned.

"Certainly."

Rising from his chair, Aman began to stroll, encircling the room as he talked. "According to Mister Latham, he did not leave his hospital room during the hours in which the escape of suspected terrorist Chanda Govinda happened across the border at Jattanwali. Correct, Mister Latham?"

"Yes."

"I see." Reaching a position behind the seated Englishmen, Aman's navigation ended, Latham astutely aware of the menace he radiated. "It might interest you to know, we've brought in the farm worker who saw a white man running away from the fence line, just after the patrol unit coasted by. Normally, we ask suspects to take part in an identity parade, but alas, there are very few white men in Lahore, so on this occasion, we will ask the farm hand to make a single identification."

"Chief Inspector Aman, such an obvious put up show is *intolerable*," Kimble protested. "However, it will be Mister Latham's word against your sole witness's statement. Hardly the basis for a successful conviction in a court of law."

"We distinguish the overwhelming weight of circumstantial evidence is enough to warrant both an arrest, and a conviction," he dogmatically retaliated. "Mister Latham had the means and the motive to act as Chanda Govinda's accomplice."

"What do you mean by, the means and the motive?"

"He could have easily slipped out of his bedroom window, without hospital staff noticing, to aid the suspected terrorist, and like Miss Govinda, he is a Christian."

"*Ohh*!" Tossing his head to one side in a show of disbelief, the diplomat retorted, "I consider such a disingenuous and weak premise to be well beyond the realms of even the most tenuous circumstantial evidence."

"Maybe so, but our witness will prove the theory."

"Very well," Kimble curtly conceded. "Produce your witness, and let's go through this charade."

Aman made an intercom call, and shortly after, an armed guard brought the farm worker into the interview room. Latham had not really taken him in during his period of concealment on the scrubland between the fence line and the road, his only concern being a smooth trek to the car, undetected. Even when the farm worker suddenly reemerged, he had barely glanced at him before taking off for the Avenger. Now he studied him closely, trying to find something recognisable in his features, but nothing came to mind. The man stood before him, could have been anyone the Lahore Police chose to bring in.

"Please stand, Mister Latham," Aman directed.

He did so, the witness gazing at Latham, as the Chief Inspector began to query him in Urdu.

"Chief Inspector Aman, "Kimble broke in, "may I ask you to speak to this man in English, and for him to make his replies in English."

"His English is not very good," Aman counselled, "but yes." Glaring at the farm worker, he ticketed, "is this the man you saw on the scrubland between the fence line and the road at Jattanwali?"

Scrutinising Latham, the bystander blinked, his kisser a cloud of conjecture. "I'm not sure...maybe. He has a similar build, but..." Incertitude overtook him, his lineaments fractured by anguish, his hands shaking. "...I hardly saw his face. He vanished like lightning...I, er..." His account stalled.

Aman barked something in Urdu at the uncertain witness, making him cower before he spewed out his remembrance in a gibberish tenor.

"English, if you please," Kimble pleaded.

Taking the farm worker gruffly by the arm, Aman tested, "is *this* the man you saw?"

"I er..." Squealing under the policeman's grip, he came across as close to breakdown. "...I'm not sure...he could have been." The grip tightened producing the required outcome. "*Yes*, that is the man."

Releasing the witness, the farm worker fell to his knees, resultant from a combination of pain and anxiety.

"Chief Inspector Aman, your interrogatory technique is nothing short of coercion," Kimble complained, "a testament obtained under extreme physical and psychological duress. It will *not* stand up in a court of law."

"Maybe not in England, Mister Kimble, but Pakistanis are in no mood to let a Westerner go without penalisation for helping an Indian terrorist to escape justice. Our judiciary is very sensitive to public opinion. I'm sure you can work out when this case goes to court, the whole country will be baying for the maximum sentence permissible."

"You keep on intimating, even advocating this Indian woman is a terrorist. Do you have any tangible proof to uphold your claim?"

"Her family has a long history of plotting insurrection acts against the State, and she is suspected to be a member of the Indian Punjab Reunification Movement."

"Suspicion is one thing," Kimble ardently persisted, "proof is another, and remains the only tangible factor irrevocably essential for any criminal conviction." Pausing to recover his calm, he submitted, "it even applies in Pakistan. As to Mister Latham's alleged partnership in Miss Govinda's escape, it still remains as speculation, despite the somewhat strained testament of your witness." Casting an eye over the disheveled testifier, he then grimaced at Aman. "This fellow is scared out of his wits. Any half-decent lawyer could easily expose his testament as near-to police intimidation and coercion in a court trial. In any case, axiomatically, he does not appear to be wholly convinced Mister Latham is the man he claims to have seen in the place where the escape took place." Standing up, stony faced and decisive, he proclaimed, "this charade is over, Chief Inspector. We've complied with your requirement. It's time for us to go."

"You are free to leave, Mister Kimble," Aman announced, "but we shall be detaining Mister Latham until this matter is resolved to our satisfaction."

"Chief Inspector Aman," Kimble hollered, "I must protest in the *strongest* terms. This is an outrage and contravenes the terms of the Geneva Convention. Unless you allow Mister Latham to leave with me, I will be raising the issue with the British High Commission in Islamabad, as a transgression of the diplomatic code, and seeking instructions from Her Majesties Government on the matter."

"You must do what you must do, Mister Kimble." Noticing the British diplomat staring at a document marked confidential, laid open on his desk, he flicked it shut and eyeballed him. "I must do, what must be done. My duty is to arrest Mister Latham for aiding and abetting a terrorist, while we make further enquiries into the Chanda Govinda episode."

~ * ~

Down in a stifling, dank and dirty detention cell in the police station's basement, Latham nestled his head in both hands, meditating his display of chivalry had at best been ill-conceived, and at worst, foolhardy.

Flipping the karma coin, he bolstered his morale, recognising he'd done the right thing, and Fiona would have been proud of his generous undertaking. Cogitating on her memory, he lapsed into grief, plunging into a morbid shape, and agonising for the umpteenth time, their lives together had been achingly brief.

Like a real-life chance meeting from a World War Two film *noir*, Dale Latham met Fiona Howard at a RAF Coltishall officer's mess party in August 1978. Though a regular parade of girlfriends had passed through his parents Cheadle Hulme house, since joining the service, his girl conquests had been far and few between, a combination of dedication to task and the dependable knowledge of being transferred to any point of the compass, often at short notice, precluding intense relationships. Albeit, the picture of a goddess-like creature enchanting a passel of RAF officers made for a step change.

A local lass, born into a retailing family, Fiona hailed from Little Plumstead on the outskirts of Norwich. Exposure to a plethora of widely differing people and experiences in her formative years had imbued her with a confident, sparkling personality. Better still, by her late teens, she had bloomed from blonde-haired, doe-eyed, gangling youth into a whole gain fashioned, vivacious siren. Though Fiona's twin attributes made her very popular with the young men of the area, her dance card permanently full, she never engaged in long endeavours, Mister Totally Right not coming into her purview.

When Dale Latham approached her, equipped with a magnetic smile and carrying two glasses of punch, he grasped her complete attention in a jiffy, other self-styled beaus dropping by the wayside or excusing themselves. Never taking their eyes of each other, by the end of the party, the pair had shaped an attachment, its maturation crisply flowering into mutual love. Less than a year elapsed before the couple married at St. Giles Church Norwich, where Fiona had been baptized and attended bible classes on her journey to become a devout Christian.

Every aspect of their lives went swimmingly well, Fiona adapting to Dale's RAF responsibilities, him in turn respecting and even taking part in her Christian activities. Born in 1981, Nicol completed their delight, Penny following in 1983 further adding to their joy. Then disaster struck a few years down line, Fiona suddenly succumbing to illness. Diagnosed with a blood disorder, it led to a blood clot on the brain, and her premature death. Devastated, Dale's world came crashing down.

Remembering the sequence of trials originally overwhelming him with immense joy, then driving him into complete despair, he reflected on his life with Fiona, pondering about the enormous chasm between the diametrically opposed poles, and trying to rationalise why she had been taken. His present circumstances and detainment in a claustrophobic cell amplified the polarised dichotomy.

Before being taken down to the basement, he petitioned Kimble to call his sister Amelia, and Matthew Chapman at Armstrong-Eliot, to advise them of the current situation, knowing the diplomat capable of pitching it in such a way so not as to cause dismay. Now he wondered in what way they'd react, and how Amelia might pass on his unforeseen extended stay in Pakistan to Nicol and Penny, without alarming them. In any event, his immediate soup darted back into the forefront of his mind again overpowering parenthood misgivings.

~ * ~

True, he had never come close to an air accident prior to the Puma ruin, but he had just about survived a harrowing endangerment, when on secondment from the RAF assisting aircrew operations in Uganda.

After Milton Obote assumed the Ugandan presidency, concurrent with the fall and exile of the tyrant Idi Amin, former Amin allies headed by Brigadier Moses Ali formed the Ugandan National Rescue Front to oppose Obote's administration. Located in Uganda's West Nile sub-region, the armed rebel group regularly attacked Ugandan armed forces and committed atrocities against civilians instrumental in Amin's overthrow. Obote ordered the rebels to be destroyed, but Ugandan armed forces soon found the UNRF were highly mobile, briskly moving out of range of ground-based tank, howitzer and mortar fire. Worse, they took up positions in civilian areas.

Not wanting to incur civilian fratricide leading to more advocacy for the renegades, Obote took advantage of Commonwealth membership and sought military advisor patronage from MoD. Latham was dispatched to Kampala immediately after his second Red Flag triumph, with a brief to appreciate the crunch, report back to MoD, and provisionally advise the Ugandan Air Force in the figure of air-to-ground tactics in the interdiction zone. By then, the rebellion had escalated into the Ugandan Bush War, Obote desperate to quickly defeat the UNRF, and put a lid on the conflict.

In those days, the RAF's inventory of air-to-ground weapons included the AGM-62 Walleye II Fat Albert television-guided glide bomb, with onboard guidance avionics. Designed to hit targets with minimal collateral damage, it suited Obote's anti-civilian fratricide policy. The smart bomb had no propulsion mechanism, but it could be maneuvered via television assisted guidance during its glide from a launch aircraft to the mark. As the pilot dove towards the objective, a television camera in the nose of the bomb transmitted images to a monitor in the cockpit. Once the pilot acquired a sharp image of the target on the monitor screen, he allocated an aim point and released the bomb, the projectile continuing to fly towards the appointed object under freefall atmospheric influences.

Part of Latham's brief centred on assessing the suitability of Walleye in the interdictor zone. Shown photo reconnaissance of the target rebel sites by the Ugandan Air Wing, nonetheless, under orders from MoD, Latham needed to make his own stocktaking to ensure minimal collateral damage. A makeshift helicopter landing pad had been set up in bushland to the west of Atiak, less than 10 miles from the UNRF strongholds further west in Onigo and Adjumani. Latham traveled from Kampala to the Air Wing airbase at Gulu in a military transport aircraft, and onwards to the forward landing site in a Bell 206 helicopter.

Prior to his arrival, airborne Air Wing assets had been reconnoitering UNRF activity in Adjumani, location of the rebel hierarchy HQ, without incurring much hostile ground-to-air rifle fire. Ergo, they submitted it was proportionally safe for Latham to make his appreciation.

After further discussions with the Air Wing relating to the enemy's deployment and strength in Adjumani and Onigo, Latham felt sufficiently briefed to make his evaluation. Early the following morning, the reconnaissance mission commenced, Latham in the observer seat of a Bell UH-1 Iroquois 'Huey' helicopter. Within minutes they were overhead Adjumani, their presence attracting uncoordinated, sporadic rifle fire, as Latham inspected rebel positions with binoculars and the pilot worked the photo-reconnaissance apparatus. Latham noted the bulk of the renegade forces were congregated in three distinct areas; a combined HQ-logistics centre with an assortment of ground attack vehicles incorporating howitzers and armoured cars, and two areas billeting troops, each he estimated to comprise a battalion, with four companies, a total of 800 to 1,000 fighting men. Flying on to Onigo, Latham made similar counts in terms of logistics centre armament and manpower numbers.

Astonished by the rebel strength, after rapidly wayfaring to the forward landing site, he linked back to MoD via Ugandan Air Force secure communications saying, Walleye attacks on the logistics centres were justified, senior Ugandan Air Wing officers highly delighted with his sanctioning of the weapon.

As he made ready to return to Kampala, Air Wing soldiers, acting as sentries on the landing site periphery, transmitted on their walkie-talkies that a large force of UNRF soldiers headed towards them from the north. Minutes thereafter, they were under attack from mortar fire, the Huey and the 206 helicopters destroyed in the bombardment. Air Wing servicemen bundled Latham into a scout car along with two officers, posthaste its driver heading south out of the landing site with three other vehicles, as rebel forces pressed home their attack, more mortar shells reigning down about the convoy.

Dispersing, so as not to allow the enemy concentrated fire, the four vehicles fanned out into the bushland, Latham's scout car driver heading for some comparatively open ground to afford increased speed. Ahead lay some thicker bush, and beyond, the road to Atiak. Conscious the enemy could pursue the escaping vehicles, the senior officer in Latham's scout car made a radio call to the Air Wing airbase at Gulu, apprising them of the standpoint, and requisitioning air support. Airborne within minutes of the incoming request, a flight of Hueys headed north-north-west towards the bushland, where the land vehicles had dispersed.

As Latham's scout car slammed into the thicker bush, its speed markedly retarded. Behind, rebel forces sprinted across the open bushland in pursuit of all the Air Wing vehicles, some desisting to set up mortar stations, and bombarding the thicker bush to their front. One shell exploded beside Latham's vehicle, its driver's reaction turning the vehicle away from the burst but into a 6-foot deep gully, rendering it fast in a thick morass of bush vegetation. Latham and the three other occupants scrambled out the stricken vehicle, and up the acute-angled side of the gully. In the distance, they saw UNRF troops bearing down on them, firing as they went.

Drawing their sidearms, the two officers and the driver prepared for the attack. Although Latham had undergone pistol tuition, RAF crew did not carry firearms during airborne and ground operational duty. Noticing he had no weapon, the senior officer handed him a spare Colt 1908 semi-automatic handgun. Opening fire as the enemy came within range, the on-coming rebels dropped down to terra firma before gunning back at the stranded quartet with automatic-rifle fire. The stalemate continued until Latham and his comrades heard the unmistakable reverberation of helicopter rotor-blades beating against the airflow from the south. Moments later, a Huey drifted overhead, spraying the rebels with machine gun fire, sending them into retreat.

After the renegade tumult died down and surviving forward landing site platoon members had been rescued by more Air Wing helicopters and deposited at Gulu, Latham began to take in he might not have survived the encounter.

Within the confines of his Lahore Police cell, he revisited the Ugandan sortie, ruminating after such a fortuitous escape, he could not rely on lady luck to bail him out again. To extricate himself from Aman's shackles, he needed some form of concerted reinforcement from the British High Commission, Bill Kimble his specific instrument to devise and execute the necessities to resume his freedom.

~ * ~

Back in Karachi, Kimble briefed Deputy High Commissioner John Soames.

"Before leaving Lahore, I talked to Landon Fawbert at the Consulate."

"What's his take on the Latham deadlock?"

Gimbal-eyed and blowing out uneasily, he made his anxiety crystal clear to Soames. "Though there is no solid case against Latham, Fawbert told me it's not unknown for the police to fabricate incriminating data, holding up in court. Worse still, Chief Inspector Aman remains intransigent." Joggling his head, he admitted, "I'm still trying to decipher exactly why."

"I see. What's his supposed motivation?"

"Well, at best, I've made out that subsequent to the Pakistani Army Puma being downed at Lahore Pakistan AFB, he is trying to make political capitol out of the escape of the suspected Indian terrorist Chanda Govinda across the border into Punjab, on the basis the PRM were responsible for the attack. Though everything points towards Muslim terrorists being the cause of the strike, plausibly the Taliban, as we discussed prior to my visit to Lahore, he refuses to rule out the PRM, apparently still manned by Indians caught on the wrong side of the border after the 1947 partition."

"Mmmm," Soames uttered whilst musing on the thorny pickle. "But what is he after? Promotion, more influence...*more* dominance?"

"I asked Fawbert the same question. It transpires Aman has ambitions to enter the political arena, and reputedly, he is no defender of President Khan, Prime Minister Bhutto and the Pakistan People's Party."

"A Muslim zealot then, even a fanatic?"

"Fawbert believes he has a very close fellowship with the radical mullah brigade, and wants to see Pakistan made into a fundamentalist Islamic Republic in the style of Khomeini's Iran."

"Isn't it rumoured the radical mullahs have tight links with Muslim terrorist organisations like Hamas and the Muslim Brotherhood, even the Taliban?"

"Indeed it is, John, and that in itself begs the quiz, could Aman be purposely misdirecting police investigations away from Muslim terrorist groups, and in the direction of soft prey, like the PRM?"

"Possibly, and in time-honoured tradition, a sacrificial lamb arrives gift-wrapped in the form of Latham, Aman artificially fusing the two strands together and claiming the Armstrong-Eliot man is a PRM sympathizer."

"There's something else."

"Oh."

"While Latham and myself were in Aman's office, I caught sight of a document folder marked confidential, it's cover also embossed with the Pakistan Army Corps Military Police motif."

"What do you envision it contained?"

"Normally, I'm not a betting man, but I'd bet the farm it held the official provisional accident report on the Puma infraction compiled by Colonel Sharif, the Pakistani Army Corps Military Police officer leading the crash investigation."

"Hhmm, I wonder what it said." Drumming his desk with his fingers, Soames considered the possibilities. "The case could be argued, Aman arrested Latham conditional on the chronicle carrying testimony of PRM entanglement."

"Equally," Kimble foreshadowed, "if it fingered the Taliban, Aman might have wanted to get Latham into custody before publication, allowing him time to establish depositions to convict him."

"Possibly. Let's park the guesswork for the time being." Rising from his seat, Soames clapped his hands as if using the gesture to fire up his cognitive clout. Taking a few steps towards his office window, he stared out at Moin Akhtar Park in the near distance, and the traffic and passers-by on 5th Avenue, his considerate posture alerting Kimble to a possible directive from him. "The central issue remains, what are we going to do about Latham?" A rhetorical ask, he turned to face Kimble. "As I see it, we can't hope he escapes his confinement of his own volition. There has never been a case of a European detainee liberating himself from the Pakistan Police. Besides, it'd only suggest he is guilty of the charges against him, and thereby, we could not formally serve him to leave Pakistan." Placing his palms open, he debated, "equally, us trying to bribe a policeman, using a third party not directly connected with the British High Commission to let him escape, effects the same impasse. Consequently, there are only two possibilities. One, we exert diplomatic pressure to ensure his authorised release, or two, we do nothing, and let Pakistani justice take its course. Nevertheless—" Pressing his lips together, he discharged a reserved regard. "While you were up in Lahore, I alerted not only Armstrong-Eliot about Latham's predicament, but with him being ex-RAF, MoD as well."

"I see." Kimble's face shrank into a grave register. "Do I detect MoD has concerns about Latham's difficulty?"

"Dale Latham had top-secret security clearance whilst serving as an RAF officer, and he is still on the reserve list. During his time in the service, he had access to some very sensitive and hush-hush data, especially about airborne weapon delivery systems and smart weapons, plus military battle plans, still current. If he were to fall into the hands of let's say, elements opposed not only to the Pakistan Government, but the precepts of NATO and the security of the United Kingdom, it could make all three vulnerable."

"Yes, I see what you're driving at. So er—" His countenance lightened. "Are you hinting Latham will need to be extricated from his incarceration, come hell or high water?"

"If this thing does go to trial, there is no telling where it might lead. The Pakistanis are aware of his background, and his comprehension might be deemed to be important to their own military agenda. They do have a reputation for extracting information from those falling foul of their legal framework. Even worse, if Landon Fawbert is right about Aman, Latham could end up in the hands of Muslim terrorists via some undercover backdoor route. Either way, our interests will be put at risk, so somehow, we must make sure the Pakistanis lawfully release Latham. Failing such a measure—" Frowning, he bore a disconcerted mug. "It wouldn't stagger me if MI6 are brought into the equation."

"You mean..." Kimble's face lapsed into an ashen complexion. "...to liquidate Latham?"

"Let's not pretend it has not taken place before under similar circumstances. If MoD reckon Latham's classified knowledge to be something enemy forces opposed to NATO and the interests of the UK can use as leverage to put our security in jeopardy, MI6 will be brought into play."

His spirits still descending, Kimble tabled, "we'd better dream up something alleviating the possibility, and quickly."

"Well—" Soames' carriage segued into a rosier pattern. "The one piece of fairly hard collateral we do have is, Pakistan Armed Forces are desperate for acquisition of the Armstrong-Eliot theatre-battlefield sensor technologies. Since they are subject to the terms of an HMG export license, granted by the Department of Trade under advisement from MoD, we could make granting factored on Latham being freed under the guise of UK national security. True, the Pakistanis might go to the Americans or the French for the procurement, but before Latham and his colleague Rendall Gilmour arrived in Karachi, I talked to both Brigadier Cham and Vice Admiral Mahmood to test their appetites. They told me, sensor technologies are critical for Pakistan Armed Forces to empower their weapon delivery platforms with optimum fighting capabilities, enabling them to counter the threat from insurgents. Their preliminary evaluation of all the available, proven in-service options puts Armstrong-Eliot head and shoulders above the international competition." Sending Kimble a buoyant mien, he notarized, "this is the practical leverage we can bring to bear. I'm not sure if it will be enough to result in Latham's release, but at least it will get the ball rolling."

"Yes, I applaud the reasoning, but do Cham and Mahmood have sufficient influence across the Pakistani government spectrum to hold sway on them wanting the Armstrong-Eliot equipments?"

"Well, put it this way, owing to Operation Desert Storm, at this juncture, neither the Americans nor the French are merited highly in Pakistani political circles. Come to that, nor are the British. Albeit, we have a long and established diplomatic history with Pakistan, and most high-level Pakistani civil servants and field-rank military officers have an affinity with England, because we trained them. It might be a case of the leopard with the least spots."

"Yes, I see your line of reflection," Kimble accepted, his intonation surging into optimism again. "Can I take it you will be talking to Brigadier Cham and Vice Admiral Mahmood imminently?"

"Verily, you can, Bill."

~ * ~

In his 56th year, John Soames possessed an enviable diplomat's CV, boasting fertile British Embassy and British High Commission posts throughout Europe, Asia and Africa. An Eton then Oxford scholar, he joined the Foreign Office with a degree in classics and complete fluency in the French, German, Spanish and Arabic languages. Assigned to the Whitehall French desk in 1960, the Foreign Office briskly took advantage of his language skills, dispatching him to Switzerland as Third Secretary for Cultural Affairs. His career progressed through a succession of second and first secretary appointments for either cultural or commercial affairs, all the way up to head of mission. In his current deputy high commissioner post for three years, he had cultivated good to great rapport with Pakistani politicians, senior bureaucrats and field rank military personnel.

Charged with vim, Soames met with Cham and Mahmood to discuss Latham's tight spot, subtlety articulating a dependency between his release and the Pakistan Armed Forces acquisition of the Armstrong Eliot theatre-battlefield sensor technologies. Worldly in their outlook and never slow to catch on to an overture, they agreed to buttonhole the Ministry of Law & Justice in Islamabad, with a view to resolving Latham's position, Soames leaving their meeting convinced of the agreement producing fruit.

True to their word, Cham and Mahmood made their pitch to the Ministry of Law & Justice, stating only circumstantial evidence existed against Latham in the escape of the presumed PRM member, Chanda Govinda. Agreeing in principle, Jitender Shadid, Permanent Secretary to Minister Sardar Kanaan, took an action to discuss the *quid pro quo* arrangement with him.

A few days crept slowly by before Brigadier Cham got back to Soames saying Kanaan had discussed the Latham dilemma with other ministers and influential government advisors, receiving some push back in response to the proposal. Cham went on to explain there were elements in Government favouring the precepts of a full-blown, fundamentalist Islamic State, the democratically elected authority to be replaced by a ruling council of mullahs. This group opposed Latham's release on the basis their doctrine allowed no tolerance for Western Christians interfering in Pakistani business.

Briefing Kimble, Soames told him, "it seems Chief Inspector Aman has friends in high places. Ministry of Law & Justice Minister Kanaan isn't finding total substantiation for our Latham proposition. What we really need is irrefutable facts to exonerate him of all suspicion." His physiognomy filling with wanting, he prodded, "got any ideas, Bill?"

"As a matter of fact, yes. Neglecting Aman arresting Latham independent of whether or not the PRM participated in the Puma apocalypse, the crux of the charge against him relies on proving Latham assisted a member of the PRM to escape across the border, and the same organisation are proved to have brought down the Puma at PAFB Lahore." Pausing, he then went into a prescriptive vent. "I suggest we contact Colonel Sharif with a goal to see the official provisional crash recount. I got the impression from Latham's description of him, he is not an Islamic State sympathizer. If he is neutral when it comes to publishing the crash investigation findings, perhaps it will benefit Latham's case."

"You mean, purvey proof positive a weapon the PRM could not have possibly obtained downed the Puma, and confront Aman with the attestation?"

"Yes. Latham put forward a Stinger brought it down. I've done some checking up on the PRM. They have little funding, and are not backed by the Indian Government, therefore it's unlikely they could have acquired a ground-to-air missile launch system. Technically, they have a passive agenda, making the occasional public protest in the form of a rally and representations to Pakistani government functionaries that are always rejected."

"And those acts are the extent of their endeavours?"

"They are, as far as I can make out. True, some 20 to 30 years ago, the PRM were more hostile, but the form manifested itself as tit-for-tat reprisals, when Indians were persecuted by Pakistanis, and the authorities did nothing about it. But it transpired as fisticuffs, not the release of ground-to-air munitions." Hunching his shoulders, he conceded, "I don't contest, behind the public facade, the PRM get up to some heavy-duty stuff, but to date there is no documented criminal activity."

"You mean, only surmise exists?"

"I came across some intelligence partially connecting the deaths of some Muslim zealots to a PRM faction. Nevertheless, nothing has been verified, and some analysts attribute the deaths were sequel to inter-Muslim tribal squabbles, harking back centuries. The Balochs do not get on with the Gujaratis, and the Kashmiris have long-standing disputes with the Punjabis. It's an eminent fact."

"Mmmm." Aroused by the appraisal, Soames soared into remedial mode. "If the record you saw on Aman's desk is a published preliminary air accident crash log, it will contain a theory as to the type of weapon fired at the Puma. In fact, the air accident investigation team must have collected material exhibits. Exploding missiles always leave traces on their targets, and fragments are dispersed in the hit-zone area." Pleased with his summary, he dwelt to evolve the postscript action. "I want you to go back to Lahore and talk to Colonel Sharif. Maybe he can accommodate the collateral needed to ease the chains on Latham."

~ * ~

With determination colouring his palette, knowing the outcome to be vital in securing Latham's release from police custody, Kimble arranged to meet with Sharif at Pakistan AFB Lahore.

Picking him up at the airbase sentry station, Sharif's aid escorted him to a large hanger, where Colonel Sharif and the crash investigation team were stationed, Kimble noticing parts of the stricken Puma strewn over the hanger floor, technicians still pouring over them.

After some light introductory chit-chat, Kimble shifted the conversation into calling territory. "No doubt you aware of Dale Latham's plight, Colonel Sharif?"

"Indeed I am, Mister Kimble. News travels fast in Pakistani military and civil policing circles. And to be sure, my accord duties with Chief Inspector Aman in respect of the Puma iniquity have necessitated a sharing of information between the Lahore Police and the Air Force air accident wing, enveloping Mister Latham's arrest."

Right away, flashes about the case file he had seen on Aman's desk alighted in the forefront of Kimble's mind, Sharif's reply confirming the file to be an official provisional accident recital.

"Tell me, Colonel, has the accident investigation team formulated a preliminary ruling germane to the munition responsible for bringing down the Puma?"

Assuming a cautious disposition, Sharif sat back. "Mister Kimble, why are you tabling the query? What is its significance to you?"

"I see no point in being coy. It might help alleviate Mister Latham's torment."

"How?"

"The Lahore Police have made an unsubstantiated conjunction between the Puma attack and the PRM. They are also saying Mister Latham abetted one of its members to illegally cross the border to India. Blatantly, it is conjecture. If verification were to come to light, the munition striking the Puma was fired by some other, as yet to be openly determined group, it'd pump up Mister Latham's case immeasurably."

"I see. And which group if not the PRM, do you theorise is responsible?"

"Colonel—" Pulling together all his diplomatic wit, he contrived an insightful face. "It's a matter of record, the PRM are a passive organisation with little funds, and no capability to acquire surface-to-air missiles, let alone possess the proficiency to fire them. On the other hand, surface-to-air attacks by a whole host of dissident Muslim terrorist organisations are well logged and indexed." Purposely dwelling, he let the allegation sink in. "Adopting a dispassionate stance, you'd agree in the light of recent terrorist operations originating from north of Pakistan, the Taliban are the most likely group to be responsible?"

"I cannot deny it is a prospect, and presumably you're keen to ascertain if the air accident investigation has revealed the particular type of ground-to-air missile fired at the Puma?"

"Very much so. The Taliban are well funded, and have access to shoulder-mounted SAMs, specifically the Stinger."

"Mmmm. When I met Mister Latham in the Combined Military Hospital, he also expressed a Stinger had been responsible." Realising Kimble led up to something, he quizzed, "but what are your expectations of me?"

"As I indicated earlier, Colonel, if you could allow me access to the preliminary findings of the air accident report, it might confirm the supposition in reference to a Stinger."

"I see." Rising from his chair, Sharif started pacing about his office, hands behind his back in the military fashion aiding his deliberation. "You put me in a difficult position, Mister Kimble."

"How so?"

"I am not a political animal. However, Chief Inspector Aman is, and I am sure the British High Commission has made the necessary researches to determine what level of supremacy he exerts with the Ministry of Law & Justice."

"Yes, we have taken those measures."

"So you will be under no illusions as to his, shall we call them, political ambitions for Pakistan."

"We have been made aware of his leanings towards the State being governed by fundamentalist mullahs."

"A minority creed, but one seducing champions in powerful domains, as well as in the more zealous parts of the populace, since Operation Desert Storm. I do not subscribe to this doctrine. I am a democrat and uphold the principles of a government elected via the ballot box."

"Do I take your declaration to imply you are willing to comply with my plea?"

Taking stock of proceedings, Sharif then grinned at the Englishman. "Come, let's inspect the crash site."

Crossing open land between the hanger and the damaged helicopter landing pad where the Puma had hurtled to the ground, Kimble began to invoke the turn of happenings leading to nine men losing their lives, and five being hospitalised, Latham among them. Staring up at a notional coordinate in the sky, 300 feet above ground level, he visualised the hovering helicopter preparing to descend. He then peered towards partially hidden buildings and rough earth at least a mile away where the SAM must have been fired from.

"You are visualising the attack, Mister Kimble?"

"Yes." Shaking his head, he flinched. "They couldn't have stood a chance. The SAM must have been upon them within 2 seconds from launch."

"A classic Stinger operation."

"Absolutely." Kimble refrained from walking, a bedevilled visage crossing his face. "Colonel, are you saying, the SAM was a Stinger?"

Sharif faced him. "I'm not saying anything yet. Come, let's continue on."

Minutes afterwards they came upon a section of burnt and blistered grass and soil, cordoned off with Air Accident embossed tape.

"We estimate from ground witness statements, it took no longer than 10 seconds for the Puma to hit the ground after the SAM struck. But for latent energy in the rotor blades cushioning the descent, and the fortunate occurrence the fuel tank did not explode, there'd be no survivors." Denoting with his swagger stick he illuminated, "those areas of burnt ground were caused by the missile setting light to flammable parts of the helicopter. The parts were still aflame when rescuers pulled the air crew and the passengers from the wreckage embracing Mister Latham."

Glowering at the lugubrious depiction, Kimble scanned all-round the cordoned off area. "I'd wager your team recovered splinters from the attack missile."

"Yes." Browsing the charred debris, he then explored into the distance. "And, they were scattered beyond this cordon."

"So—" Kimble's inflection billed into rosy. "Regressing to the theme I posed in your office, were your team able to identify the missile type?"

"At the north end of the air base, over half a mile from the crash site, a member of my team picked up a fragment of the munition on open land, not far from the perimeter fence. It retained the singed and indistinct opening six letters of a serial number. After cleaning the fragment in an alkaline solution and examining it under a microscope, a technician exposed the number, 964623." Sinking into a pensive mannerism, he left Kimble undecided if he'd continue. Adopting a resolute puss, he then divulged, "we checked the number with US DoD government furnished equipment records at the Pentagon. The Americans issued surface-to-air missile serial number SAM 964623762094-010-900 to the Mujahideen in 1986, along with a FIM-92 Stinger man-portable air defence system."

"Of course, to counter Soviet gunship operations during the Soviet War in Afghanistan. The DoD GFE programme allowed the supply of quite a number of Stinger systems, and SAMs."

"Quite. In more recent times, it's self-evident the Mujahideen have made friends with other radical Islamist groups, encompassing the Taliban, and of course the latter are situated in Afghanistan."

"Mmmm. You may recall Latham proposed the Taliban to Chief Inspector Aman as a conceivable originator behind the Puma attack?"

"Well, with the explosion traces to hand, his deduction appears to be most likely."

"May I enquire if both the SAM serial number and the Taliban being the most probable group responsible for the terrorist incident, are implicit in the preliminary air accident narration?"

"Yes, they are. Notwithstanding, we need proof positive." Downshifting into a ritual tack, he specified, "since identifying the Stinger missile origin, both the Pakistan Army Corps Military Police and the Pakistan Intelligence Services have been trying to track down those involved in firing the SAM. To date, we have come up short, but via infiltration into the Taliban and other disaffected groups, we hope to pinpoint the culprits, and bring them to justice." Slinging a cheerless gawp at Kimble, he pronounced, "I perceive what you are going to ask me next. Can you have a copy of the official preliminary air accident chronicle."

"Yes, you've read my intention."

"Though I oppose Chief Inspector Aman's and the radical mullahs' agenda, I am a careful man when it comes to incurring their displeasure. I'd suggest you undertake proper channels in order to see the paper."

"Do Brigadier Cham and Vice Admiral Mahmood have sufficient smack to present the British High Commission with the data?"

After considering the pivotal inference for a trice, Sharif replied, "Cham and Mahmood fly high above any threat to their standings from lesser beings like Aman. If you could get their patronage, I am sure I will receive a direct order to provide the exhibit."

~ * ~

Whilst in Lahore, Kimble called in at Police HQ to see Latham, the desk sergeant escorting him down to the cells. Conscious not to let the cat out of the bag apropos the air accident dictum in the presence of the police, he broached, "Mister Latham looks a bit pasty, Sergeant. Can I take him to your exercise yard for a breath of fresh air?"

Okaying the wish, the desk sergeant led the two Englishmen into a yard surrounded on three sides by the police building and a large reinforced-steel gate on the fourth. After assigning two armed policemen to guard stations, at either end of the gate, he left.

"I take it the fresh air ask was a ruse, Bill?" Latham murmured.

"Mmmm. Your cell is probably rigged with microphones, and I have some encouraging information, I don't want the police to overhear." Gawking at the guards, he entreated, "come, let's walk around the yard periphery."

Kimble outlined the *quid pro quo* strategy agreed with Soames to get him acquitted, and his conversation with Colonel Sharif, stressing the dependency on legally receiving the preliminary air accident document via either Brigadier Cham or Vice Admiral Mahmood. He did not recap on Latham's top-secret security clearance classification or mention the potential complication of MI6 coming into play.

"Founded on previous sagacity, I knew the SAM had to be a Stinger," Latham reiterated.

"Quite. Now, what I want you to do, Dale, is stay calm, and wait for all the interrelated cogs to slip into place. As soon as we ceremoniously have the recital, the British High Commission will bring pressure to bear on the relevant Pakistani agencies for your release, on the basis the PRM were not responsible for downing the Puma, and your so-called liaison with Chanda Govinda is purely circumstantial. Thus, it leaves Chief Inspector Aman with no solid grounds to hold you on."

"Sounds marvelous, Bill, but don't underestimate Aman. I have a boding he is operating from a position of strength."

Though Kimble knew it to be true, he did not confirm the guess, knowing it best to keep Latham's spirits high. "I'm sure, we will prevail."

Halting perambulation, Latham said, "there's another aspect to take into consideration."

"Oh?" Glimpsing at the guards, he made sure they were disinterested in their conversation. "Come on, keep walking or the sentinels might become suspicious."

As they moved on, Latham delivered the diplomat a contrary kisser. "Off the record, this could be an appropriate time to unofficially tell you about the meeting Rendall Gilmour and myself had with Cham and Mahmood back in Karachi."

Kimble quailed. "Does it have a bearing on what we are discussing?"

"It could do."

"Alright, let's have it," he reluctantly cooed. "But whatever you tell me, please make sure it stays under wraps in the future."

"Cham and Mahmood more than hinted management consultancy fees were an expectation as part of a contract award to Armstrong-Eliot."

"I see."

"I'm telling you this, Bill, because pitching for the preliminary air accident log may or may not work in my favour." He clouded over. "They could see it as an opportunity to lever an advanced management consultancy fee, and converge on Rendall Gilmour to test the temperature of the water, producing an unprecedented happening. You see—" Grimacing, he bared his teeth. "Contracted management consultancy fees are covered as line items in the project account and end up as admissible costs on the company balance sheet. Any disbursement given prior to contract award falls outside of Armstrong-Eliot's MO, and thereby will definitely not be allowed for fear of creating a precedent and falling foul of bribery and corruption accusations by the company's auditors, when such payments came to light in the profit and loss columns of the annual report."

"Yes, confidentially, I am well aware of the practice, and I do take your point. Let's just hope Cham and Mahmood don't get greedy, and take a long-term perspective about management consultancy fees, aka, inducements, and in the meantime, come up trumps in respect of the preliminary air accident recount." Stopping he changed the subject matter. "How are you coping being cell bound?"

"Solitary confinement is difficult, mainly because it fosters too much time to think and assume the worst. After you left Lahore last week, Aman had me fingerprinted, then implied fingerprints found in Chanda Govinda's apartment matched mine."

"How did you respond to the accusation?"

"I repeated I was not involved in her escape to India, and thereby had never entered her apartment, so the fingerprints found could not be mine."

"I imagine he didn't believe you."

"Of course."

"Well, as I have indicated before, I won't query anything that might incriminate you, so the fingerprint ruse will remain a red herring as far as the Foreign Office are concerned."

~ * ~

Back in his cell, Latham mentally went over all the permutations that might be derived from the British High Commission operation to extricate him from his detention. He had not told anyone about his true involvement in aiding Chanda Govinda to escape across the border, least of all Bill Kimble. If the escapade stayed unproven by the Lahore Police, there'd be nothing gained in confessing his part in the getaway. For him, it'd only open personal ramifications with both the Foreign Office via the British High Commission, and more critically, Armstrong-Eliot. The Foreign Office could take away his passport, making him a useless resource to the company, his dismissal directly following. Not relishing the prospect and rendering the finding of another sales-consultancy job in the supplier defence sector near to impossible, placing at risk his financial responsibilities to his sister Amelia for the upkeep of his daughters Nicol and Penny, he dismissed the barbed inclination.

But might he be worrying unnecessarily? Aman had confronted him with the farmer who had seen someone at the Jattanwali fence line, but apart from the Chief Inspector's blatant coercion, he did not voluntary identify Latham to be the person. Since, six days had passed with no further witnesses brought in. Of course, there weren't any. Nevertheless, could Aman manufacture a witness, persuading him by threats or bribery to finger Latham? The heartless likelihood tarried anonymous.

Apart from the witness element, Latham considered imaginable outcomes to the British High Commission plan of attack. With the air accident chronology as a defining fulcrum point, the forces of logic stacked up in his favour. Supplemented with HMG making an export license for the Armstrong-Eliot theatre-battlefield sensor technologies contingent on his release, seemed to make his discharge a certainty. Even so, despite all the positive dynamics he gleaned from Bill Kimble's briefing, politics could play a significant part in the release procedure, plausibly Aman conjuring up some form of counter not allowing it to happen.

Stretching out on his bunk, Latham realised more bridges had to be crossed before he saw the light of day again on a regular basis. Failing a successful sequel of the task ahead, only the unending, fettered sovereignty of a dark and sweltering Pakistani prison awaited him, without the tempering of tonality constraint.

Chapter 11: Resolution

Soon after Kimble returned to Karachi, Soames made representation to Brigadier Cham regarding the vital preliminary air accident data, the soldier reciprocating saying, Vice Admiral Mahmood and he were in toto cognizant with the Latham brainteaser, and intended to do everything within their sways to ensure a copy of the file wound its way into the Deputy British High Commission Karachi. Within 48 hours, it arrived on Soames desk. Armed with the crucial collateral, Kimble flew back to Lahore to secure Latham's release from police custody.

Agape that the British High Commission had managed to obtain the preliminary intelligence, at the onset the usually unshakeable Chief Inspector Aman blathered in response to Kimble's demand.

Regaining his composure, he insisted, "this document is a sideshow of the real crux why we are detaining Mister Latham—"

"Chief Inspector," Kimble tersely interrupted, "when you arrested Mister Latham, you expressly allied the Puma air attack to his alleged association with Chanda Govinda, her theoretical membership of the PRM, and her escape across the border." Picking up the instrument from Aman's desk, he touted, "this registration makes transparent a SAM Stinger missile brought down the Puma, and the only terrorist group having access to such a weapon via the Mujahedeen, are the Taliban. Effectively, it torpedoes your assertion the Punjab Reunification Movement were responsible for the juncture, and thereby there is no correlation between Mister Latham and the PRM."

"Might be so. Anyways, this is a preliminary report. If further exhibits come to light as the crash team investigators shift through the wreckage, the final document could make alternative conclusions."

"Chief Inspector," Kimble steadfastly rebuked, "we both know the possibility is highly unlikely. With respect, you are grasping at straws in your drive to sustain Mister Latham's detainment."

Annoyed, Aman wrinkled his brow, recognising his game plan for bringing Latham to trial had been at least partially invalidated. "Putting the anticipation aside for a moment, there is still the matter of Mister Latham's nexus in the escape of Chanda Govinda. You might surmise it is guesswork on our behalf, but there is enough circumstantial evidence to hold him until we have completed our investigations."

"Under the circumstances, Chief Inspector," Kimble argued, "at the very least, Mister Latham should be released from custody on bail."

"To effectuate such an undertaking, Mister Kimble," he threw back, "a lawyer will need to make an application to a circuit judge, and be heard in the Lahore High Court."

"Very well, the British High Commission will hire such a lawyer to make the application."

~ * ~

Eventuating from Aman's riposte, Kimble went on to see Landon Fawbert at the Lahore British Consulate, briefing him on the latest state of play in the nature of the Latham quandary.

Fawbert had owned a number of Foreign Office off-shore posts prior to being assigned first secretary for commercial and diplomatic affairs at the Lahore British Consulate. A dapper man with a sharp mind and a high regard for protocol, he joined the Foreign Office after graduating from the LSE with a degree in international affairs. During his career, he had gained a reputation for reading tricky situations correctly and handling arduous assignments, ideal prerequisites for dealing with the fast-developing Latham case.

After Kimble briefed him about Latham's predicament a few weeks earlier, before flying to Karachi, he had responded by arming Kimble with his take on the scrape. Subsequently, Fawbert made discreet enquiries with contacts in the Pakistani government administration, pertaining to current policies on foreigners assumed to be involved with anti-establishment organisations, including the PRM.

"Anchored on what I learnt from government sources," Fawbert retold, "in the current political climate, homeland intelligence agents and the police are showing little latitude for giving suspects, inclusive of foreign nationals, the benefit of the doubt if they are purported to have dissident alliances. Aman is not the only hard-faced policeman taking this policy to its limits." Offering a considerate expression to Kimble from across his desk, he solicited, "we will need to be careful selecting a lawyer to represent Latham's application for bail. In the past, cosy affinities between judges, briefs and senior policemen, have seen applications for bail turned down and suspects incorrectly imprisoned."

"Yes, the gerrymandering practice is infamous. The framework can be manipulated to generate the upshot the police covet, especially when there is a political angle, and evidently, Latham's misfortune falls into the discriminatory category."

"*Oh*," Fawbert juddered out. "Why?"

"We've been working the Pakistani establishment using Brigadier Cham and Vice Admiral Mahmood as conduits. Unfortunately, or rather, predictably, the well-meaning labour manufactured push back from opposing quarters."

"Those wanting to see Pakistan turned into a full-blown, fundamentalist Islamic State, run by the mullahs?"

"Yes. They are a minority, but they have out-of-proportion clout. Irrespective of us making supply of the Armstrong-Eliot theatre-battlefield sensor technologies dependent on Latham's release, as opposed to being clear-cut, its touch and go concerning his fate. At the end of the day, the political sphere of influence could override Pakistan Armed Forces military requirements. Though the French and the Americans can only offer inferior substitutes for the Armstrong-Eliot systems, the politicians might force Pakistan Armed Forces down either route."

"I see. Well—" Swinging about in his captain's chair whilst making cerebration, Fawbert then focused on a cabinet on the far side of his office containing dossiers on local Pakistanis providing various functions to the consulate, encompassing legal services.

"Landon," Kimble prompted, observing his inertia. "What are you thinking?!"

"I'll check our files, but I know in advance Babar Dhariwal is the one lawyer we've distinguished with a reputation for integrity. However—" Rubbing his chin, he contemplated further. "Selection of the circuit judge hearing the case will be down to the Ministry of Law & Justice. Bail pleas are held daily. They can be a bit hit and miss, dependent on who is in the chair. Dhariwal could advise if the sitting judge can be trusted to be impartial."

"Hhmm." Ruminating on a workup, Kimble's eyes flashed about as if fishing for the optimum package of measures. "Can you set up a meeting with Dhariwal?"

"I can do much better. I'll arrange for us to have dinner with him this evening, here at the consulate."

~ * ~

Straight off, Babar Dhariwal struck Kimble as being an atypical Pakistani. Far from the scowling and brooding archetype identified with the conspicuous majority of Pakistani men, he emitted an outgoing and congenial individuality, a glow unfluctuating on his face throughout conversation. Kimble refereed him to be persuasive, and feasibly had a winning way about him with judges and juries alike. He reminded him of some Pakistani senior civil servants and field-rank military officers he had met during the course of his duties, either influenced by British culture or the recipients of British training.

"Tell me, Mister Dhariwal," he implored, during pre-dinner aperitifs in the consulate's sumptuous lounge, "have you ever been to England?"

"Indeed I have, Mister Kimble. I graduated from the University of Exeter with a law degree."

"Mmmm, I thought as much. You have the mark of an English gentleman about you."

"Purely down to my grounding, whilst I attended Exeter. You see—" Coming over as gracious and convivial, his frothy ambience melted any further preconceptions. "I grew up in a traditional family, with demarcation lines for the genders and a life guide defining acceptable behaviour as laid down by the Koran. I found it all very regimented and restrictive. An epiphany moment, Exeter liberated the gregarious side of my nature, saturating me with confidence."

"Has your emancipation helped you in your chosen profession?"

"It has. Often, my clients have poor regard for the law and the judiciary, picturing both are biased against them. I try to infuse them with the self-belief they are capable of defending themselves in a law court, by being honest and fearless." Grinning devilishly, he qualified, "given they are innocent. And for my part, during court sessions I try to make a bond with both the judge and the jury, and if apt, bring some levity into play. You see, in principle, administering the law is a portentous duty, and those coming into its domain feel they must also adopt a solemn stance. Of course, I do not advocate flippancy, more a desire to encourage those on trial to let their natural disposition shine. It's a well-known celebrated benchmark that juries make consideration not just based on the facts brought out by both prosecuting and defending counsels, but also on how the defendant comes across in terms of personage."

"Mmmm, you appear to be very conversant with your trade," Kimble complimented. "Let me put our cards on the table. Mister Fawbert and I have a potential client for you." Facing his colleague, he advocated, "Landon, please acquaint Mister Dhariwal with our problem."

Fawbert profiled every detail on the Latham conundrum, punctuating his review by stating the British High Commission needed a lawyer to make representation in court to attain the detainee's bail. "Our main dread," he enlightened, "is Latham being put before a circuit judge who has a political agenda, and concealed sympathies for Muslim extremists and terrorists."

"I'm accustomed to all the circuit judges working the Lahore High Court," Dhariwal established. "Regrettably, some are as you describe, but most are either neutral or defend the status quo. They have no wish to live in a fundamentalist Islamic State run by the mullahs."

"We understand Haroon Sangrasi is the circuit judge sitting next week," Kimble pitched. "Can you give us a thumbnail sketch of him?"

Searching for a judicious response, Dhariwal cogitated on the request. "Hhmm, not the ideal. He *is* staunchly against any form of terrorism, and those associated with it, but on the positive side, he abhors the mullahs, so it's unlikely Chief Inspector Aman can play the Islamist card before the hearing."

"Do I take you to mean, the police discuss cases with the judiciary as a matter of course, before hearings take place?"

"Purely unofficially, Mister Kimble, and only when the police have a singular interest in seeing the detainee remains in their custody."

"So Aman will accost Sangrasi about Latham's case?"

"As I say, it is credible, but Sangrasi will be conscious of Aman's extremist Islamic State leanings, so it is likely he will deduce Aman has an ulterior motive to further his adopted cause." Resting, he vented a steely blaze at Kimble. "It will bolster your case tremendously, if you can field a character witness for Mister Latham, preferably a Pakistani of some standing."

"Mmmm. Latham has very good fellowship with Lieutenant Colonel Ghulam Bishara, Head of Battlefield Surveillance Systems Directorate, Pakistan Army, at JSHQ Rawalpindi."

"Excellent. High-ranking officers are ideal."

"Right." Kimble turned to Fawbert. "Landon, you make an application for bail, utilising Mister Dhariwal's talents. Meanwhile, I'll contact Colonel Bishara, petitioning him to speak on Latham's behalf at the hearing."

~ * ~

The following Monday, armed police officers escorted Latham from Police HQ to the Lahore High Court. Kimble had flown to Karachi the morning after he met Dhariwal, so Fawbert had visited Chatterjee Road with Dhariwal to issue the request for bail certificate issued by Judge Sangrasi, and to introduce Latham to his lawyer.

Standing in the dock, Latham gazed at Dhariwal in his defence position, then at Fawbert sat slightly behind him. Both retorted with dauntless faces. Scrutinising all quarters of the court room, Latham clocked Chief Inspector Aman alongside prosecuting counsel, Mister Hingora, various court functionaries, and a few people in the public seating area, embracing Ghulam Bishara. Expanding his study, he locked onto a tall white man, dressed in an off-white suit. *Must be a journalist*, he derived.

Proceedings opened at 10:00 am, with the clerk of the court reading out the charges against Latham, and Mister Hingora acquainting Judge Sangrasi with the stage setting behind his arrest and detainment in police custody. With reference to the available data, though it be circumstantial, he emphasised the police believed the accused to be guilty of aiding and abetting a probable terrorist to escape across the border. Closing by opposing application for bail, Sangrasi noted down the objection.

Defence counsel Dhariwal then challenged the assertions made, Latham's presupposed alliance with Chanda Govinda in particular. He further stated the police had no solid corroboration against the accused, and had not charged him. Under the circumstances, he nominated Latham be set free under bail conditions.

Quizzing the accused as to his purpose for being in Pakistan, Latham replied to the judge by explaining the nature of Armstrong-Eliot's business, and his engagement with Pakistan Armed Forces. Satisfied with the explanation, Sangrasi told the clerk of the court to call the accused's character witness to the stand.

After Bishara verified his post with Pakistan Armed Forces, Sangrasi probed, "what is your connection with the accused, Lieutenant Colonel Bishara."

"I have known ex-RAF Wing Commander Dale Latham since May 1986, when he visited the Pakistan Army Aviation Wing at AVN Base Multan. At the time, Mister Latham headed sales for Dandridge's sensor systems division. We met again at Dandridge in West London, June 1987, and more recently, just a few weeks ago, when he visited JSHQ Rawalpindi on behalf of Armstrong-Eliot."

"And how'd you describe Mister Latham's persona and temperament?"

"Dale Latham is a trustworthy, honourable man, rare attributes in an age of skullduggery and double-dealings."

"I see." Sangrasi recorded a few salient remarks before addressing the prosecuting counsel. "Mister Hingora."

Counsel for the prosecution stood and glared at the witness, his demeanour belligerent, dismissive. "Lieutenant Colonel Bishara, has what you have heard regarding the charges against Mister Latham surprised you?"

"Yes. Very much so."

"So, you don't concede there could be a dark side to Mister Latham's personality?"

"Incontestably not."

Skeptical, Hingora exchanged a few whispered words with Aman, Latham eyeing them suspiciously.

Resuming, counsel for the prosecution queried, "can you really have formed such a favourable conviction of the accused, fathered on three meetings?"

Clearing his throat, as if affronted by Hingora's cynicism, Bishara then clarified, "I have been with Pakistan Armed Forces for over 30 years. During my tenure, I have learnt to gauge both Pakistani nationals and foreigners with impartiality. Often, first impressions are proved to be true over succeeding years. My initial imprint of Mister Latham has endured as I stated, trustworthy and honourable. My appreciation has been perpetual, without reservation."

Pouting dismissively in response to the intrepid reply, albeit, Hingora disciplined himself not to counteract the assertion. "Thank you, Lieutenant Colonel Bishara."

Standing Bishara down, the judge allowed Hingora to continue arguing as to why the accused should be denied bail. Appropriate to the severity of police misgivings against him, Hingora stressed it was not in the public interest to allow a probable enemy of the state the opportunity to escape justice, his rhetoric fiery with unbridled belief. Astounded by its ferocity, Latham anxiously eyed Dhariwal, the defence counsel hand gesturing for him to stay calm.

By contrast, when Sangrasi called counsel for the defence to make his argument, Dhariwal remained light of tone and fleet of foot, his entreating mug endearing him to the court. Contending his client resided merely as a victim of circumstance, in the wrong place at the wrong time, and pinpointed by the police because they had failed to apprehend the real miscreant, if in truth such a person existed, he effortlessly pulled Hingora's conjecture apart. During his reasoned monologue, Latham discerned Aman surging into the jitters, his eyes burning with venom, his hands clenched together exposing pressurised veins.

After the judge had asked the accused a few more questions, verifying his background and presumed previous clean bill of health with the law, he summoned counsels for the prosecution and defence to make concluding statements, Hingora pressing for bail to be denied, Dhariwal safeguarding the court the British Consulate had agreed to be responsible for Latham's bail conditions to the letter.

Calling the clerk of the court to the bench, Sangrasi spoke to him under his breath, Latham left beside himself apropos the outcome of his hearing. Facing Dhariwal and Fawbert expectantly, in response, counsel for the defence extended him an encouraging cast.

Breaking from hushed conversation, the judge addressed the counsel for the prosecution. "Mister Hingora, on balance, I have heard nothing suggesting the accused might abscond if set free under bail conditions. Bail is set at 1milion rupees. The Lahore Police will continue to keep Mister Latham's passport until their explorations are complete pertinent to Chanda Govinda's illegal defection."

His hammer came down on the gavel, and the clerk of the court commanded, "all rise."

After louring at Latham, Aman quickly left the court, Hingora in tow.

Seconds elapsed before Dhariwal and Fawbert jubilantly made for the dock.

"You can come down now, Mister Latham," counsel for the defence offered with a broad smile.

Stepping down Latham wondered, "what happens now?"

"Mister Fawbert will pay the ticket to the clerk of the court. In turn, he will supply the terms of your bail to us and the police. It will most probably say you are to remain at the British Consulate, and you must check in with the police periodically, until their investigations are complete."

Laying a compassionate hand on Latham's shoulder, Fawbert prescribed, "come on, Dale, I'm sure you'd welcome a hot bath, followed by some quality food and a soft bed at the consulate. We'll also deck you out in some new clothes."

"Yes, but to begin with, I must thank Lieutenant Colonel Bishara."

Elated, Latham walked into the public area where Bishara stood smiling warmly at him.

"Well, Dale, I didn't expect to meet you again so soon, and under such trying singularities."

"My dear Ghulam, thank you for your impassioned and resolute character statement. It's what swung the judge to allow bail."

Glancing up and down the courtroom, Bishara examined for snoops. "Come, let's get further away from the court administrators."

Following him to a quieter part of the public area, Bishara rested by the exit door then turned to face Latham with a grievous phiz.

"Dale." Eyeballing the Englishman with both reverence and a ration of rebuke, he then ratcheted down his obvious tilt at mild castigation by adopting his usual sanguine personality. "You are a good and compassionate man, so I'd not be dazed if you came to the aid of a distressed woman. I'll refrain from asking you to confirm or deny the charges against you in respect of aiding Miss Govinda, but I'd caution you to be very wary of incurring Chief Inspector Aman's displeasure." Darting his eyes about, he reconnoitred to ensure they still had privacy. "Before traveling to Lahore, I canvassed opinions on him from some contacts I have in the Ministry of Law & Justice. I can't tell you what I discovered, but I will say, it disturbed me. He is a very clever man playing the political structure to get what he wants. He is well connected with some government opposition politicians both in Lahore and Islamabad. Whatever he suspects you off, do not treat it lightly. I'd also advise you to marshal the full force of British High Commission resources to extricate yourself from this mess pronto."

Latham lowered his head. "I take your point, Ghulam. But please believe me, Landon Fawbert and others have been shifting heaven and earth on my behalf."

"Are you unambiguous the Lahore Police won't find any incriminating evidence?"

"Yes."

Breathing out a sigh of relief he trilled, "well my friend, let us hope when we meet again, it will be under a less onerous *mise en scene*." Squinting at his watch, clearly pushed for time, he frowned. "I really must go. Good luck, Dale."

After shaking hands, Latham watched him leave the courtroom. Refacing the bench, he saw the gent in the off-white suit he had noticed at the start of the hearing had abided in the public area. Concentrating on him for a few instants, he took in the man's angular facial features and unmistakable detachment to his stare, then peered away on hearing Fawbert call to him.

"Dale, we need you to attend the clerk of the court with Mister Dhariwal. They want you to sign a few papers."

Joining them, Latham glimpsed back into the public area, but the man in the off-white suit had gone.

Chapter 12: Bail

Settling into his consulate quarters, partial relief gushed through Latham, the Lahore Police not confronting him with any further witnesses or incontrovertible actualities appertaining to his hypothetical tie in Chanda Govinda's escape, instilling him with pregnant hope. Nevertheless, he revisited notions about Aman manufacturing evidence and presenting false witnesses, in his drive to make an example of him. In exchange for allowing an export license for the sale of Armstrong-Eliot battlefield target sensor systems to Pakistan Armed Forces, the British High Commission had played all their cards, principally arousing his release, and if not charged, complete exoneration to the *quid pro quo*. Legitimately, they could do nothing more. Realising he needed to play the waiting game until Aman informed the consulate *vis-a-vis* completion of detective work, he decided to contact his family and Armstrong-Eliot, telling them the good news about his bail.

Later in the day he telephoned Amelia.

"Dale, after receiving a call from Mister Kimble about your police detainment, we've been so worried about you. Though he made it out to be a minor issue, my instincts told me it lodged as something more serious."

"What have you said to Nicol and Penny?"

"Only that due to commercial drivers, you have been delayed in Pakistan for longer than expected."

"Did they buy it?"

"So far, but if this dilemma continues, at some stage I will have to confide in them. When do you expect to book a flight to Heathrow?"

"Hard to say, Amelia. It all depends on when the Lahore Police terminate their investigation."

"Are you aware, a chronicle in last Thursday's Telegraph pertained to an unnamed British businessman arrested and taken into custody by the Lahore Police?"

"No."

"It came via a Reuters feed from a Pakistani Government spokesman. On the back of it, no doubt the British press will sense a feeding frenzy." She broke off, Latham detecting some reserve in the making. "Did your court display attract newsmen?"

"Not sure. There were no photographers or journalists pressing my defence counsel for a statement at the end of the hearing, however..." He scowled.

"*Yes*," she goaded, sensing reservation in his voice.

"I did see one white man in the court public area."

"Ahh, he must have been a columnist."

"Maybe, but if so, why didn't he call for an interview or a statement?"

"Dear God—" He depicted her hunching her shoulders. "I've got no idea, Dale. You tell me."

"I can't, and the sighting has left me with a strange presage, but plausibly I suppose it's nothing."

"You don't sound very sure of yourself. Did you ask the British High Commission representative about this man?"

"I intended to, but he vanished."

"Well, what worries me is, if he is a pressman, the daily's will be full of the case, and now they'll know your name. Nicol and Penny are bound to pick up on the detail."

"Yes, and it's to be avoided. I'll call you tomorrow to see if it proves to be the case."

Closing the call with some small talk, next Latham telephoned Matthew Chapman at Armstrong-Eliot.

"I'd imagine MoD have been keeping you up to date with my affliction via the Foreign Office?"

"Yes, Dale. We've been fully briefed. What's the latest?"

Latham recalled the bail hearing details, finishing by saying he'd be resident at the British Consulate Lahore until the police finalised their enquiries.

"How much longer do you estimate this stalemate to go on?"

"*Huh*, I called my sister before telephoning you. She tabled the same query. I wish I knew, Matthew." Dithering, his cadence germinated into a fraught rasp. "Consequently, I'm increasingly concerned about my future with the company."

"Your job is safe for the time being. Rendall Gilmour is covering your responsibilities and customer base. Having said that, I'm going to find it difficult to convince the board of directors to maintain this state of affairs for much longer. It's nearly three weeks since you were arrested and detained by the police. I'm sure the board can be persuaded to view you favourably for another few weeks, but from then on, don't count your chickens."

"Yes, I reckoned you might say something along those lines."

"Hospitalisation after an air accident can be tolerated, but I rather think your troublesome obstacle has come about sequent to a personal union, well out of the sphere of your company duties."

"I'm not going to argue the asseveration, Matthew. I'd just like to be reassured you will continue to champion me for as long as you can."

"You have my word, Dale. Keep your pecker up, and call or wire me as soon as the impasse is resolved."

"Will do."

Ruffled and jumpy, the next day, Latham called Amelia again.

"Anything more in today's newspapers?"

"Not a sausage. Clem bought The Times, the Guardian and the Daily Express, as well as the Telegraph. We combed every international section, but the news from Pakistan did not make any mention of an Englishman being in court."

"Well, it rather proves the hypothesis. The white man in the off-white suit could not have been a correspondent."

"Mmmm. Maybe he lives in Lahore, and has a fascination for court cases?"

"Possibly, but if it were true, he'd have had a suntan. It's impossible to avoid a suntan if you are out here for any length of time. This chap appeared to have just stepped off the flight from London, his skin tone as pale as oriental lilies."

"Well, you'll have more important issues to absorb your time, rather than figuring out the origins of a complete stranger in a Lahore courtroom."

"Yes, you're right, Amelia. Plainly, it's just me being paranoid, a symptom resultant from my incarceration."

His meditations still dogged by the unexplained stranger; Latham addressed Landon Fawbert on the subject.

"A tall, white man in an off-white suit?" Fawbert dubiously reiterated.

"Yes, with angular facial features and blond hair, aged about 30. He sat towards the back in the public area behind the prosecution team."

"Can't say I saw him. Besides, I concentrated on proceedings. But er—" Baring his teeth, not in the accepted hostile fashion but more prompted by apprehension, he beseeched, "why is this sighting patently causing you anxiety?"

"I just can't rationalise it, Landon, other than seeing what, on the face of it, is a curious court hawk of European origin, I've failed to fathom my vague intuitions."

"Well, erm...*hah*—" He beamed at Latham. "Forget about this phantom. Just gird your loins for whatever comes out of the police investigation, and hope it is negative."

"Yes, it's what I kept telling myself, whilst caged in that grime-ridden police cell."

~ * ~

Over the course of the next week, Latham reported to Police HQ every day, accompanied by Fawbert; the terms of his bail necessitating the daily check-in. On the fourth day, when the Englishmen left Police HQ, as usual Fawbert turned left to retrieve his Rover 827 with diplomatic plates, leaving Latham waiting outside its main entrance on Chatterjee

Road, idly monitoring street life hustle and bustle. Never one for extreme regularity, the daily demand had started to grate on Latham. It seemed no sooner had he completed the obligation then the blessed process began again. Casually gawping at passing road vehicles, the odd donkey-drawn conveyance, and a throng of people going about their everyday routines, it dawned on him they were all completely free, whereas he abided tethered to a metaphorical leash, a virtual prisoner with very limited liberties.

Shaking his head at the recognition, coincidentally he clocked a man dressed in an off-white suit, staring at him from the opposite side of Chatterjee Road, some 30 yards away, the man's image, *inter alia* his angular face and blond hair coming into full focus for a few moments, every 10 to 15 thudding heartbeats, when passers-by exposed him. As the man continued to pour over him, Latham's jaw dropped in amazement. Next, he heard the toot-toot of a car horn and turned to see the Rover pull up in front of him.

Swiftly opening the passenger door, Latham yelled, "can you see him?"

"What?"

"The man I saw in court is standing on the opposite side of the road." He pointed. "Look." But the man had gone.

Fawbert peeked in the given direction. "Get in the car, Dale."

"But he was there I tell you."

"Get in the car."

As the Rover pulled away, Latham perused Chatterjee Road hoping to see the bogeyman.

Stealing a glimpse at his companion, Fawbert labeled, "this obsession is fast entering phobia territory, Dale. Lots of men wear off-white suits in Pakistan."

"This was a white man."

"Some Pakistanis have light complexions and are easily mistaken for Europeans."

"I'm telling you, Landon, it's the same man I saw in court. He stared directly at me, as if transmitting a message."

"Don't be ridiculous. This milieu is getting the better of you. You need to calm down and relax."

Frustrated, Latham did not argue the averment, but persisted absolutely sure of the identification. *Why did that man survey me?* he pondered. *What does he want?*

~ * ~

Anonymous to Latham, back at the Consulate, Fawbert called Bill Kimble at the British Deputy High Commission, Karachi.

"My impression is, Latham is losing it, Bill."

"What's made you come to such an ungenerous conclusion?"

"He has delusions about a white man he saw at the bail hearing dogging him."

The line went quiet.

"Bill…"

"Sorry… just deliberating. Tell me more."

"He claims to have seen a white man dressed in an off-white suit in the court public area, and today, when we went to Police HQ for his daily enrolment, allegedly, the same man stood on Chatterjee Road, spying on him. Professedly it's nothing, but what's your take?"

"Hhmm, let me call you back. I just need a few minutes with John Soames to discuss the matter."

Baffled by Kimble's apparent awkwardness, his response inciting more issues than it answered, Fawbert slowly replaced the telephone receiver, the minutes turning into over an hour before Kimble telephoned him back.

"Landon, I need to tell you something in confidence over the scrambled link. Can you go to the security room at the consulate, and I'll call you back from our security room."

Howbeit befuddled, Fawbert complied with the command.

"To say the least, what I have to tell you is sensitive," Kimble began when they reengaged, his idiom so sincere he had Fawbert guessing as to what might be divulged. "So please keep it to yourself. The fewer people who know, the better."

"Go on."

"After the police took Latham into detention, Soames and I discussed the implications *vis-à-vis* his security status. While with the RAF, Latham's top-secret security classification gave him access to highly sensitive, on a need-to-know basis data, especially about airborne weapon delivery apparatus, smart weapons, and battlefield strategies, some still current. If he were to be lawfully imprisoned, it makes him vulnerable to coercion from the Pakistani authorities, and, a potential mark for terrorists, should sympathizers in the Pakistan government structure allow him to be kidnapped. With his branded allegiance to the institution of a mullah-run Islamic State, Chief Inspector Aman could be a candidate, allowing the latter action to arise."

"I see." Still not entirely cognizant with Kimble's line of thought, Fawbert flexed his facial muscles. "So, what is this preamble leading up to, Bill?"

Almost feeling Fawbert's disconcertion welling up, Kimble clarified, "when we acquainted the Foreign Office about the Latham pickle, they contacted MoD. In turn, we suspect with Latham's top-secret security classification in mind, MoD made MI6 aware of the emergency."

"You don't mean to tell me—" Alarmed by the opus of his adverse ramifications calculation train he halted. "Are you implying Latham is being shadowed by MI6…" Further floored by the distasteful conviction, he lingered then unsteadily completed the certitude. "…and the white man Latham claims he saw, is an MI6 operative?"

"Well, yes."

"*Good god*," he exclaimed. "He's not a liquidator, is he?"

"We can't confirm for certain, Landon, but it's not nameless for UK nationals with top-secret security classifications to be taken out by MI6, if they arbitrate the person under surveillance cannot extricate themselves from the hole they're embroiled in."

"*Oohh*!" Fawbert's eyes blinked from side to side as he took in Kimble's reckoning. "Do you perceive Latham has made the coupling?"

"No, not yet, or he'd have made his fear clear to you."

"And presumably, if this person is an MI6 agent, he has not registered with the British High Commission in Islamabad?"

"I called Augustus Dawson to see if he had received an authorised notification from MI6, but he replied in the negative. MI6 are a law unto themselves. Protocol does not necessitate they contact overseas British high commissions and embassies when on a mission, and, we do not have the remit to demand appreciation of their purpose or power to reign in their activities."

"Dear me—" Breathlessness devoured Fawbert. "What a terrible pinch. What on Earth are we going to do, Bill?"

"Soames wants you to sit tight for the time being. Say nothing to Latham, and if he makes the MI6 linkage, say he is incorrect. He's a smart cookie, so he won't credit you, but…it's the official line, Landon."

When Fawbert left the consulate security room, the increased, languid pulsation of his jugular against his starched shirt collar caused by Kimble's news making for increased blood pressure, necessitated him to undo his top button. Taking a few deep breaths, he recomposed himself before returning to his office.

Sure enough, he had heard rumours about MI6 liquidators, but this transpired as the foremost occasion it had touched his patch. Though a very experienced diplomat, used to resolving all kinds of commercial, cultural and personal matters, the Latham fix had slipped into an altogether more tenuous category. If the Lahore Police found a way to convict him, be it real or rendered, he knew MI6 would engineer a method for eliminating him, possibly in such a way to come across as an accident, rather than death on the end of a sniper's bullet, or a poisoned umbrella tip. But all the theorising paled at the prospect of Latham making the bridge between his top-secret security classification and the white man in the off-white suit being an MI6 agent, then confronting him with it.

"How do you console a man destined for the drop by his own side, if the Pakistani legal directorate finds against him?" he asked himself.

~ * ~

For what bore the hallmarks of an eternity, Fawbert continued to escort his charge to Police HQ for his daily recording, on every instance Latham constantly on watch for the chimera who had eyeballed him on

148

Chatterjee Road. He did not see him but sensed someone spied on him from a concealed position, his studying of the crowd and darting eye movements alerting Fawbert's scrutiny. Deciding to ignore Latham's behaviour in case it led to a protracted conversation, culminating in him making a conceivable MI6 interdependence, Fawbert did not discourage him. Instead, he ushered Latham in and out the Police HQ, without disbelieving his forebearance to clock his shadow.

The tedious commitment continued for a few more days, then out of the blue, Chief Inspector Aman's aid materialised during the next check-in, summoning the Englishmen to Aman's office.

"I have to tell you, Mister Latham," Aman began from behind his desk, "we are still not satisfied with your story relating to your guild with Chanda Govinda. Granted, I will concede most probably, the PRM did not perpetrate the SAM attack on the helicopter at Pakistan AFB Lahore. However, our examinations reveal you were the only white man Miss Govinda had any contact with during the period immediately prior to her illegal crossing of the borderline into East Punjab. Brokered on the statement made by the farmer, seeing a white man in the fence line vicinity, and who thereafter evaded the chasing border patrol, by default, you remain our prime suspect."

"But Chief Inspector," Fawbert retorted, "the farmer did not positively identify Mister Latham when you brought the two of them together, and I presuppose since you have not confronted Mister Latham with other witnesses or unequivocal particulars, nothing to incriminate him has come to hand?"

"Your speculation is now beside the point, Mister Fawbert. Suspicion braced by logic is enough to indict Mister Latham for a court trial." As Aman cast a disparaging mien at him, the blood began to drain from Latham's face. He could see himself being convicted and spending no telling how many years behind bars in a foul Pakistani prison. "Howsoever," Aman continued. Standing up, he turned and lamped at a map of greater Lahore on his office wall, his intention, to prolong the tension. Avoiding the Englishmen's eyes, he aired, "it seems Mister Latham has friends in high places, principally with Pakistan Armed Forces. I have been instructed by the Ministry of Law & Justice not to charge Mister Latham unless the charge can be substantiated with witnesses in court." Facing the Englishmen, he reluctantly ratified, "unless new evidence is established up to and including the maximum time we can have him in virtual custody, I am also ordered to release him from his bail conditions." Wittingly hanging out the promising edict, he then conveyed, "his detention time expired at midnight yesterday."

Astounded by the admission, Fawbert rippled his brow. "You mean, Mister Latham is free to go, and you will return his passport?"

"He is free to go, but his passport will be given to him at his overseas airport departure point. In the meantime, we will continue to track down fresh witnesses and hard exhibits connecting Mister Latham with Chanda Govinda's escape."

"I see."

"Before you leave this building, Mister Fawbert, see the desk-sergeant and he will go through the process of releasing Mister Latham from his bail conditions."

Still rattled by the startling plot twists, Fawbert gathered his judgments before responding. "Right...erm—" He glinted at Latham, also dumbfounded by the directive. "Let's get on with it."

~ * ~

On leaving Police HQ, for once, a gleam covered Dale Latham's face. Emerging into pure daylight, he buoyantly peeped upwards at a cloudless blue sky, a ginormous load having been lifted from his shoulders. Evaporating from the forefront of his mind, for once he did not browse the foreground in search of the banshee, a.k.a, the mysterious white man in the off-white suit. Already he saw himself climbing aboard a British Airways 747 and heading back to Blighty.

Meanwhile, as Fawbert retrieved the Rover, he remained flummoxed by Aman's tame backdown without objection to Latham's good fortune. *Could his release be that simple?* He premeditated not. Perhaps the policeman played another card, something more clandestine to keep his suspect loosely within his grip.

Driving back to the consulate, Fawbert put his surmises aside. "Well, Dale, you must be ecstatic."

"I'm still trying to resolve what just happened, but—" He beamed at Fawbert. "I've decided to stow away my reservations and bask in my new-found freedom away from the bail criteria."

"Yes, er," he near-to comically exalted, "Her Majesties Government will be pleased to retrieve our one million rupees bail bond."

Back in one of the consulate's first floor reception rooms towering over Mozang Road, Latham's high-spirited mood bloomed. "This really is a red-letter day," he enthused. "For a while, I perceived I'd never see England again."

"Yes, a most welcome but unforeseen reversal of fortunes," Fawbert accredited, trying to reflect Latham's joy. "But I'm still wondering what really prompted it."

Not taking in his reservation, Latham effervesced with more elation. After setting out his blueprints appertaining to resumption of his family and professional life, he quizzed, "what's the procedure from here, Landon?"

"Well, erm—" Coughing as if to regulate himself back into formality, he donned an approved posture. "As I understand it, you'll need to be debriefed by John Soames in Karachi, and of course arrangements have to be made with the police for the restoration of your passport at Jinnah International Airport." Forcing a bright countenance before dropping his manner into a lower register, his scepticism about Latham's release still budding, he verified, "but er, I'd speculate within a week you'll be touching down at Heathrow."

Latham clapped his hands. "Oh my word, wonderful." Bouncing about the reception room he envisioned the near future, then quite at random, squinting out of one of the windows against the sun, for the briefest of moments, he saw the man in the off-white suit. "*Mother of God!*" he bellowed, luring Fawbert's absorption.

"What?"

"He's down there on Mozang Road."

"Who is?"

Facing Fawbert, his jubilant footing rapidly decaying into unease, Latham trumpeted, "the *man* in the off-white suit."

Scurrying over to the window, Fawbert leered out.

"Can you see him?" Latham burbled. "He's on the far pavement, standing next to some parked cars."

Grimacing, Fawbert picked out Latham's spectre between people walking to and fro. "Yes, I do see him."

"You deliberated I had imagined him, didn't you?"

"True, the mind can play tricks on the senses for people caught in a police web." Overwhelmed by knock-on repercussions, he turned away from the presence. "But incontrovertibly, he is real."

"Who the hell is he?" Latham vociferously explored. "Why is he dogging me?" Suddenly, the light went on. "Just a minute..." He glowered at Fawbert. "...of course, I should have made the connection earlier. He's not a columnist for one of the dailies or a curious law court spectator, is he?" Stepping forward, he hindered just short of Fawbert, his eyes aflame with the realisation eluding him when his mind tarried cluttered with strains about a credible jail sentence. "He's a UK government man, isn't he? checking to see if I'd be acquitted, or imprisoned." Lowering his head, cognizance overtook him. "With my top-secret knowledge I'm regarded to be a security risk, aren't I?" He swung his head up sharply. "He's MI6...isn't he?"

Awkwardly, Fawbert turned away, his embarrassment plain to Latham. "We can't sanction that for definite, Dale, but he could be?"

"*God almighty!*" Convulsed, the flesh out came crashing through, Latham pouting sardonically. "For a while I lost my capacity for logic, when I dawdled so consumed with my arrest and confinement." Strolling away from the glazing, hands in his trouser pockets, bewilderment overtook him. "It's manifest now. The British High Commission informed MoD about my glitch, and bearing in mind my security classification, they told MI6." Faltering on the back of vivid attainment, he swiveled about, staring back at Fawbert searchingly. "But what is his mission, Landon? What has he been tasked to do?"

Compulsively Fawbert confided, "we can only guess about his intentions. As always, the intelligence services operate independent of the

Foreign Office. We are rarely told about their in-country activities, apart from when they need our help."

"Well, he's not here purely to observe aftermaths. Dependent on how my police enigma ultimately works out, he's here to make sure I never end up in a Pakistani prison, and I don't mean to spirit me away." His revelation flowering, he solemnly lamented, "he's here to liquidate me."

"We don't know for sure, Dale."

"Either way, I'm not going to be safe from either Chief Inspector Aman or the man in the off-white suit, until I have my passport, and I'm out of Pakistani air space."

~ * ~

After much conjecture, late in the afternoon Fawbert called Kimble in Karachi.

"We have an unpredicted turn of events, Bill," he relayed on, his voice clinical without triumph. "Latham has been released from his bail condition under behest from the Ministry of Law & Justice."

Staggered by the unanticipated rebound, he responded, "well, I must confess your news confounds me. Pakistan Armed Forces, principally by way of the offices of Brigadier Cham and Vice Admiral Mahmood must have more clout than we conceived."

"Aman is persisting his quest and has retained Latham's passport, but if his explorations yield nothing further, Latham is free to leave Pakistan."

The line went quiet at the Karachi end.

"Bill!"

"Sorry, just brooding. Tell me, with Aman's celebrated mullah-run Islamic State leanings and his presumed unceremonious confederation with Muslim terrorist organisations, might he have freed Latham in order for him to be captured by say, the Taliban?"

"A similar brainwave has crossed my mind, but I didn't want to table it. I gauged it'd sound just too fanciful." Pausing, he swallowed to discharge the tension in his voice. "There is another factor as well." He coughed, the release still incomplete. "Latham has now made the link between the man in the off-white suit and MI6."

"How?"

"The man spied on the consulate straight after Latham's liberation from his bail conditions. He saw him and the inevitable ensued."

"I see. I thought I detected some strain in your voice."

"Quite. For obvious reasons, I've lasted uptight since the sighting."

"So, erm—" Kimble contorted his face at the gravity of what he had to say next. "Latham assumes he is a liquidation target?"

"Yes. He worked out the variables and came to that conclusion. Since he is free from police custody, I saw no point in denying the possibility"

"So...we are faced with both a feasible abduction, and if Aman produces conclusive depositions of Latham's guilt, an even more conceivable assassination."

"Quite so. To say the Latham scrape has snowballed is an understatement." Dwelling to assemble a precise next set of words, he pleaded, "Bill, I need some express direction from Soames, approved by British High Commissioner Dawson in Islamabad, and, the Foreign Office."

"Right. Let me get back to you after I've had a confab with Soames. In the meantime, keep Latham inside the consulate, and raise the terrorist threat alert level to severe."

Chapter 13: Abduction

Fully focused on the campaign, Fawbert carried out Kimble's instructions, also arranging commercial air transportation to take Latham from Lahore to Karachi. Wondering what might come about next, he began to assess the Latham crisis in the mould of a haphazard airborne foul-play leading to a set of knock-on sequels, yet to be holistically resolved.

When consequential from the evolving danger to Latham he called for Chief Security Officer Doyle Blake to uprate the consulate's terrorist threat alert level to severe, a distinct vibe of restlessness swept over him. A seasoned professional with ice water in his veins, Blake had taken onboard the decree without hesitancy, his emotionless response magnifying Fawbert's looming ferment.

Before moving to Foreign Office security, Blake had been with the SAS, seeing action in Operation Desert Storm, and prior to taking up his post at Lahore, with the British Embassy Khartoum. Attacked by Islamic militants, Foreign Office grapevine chatter reported Blake and his team defeated the assault on the Khartoum embassy with consummate professionalism, repelling the assailants within tens of seconds, six jihadists dispatched to Allah, and no embassy staff injured. Fawbert hoped Blake wouldn't have to perform similar heroics at the Lahore British Consulate.

Telephoning Fawbert with his requested instructions, Kimble's message annexed further alarm to his already shaken state.

"Here's the upshot of my discussions with Dawson and Soames. Under the prevailing set of inevitabilities, we shouldn't take any chances with Latham's security. When you escort him to Lahore Airport, use the bullet-resistant Rover 800, with an armed guard following in an open-top jeep."

"Got it."

"By the way, Dawson called MI6 in London. Before taking over the Pakistan British High Commissioner post from Branden Godfrey, he had some undertakings with MI6 in his previous Foreign Office post in Prague. Despite the association, MI6 neither confirmed nor denied they have a man in the field in Lahore. Translated, it means they do. Unfortunately, the caveat precluded Dawson from dissecting the nature of the operative's mission in depth."

"So presumably, we continue to surmise the worse?"

"Yes. It's imperative Latham collects his passport and makes it onto a UK-bound flight, without any intervention from Muslim terrorists, or the Lahore Police reacquiring him. If either potentiality were to occur, the shadowy MI6 man might take action."

"I've got Latham booked on a PIA domestic flight to Karachi, departing at 08:45 tomorrow. I assume you'll meet him at Jinnah International?"

"Yes, and I have already arranged for a bullet-resistant Jaguar XJ40 and an armed guard for his escort to the Deputy High Commission."

"What do we do—" Taking in a sharp intake of breath, Fawbert broke off, fretfulness diluting his professionalism. "What do we do, if chummy turns up en route to Lahore Airport?"

"MI6 never put Foreign Office personal in the firing line. If this man in the off-white suit is going to do anything, it will be when Latham alights from the Rover, but it's highly unlikely. Obviously, he knows Latham has been released, so he'll back off for the time being."

Unconvinced, Fawbert uttered, "mmmm. What about if he takes the same flight as Latham to Karachi?"

"He could do, but liquidating a mark on an aircraft is very risky, and if caught, MI6 will not want their man facing a public trial of his own." Lingering, Kimble made further consideration. "No, I'd deem he still has a watching brief."

"Holy Moses, you've drawn up all the possibilities."

"Yes. Subsequent to MI6 virtually confirming they had a man in the field, I mooted the same issues you have slated during the three-way review with Dawson and Soames. We've addressed all the potentials."

"I've got a bad augury about this whole intrigue, Bill. I've had it since Aman fortuitously unbound Latham from his bail conditions. It feels like a set up. And now there is the categorical probability of an MI6 agent coming into play with a different agenda."

"Yes, I agree, but we have no other selection but to bring Latham back to Karachi. Just try to stay calm, Landon, and above all else, don't let Latham discern your reservations about his security."

"Right. I'll phone you when Latham is airborne."

~ * ~

Lying in bed staring at the ceiling the night before his flight to Karachi, Dale Latham persisted in two minds about his eventual official departure from Pakistan. Though Fawbert had not shared his Kimble conversations with him, the recognition an MI6 agent trailed his every move drove him to compute all the thinkable permutations. Howbeit, without discriminating Aman's sympathy for the institution of a mullah-dictated Islamic State, he did not consider plausible abduction by Muslim terrorists.

Not in his wildest fantasies could he have conceptualised the Chanda Govinda liaison leading to the present set of circumstances he now found himself entrapped within. He promised himself, if he survived the escapade, there'd be no more coming to the aid of damsels in distress on foreign soil. His competency for goodwill had utterly overwhelmed the disciplines and decision-making processes serving him well in the RAF, and at Dandridge and Armstrong-Eliot. If someone else had come to him with schemes to patronise an Indian girl illegally escape across the border, after assessing the probable adverse consequences, he'd have prescribed against the cavalier enterprise.

Why then did he so readily acquiesce to Chanda's needs? Additional to honouring the memory of his dead wife by aiding a Christian, he mediated under his physical and psychological state post the helicopter downing, he'd become more susceptible to doing a good deed for someone tending to his welfare at the Combined Military Hospital. All ifs and maybes, immaterial to what he now faced, Latham endured cerebrally agitated by his plight.

With analysis and machinations fading from his mind, he fell into a disturbed sleep, waking frequently until his room phone rang at 06:00, Landon Fawbert asking him to meet him in the consulate refectory for breakfast in 15 minutes.

Noticing Latham's forlorn puss as the pair munched their light breakfast, Fawbert enquired, "how are you feeling this morning, Dale?"

Unsettled, he replied, "I can't really say, other than a mixture of measured optimism tinged with fear."

Not wishing to indulge his charge in despondency, Fawbert asserted, "let's keep positive. We will be leaving for the airport soon. By midday, you'll be in the Deputy High Commission Karachi." Supplementing the bolstering, he laid a kindly hand on Latham's shoulder. "After debriefing, you'll be on your way to Blighty." Clocking Latham had finished his breakfast, he smiled, then urged, "come on, chin up. Let's get you ready for departure."

When Latham returned to his room to collect his baggage, Fawbert revised final protection issues with Blake.

"I've set up a safeguarding detail for escorting Mister Latham and yourself to the airport," Blake corroborated.

"You're not coming with us?" Fawbert dryly muttered.

"No. My crucial role is sustaining the consulate's security, and under Foreign Office operational procedures, when the terrorist threat alert level has been heightened to severe, the chief security officer has to remain on the premises. Don't be overly disquieted, the securing team won't let you down."

"Tell me, Doyle," he began, his features awash with circumspection, "have you ever been involved in a potential abduction scenario in the past?"

"No, but whilst with the SAS, I played roles in the freeing of British captives seized by Islamic radicals and dissidents in Yemen and Somalia."

"How erm—" He blinked, not wanting to complete the query.

"Yes."

"How did those sorties work out?"

Blanching, Blake confided, "just let's say, they were variable in the sort of achievement."

"You mean, some of the captives were killed?"

As if the very mention of captives brought back bad memories, Blake's head fell.

"Rescuing people kidnapped by political and religious groups, not having a care one way or the other about staying alive, is always problematical. Unlike criminal kidnappers ransoming a rich entrepreneur's daughter with every design of coming out alive after the melee, you can't barter with these people. Once they have what they want, usually hostages are killed. Accordingly, surprise is key for a successful raid on where the abductees are being detained. But—" He exhaled noisily. "Inevitably, because the terrorists are geared to expect a rescue attempt, it's impossible to ensure all the captives get out alive. Both the Yemen and Somalia missions resulted in the deaths of some captives."

"*God forbid*," Fawbert blurted. "I hope we don't have to resolve Latham being abducted. He's had one hell of a baptism of fire already. Falling into the hands of a fundamentalist sect might just finish him off."

"I'm not so sure," Blake optimistically opposed. "He seems to be made of the right stuff to combat the circumstances overtaking him. He'll be calling on his RAF tutelage to get him over the line for the balance of the ordeal. He's tougher than you might think."

"I suppose so, but I've derived the explicit prognostication really tearing at him is the prospect of orphaning his two daughters."

"Well—" His speech toppled into a pensive vain. "Imaginable family implications are quite normal in these situations. Loved ones play on the mind far more than uncertainties about personal safety. It's the age-old warrior conundrum."

~ * ~

Just before seven, the Rover 800 containing Latham, Fawbert and a driver pulled out of the consulate, turning left onto Mozang Road for the short trip to Lahore's Allama Iqbal International Airport, less than 5 miles away. An open-top Jeep with three armed guards followed directly behind. Appreciably numb, Latham goggled about, expecting to see the man in the off-white suit, but only passing Pakistanis came into view, going about their regular customs or rushing along to work.

At the junction of Lawrence Road with Mason Road the traffic dallied, Latham noticing a group of men with banners proclaiming, 'Death to Infidels', ransacking a Christian Church while pinning its petrified vicar against a wall. Indicating the atrocity to Fawbert, the diplomat forged a disgusted, withering face, but said nothing.

Subliminally recalling other acts of barbarity he had witnessed during his current visit to Pakistan, without doubt, Latham concluded, a wave of Islamic fundamentalism swept unabated in the streets, spurred on by Muslim zealots, the administration taking no action whatsoever to curb the outrages. He wondered how much worse it could get before the Government stepped in to stop the outrage, or, maintained a convenient blind eye.

Continuing along Lawrence Road and Jail Road, the motorcade dragged in the rush hour, increasing traffic density reducing speed to a walking pace, vehicles finally coming to a stop on the Sherpao Bridge approach, just past the busy Siddiq Trade Centre, Fawbert's and Latham's hearing drawn by irate road users' horn shrieks and exchanging moans about the standstill.

After glancing at his watch, Latham peered at Fawbert uneasily.

"Plenty of time," Fawbert pledged. "Relax, at this time in the morning the Sherpao Bridge is a traffic black spot. It will soon clear."

Reacting with a keyed-up expression, nevertheless, Latham accepted the stoppage. Then ostensibly out of nowhere, a band of men, dressed in black thawbs and black headdresses with black masks and carrying Kalashnikovs, surrounded the British Consulate convoy, aiming their weapons at the vehicle occupants, fellow road users and pedestrians left agog at the extravaganza. One of their group advanced with a massive sledgehammer, pounding the Rover 800's rear nearside passenger door window until it fractured, and he pushed it inside the vehicle.

Instantly, Kalashnikovs were trained on Fawbert and Latham, one of the attackers shouting for the central door lock mechanism to be opened. With no other option, Fawbert hesitantly nodded to the driver. Moments thereafter, the attackers had the door open and wrestled a dazed Latham out of the Rover. With the snatch over in less than 30 seconds, the assailants hurriedly moved away with their captive in-between the ranks of vacant people on the sidewalk, to vehicles parked on a narrow service road between the Sherpao Bridge flyover and Mian Mir Bridge to the north, their guns still covering the consulate detachment. Two of the raiders hustled their quarry into the back seat of a saloon.

The last thing Latham heard and glimpsed, before one of the abductors covered his head with a black muslin bag, was the caterwaul of a car careering through the traffic, its driver dressed in off-white clothing.

Chapter 14: Nowshera Virkan

Speeding away, the taker's three-vehicle cavalcade joined Mall Road via the Mian Mir Bridge link road, heading north-west. Outwardly nondescript in the barrage of early morning vehicles traveling into Lahore city centre, they settled into the average speed attendant to traffic conditions, palpably insouciant about credible police car pursuers.

Meanwhile, back on the Sherpao Bridge approach, a distraught Landon Fawbert called Blake at the Consulate on the Rover's radiotelephone, requesting police assistance. For motives he could only guess about, they did not arrive on the scene until 20 minutes later. Relaying on what had eventuated, the police officers took an eternity to grasp Latham had been abducted, Fawbert near to losing his customary cool in annoyance.

Completely blocking traffic on both sides of the road, the grab had attracted a large crowd, curious to see what might happen next. After recurrent contact with their command and control post at Police HQ, one police car headed off in the direction of the Mian Mir Bridge, leaving the remaining police officers to take statements from Fawbert and the consulate armed guards, plus tend to crowd control and road traffic duties on the Sherpao Bridge flyover, the disproportionate resource allocated to the latter steps astounding Fawbert.

Still heading north-west, the escaping vehicles proceeded into central Lahore, at length emerging onto the N5 dual-carriageway and crossing the Ravi River before joining the N60 and the AH1 motorway, to all intent and purpose, behaving no differently to other road users. At Warn Chak, they left the motorway traveling north towards Nowshera Virkan.

Throughout the journey, though horrified by his abduction, Latham remembered his RAF training, the Monchengladbach exploit in particular, and tried to bide calm. Stifled by the muslin bag, he made to lift it, only to find a rifle muzzle jammed into his midriff, forcing him to endure the discomfort. Wondering what his ultimate destination might be, he speculated if his kidnappers were the Taliban. Surely they could not be taking him to Afghanistan, over 350 miles to the north-west of Lahore? That selection stood the possibility of interception by the police and maybe the Pakistani military, assuming both had been marshaled in response to his plight. *No*, he calculated, *they must be making for a secret hideout, somewhere outlying from Lahore, with the intention of conducting their business before the Pakistani authorities launch a search and rescue mission to track the assaulter's vehicles.*

During the trek he heard no conversation from his abductors, but he felt and sensed their presence, the two sat either side of him, reeking of tobacco. He had foreseen a high-speed escape, with him being buffeted about the car. In contrast, apart from an initial burst of speed right away after the abduction, the vehicle hardly deviated from what he deduced to be regulation road speeds, with no overtaking manoeuvres or jagged movements to evade probable followers.

Replaying the nab in his mind, he rationalised just how simple the operation had been to execute, pedestrians providing cover for the gunmen, mindful the consulate's escort guards in the following vehicle would not fire into their midst for fear of creating an international incident. Soon after the getaway, he had altogether expected to hear the wailing of police car sirens in pursuit of the kidnappers. Why it had not occurred mystified him. Surely Fawbert called for police intervention within a jiffy of the snatcher's departure?

After a period of steady state vehicle movement, he perceived the car braking, and turning left off a comparatively smooth road onto a bumpy track. Eventually coming to a halt, he distinguished himself being bundled out of the car and thrust forward. Hearing a building's door being opened, his hijacker's pushing resumed, forcing him on past it's opening. Inside, a rifle muzzle poked into his lower back, guiding him, until he discerned two sets of hands push him down onto a chair and tie his hands together using the back of it as a fastening fulcrum. Again, he had not heard a single word spoken during the transition from the car to the confines of what he theorised to be a building room, silence continuing to reign from his captors.

The click of an electric switch pricked up his ears, the muslin bag removed, exposing his highly dilated eyes to white light from two pairs of third-degree lamps, his pupils reducing to their minimum in response. Snapping his head down, he shut his eyes to avoid the high-intensity glow, but a hand grabbed his hair, yanking his face up again, his eyes automatically opening in response. Acclimatising to the intense light, he picked out at least six figures silhouetted behind the glare, more shades of Monchengladbach surfacing in the forefront of his mind.

"If you are going to survive this ordeal, you will need to answer our questions fully and frankly," a disconnected voice told him.

"Who are you?" Latham ventured.

"Who we are is no concern of yours. Let me assure you up front, we have no tolerance for delaying tactics or falsehoods. If we suspect you are not telling the truth, you will be tortured, and it will not stop until we are satisfied with your answers. Do you understand?"

He gulped. "Yes."

"What is your name?"

Licking his lips before replying, the abductee stated, "Dale Latham."

"Ex-RAF Wing Commander Dale Latham?"

"Yes. Now, that is all I am going to confirm."

A gruff backhand smashed into his face from behind.

"Why are you in Pakistan?"

No reply.

"Why are you in Pakistan?" the voice sternly trilled.

Again, the merciless backhand struck Latham hard across the face from behind.

"If you know my name," he spluttered, "indisputably, you will know why I am here."

"To sell arms to Pakistan Armed Forces."

"To sell defence battlefield target sensor systems."

"It amounts to the same thing."

"What is it you want?"

"Information."

"What information?"

"We want you to tell us about how your sensor systems work, and how they can be countered. We also want you to tell us about UK Ministry of Defence strategies for war in the Middle East."

"Ohh," Latham sighed. "You chose the wrong person to abduct. By trade I'm a salesman, not a technician, and I left the RAF long ago, so I have no familiarity with any war plans."

"You are being modest. We know otherwise. You have technical expertise, and on behalf of your employer, Armstrong-Eliot, your top-secret security classification enables you to have open discussions with your Ministry of Defence."

Persisting tight-lipped, the inevitable hand swept across his face, this time drawing blood from his mouth.

"You are receiving the lighter shade of our interrogation technique at present. If you continue to be uncooperative, there are much more effective means we have to permanently disfigure you, or if necessary, kill you. I am sure you can presuppose what I am talking about."

Blood oozed from Latham's bottom lip, a shiver ran down his back, but he did not reply.

"Tell us about how the Armstrong-Eliot battlefield target sensor systems can be countered."

"I've told you, I'm on the sales side of the company. My technical understanding only runs to positioning the systems' features, benefits and advantages."

"We don't believe you. With your RAF background, you will have received technical schooling on all avionic equipments, incorporating sensor systems. Now tell us, how is it possible to counter the Armstrong-Eliot battlefield target sensor systems?"

Latham shook his head, then flinched for the awaited hand swipe across his face. It came several times, his mouth cut wider open and spurting blood, his nose also beginning to seep blood. As his heart began to beat more rapidly, he picked up on an increasing throbbing vibration in his temple and the front of his cranium cavity, the sensations confirming his worsening dread.

Like a car production line, the prosecution went on and on, his torturer repeating the same demand, Latham saying very little, the hand from behind making his face into a ghastly, bloody mess in response. Ultimately, he lost consciousness, everything venting to black.

~ * ~

Starting to resume cognizance on the bare floor of a dissimilar dark room, he detected his hands had been tied behind his back, and his ankles strapped together. As his susceptibilities revived, he suffered acute pain from his blistered face. Coughing to relieve congestion, blood spattered the floor from his internally bleeding mouth. Groaning under the soreness and irritation, his energy near to spent, he knew when his hijackers started the inquisition again he had little resistance left in the tank to counteract the brutal onslaught, and might not be able to stand firm for much longer.

Through his inflamed eyes, he picked out the room peculiarities and the odd rectangular or rhomboid shape he guessed to be furniture. With effort, he managed to roll over, recognising the outline of a shuttered window, light rays emerging at oblique angles around its top and sides. He had lost track of time, but the light shafts proved it must still be daytime. Before he could rationalise his misadventure, he heard footsteps advancing towards the room. The door flew open and two masked men dragged him away down a corridor into the grilling room, spotlights illuminating the chair he had earlier been fixed against. Tying him to the chair again, they then ripped open his shirt to expose his chest. Feeling metal ends being applied to both sides of his chest and fixed with sellotape, he also clocked two wires trailing away towards the spot lights then disappearing behind their glare. Raising his head, again he picked out the silhouettes of his interrogators beyond the lights.

"For your sake, we hope you will be more cooperative during this session. Now, tell us how the Armstrong-Eliot battlefield target sensor systems can be countered."

"I've told you," Latham managed to babble out, his speech impaired by his battered and bruised mouth. "I don't know."

Expecting a vicious swipe across his face, instead he writhed and screamed under the shock of electricity coursing through his body. When the power surge ended, he collapsed in the chair, a gruff hand hauling him up to face his tormentor.

"That was 200 volts of direct current. The machine I am operating can output up to a 1,000-volt charge of direct current. Let me impress upon you, you will not survive a 1,000-volt charge. Now, answer me."

"I keep…on telling…you," Latham stuttered out. "I *don't* know."

A fresh charge of electricity flowed into his body, for much longer than the earlier assault, Latham contorting and blaring a high-pitched scream in response.

"Tell us how your target sensor systems can be countered."

Smarting from the electrical discharge, he took in several gapes of air, the usual hand not arriving as if experience told his torturers to expect him to need time to recover before speaking. "Other than take out the platform…in which a sensor system is installed…I don't know." Spitting out, he ejected the buildup of blood from the inside of his mouth. "They are passive infrared and laser based, electro-optic and electro-acoustic systems used for target acquisition."

"We are getting somewhere. We are aware radar-guided munitions fired from air and surface platforms can be jammed with electronic countermeasures. What are the countermeasures for the Armstrong-Eliot battlefield target sensor systems?"

"You're barking up the wrong tree."

"What?"

Taking another large gulp of air, he spewed out more blood before answering. "Unlike radar ECM, passive light and acoustic sensor systems do not lend themselves to countermeasures."

Not quite true, Latham gambled his captors knew no better. They were incorrectly talking about active infrared countermeasures, used to deflect an in-coming infrared-homing, heat-seeking missile by confusing its infrared guidance system to miss the target. Armstrong-Eliot's battlefield target light-sensor systems were passive, meaning they sensed a platform emanating a heat-signature to determine their latitude-longitude coordinates against a GPS map, plus the platform type and offensive capabilities from a library of computer-stored enemy platforms, premised on the heat signature. Coupled with low-level light sensors in the visible band, expressly useful under smoke and fog conditions, the combination lit up the battlefield, enabling commanders to identify enemy displacements and capabilities, with an object to accurately launch offensive munitions. Similarly, Armstrong-Eliot's battlefield target acoustic-sensor systems were passive, meaning they pinpointed gunfire by measuring air movement.

Silence greeted Latham's revelatory declaration, followed by hushed whispers in Urdu between what he estimated to be five or six men.

"We will check out your assertion," said the disenfranchised voice. "Let us now turn to UK Ministry of Defence goals for war in the Middle East."

"I comprehend even less about current MoD affairs," he repudiated. "I'm on the contractor side of the equation. I've not had access to such information since I left the RAF in 1982 and the MoD withdrew my top-secret security classification."

"Let's see."

Another high-voltage burst surged about his body, making his muscles flinch and remain contracted.

"Well?"

"I keep on telling you..." Gargling to find his speech, he then mumbled, "I am not party to anything current."

"We don't believe you. What are MoD's plans for Afghanistan?"

"I have no idea," he lisped. "My contractor status does not make me privy to any strategic designs. Like every other MoD contractor, all I have is UK B Eyes Only security status."

Unconvinced, the torture went on, Latham's responses not satisfying his prober, the electrical charge progressively ramping up to loosen his tongue.

"Give us the intelligence we want," demanded the voice, after a 350volt charge had failed to achieve the information they wanted.

Gathering what little of his strength endured, Latham adamantly retorted, "I *don't know* the answer."

A short silence was followed by more mutterings in Urdu.

"We will give you one more chance. If you don't reply satisfactorily, the machine will be set to a 500volt charge. What are MoD's intentions for Afghanistan?"

"What do you want me to do?" Latham howled. "Invent something?"

He heard the machine being operated, and a huge pulse of electrical energy streamed into his body, making him tense against his bindings and incapacitating his ability to scream in torment. After a few heavy heartbeats, he spiraled down into a black hole coma.

~ * ~

Regaining *compos mentis,* lying on the floor in the room down the corridor, with his hands still bound behind his back and his ankles strapped, Latham felt like he had been hit by a thunderbolt. As his tingles resuscitated and his senses re-established function, he detected no light shafts radiating from the shuttered window. Clearly nighttime, he must have been out for hours. Flexing his arms up to find some comfort, paradoxically, it only produced pinching of the areas on his chest where the electrodes had been affixed. Sucking in breath in reaction, he reckoned they must be scorched.

"*Jesus,*" he wailed.

Nicol and Penny came into his mind. Might he never see them again? What had started out as a well-intentioned response to a plea for help, had cascaded into a gritty wrangle in police custody and now excruciating torture at the hands of his abductors. Genuinely, he could not answer the MoD issues posed by the chief inquisitor, and therefore a way out of his predicament tarried beyond his invention. If he made something up, providing temporary respite, only for it to be tested for validity and soon debunked by his examiners, the torture would resume without mercy. Before slipping into half-sleep, he began to resign himself to death, his resistance to agony about spent.

As the passage of time persisted, the reverb of someone opening the room door brought him painstakingly awake. *They're coming for me again,* he deduced. Through the dimness, he saw a figure kneel down beside him.

"If you want to get out of here alive," the lifesaver murmured, "do exactly what I say."

Stunned, Latham took a few moments to take in the offer. "Who are you?"

"Never mind. I'm going to release your shackles. Your wrists and ankles will probably be numb. When the blood surges back into your hands and feet, you'll feel a different pain. Don't cry out. Got it?"

"Yes."

After Latham had adjusted to freedom from shackles, by flexing his hands and feet, the liberator informed, "you're in a farmhouse on the outskirts of Nowshera Virkan. I managed to enter the back of the house via a window in the room next to this one. There are eight terrorists holding you. All of them are eating in the front room. We need to make our escape without drawing their attention. Say nothing when we leave this room. Just follow my movements. Got it?"

"Yes."

"Once outside, if we are discovered, we will have to run to my car. How do your legs feel now?"

"Not A-1, but I'll make it."

"Good."

Stepping lightly and carefully, the paladin led the way, Latham inches behind him, following suit. In the adjacent room, Latham saw a window had been left ajar, the unknown man delicately negotiating its sill and climbing outside without making a sound. Replicating the action, after Latham eased himself down from the window to the ground, he scrunched up his eyes endeavouring to bring them to full performance. Everything emerged as black and shapeless, the moonlit night sky creating a lighter shade of black like a curtain over the landscape, providing the only demarcation to gain his bearings. Instinctively, his ears pricked up to compensate for lack of visual aids. Apart from insect noises and the faraway hum of traffic in Nowshera Virkan, the night lasted still.

"Crouch down and follow me," his saviour whispered, "but be careful of your footing. There are loose rocks at the back of the farmhouse. Dislodging them will make a noise fetching the terrorists."

Cautiously, the pair proceeded away. Based on the action of his footsteps, Latham appraised the terrain went in a slight uphill direction. Stumbling a little as the gradient took a further upwards inclination, the paragon caught his arm before he fell.

"Not far to go now before we are out of the difficult bit. We are nearing a ridge. On the other side is an open field, about half a mile across. Just beyond the field limit my car is parked on a dirt track."

As his rescuer began to descend from the elevated land into the field, Latham searched for the land ridge top with his feet. Steeper on the down side than he surmised, he began to slip, until, again, his rescuer caught his arm.

At the field level, they quickened their pace. Reaching its far side, Latham's champion scanned back at the ridge then addressed him. "Hhmm, we're going to be okay. There's no clatter of them following us."

In the dimness, the outline of a car materialised, partially concealed behind a row of trees on the dirt track.

Inside the car, the protector tossed Latham a bottle of water before shining a pencil torch beam on a map, its reflection allowing Latham to make out his lineaments.

Astonished by what he saw, he stopped gulping down the liquid and stammered, "you're the man who's been dogging me since my bail court appearance."

"Yes," he replied sustaining his map study.

"Who are you?"

"I'm your guardian angel, Mister Latham."

"Are you with British intelligence services?"

"Let's just say, I work for HMG."

"Foreign Office?"

"No," he casually articulated, still examining the map.

"MI6 then?"

Peeking at his charge, he subtly replied, "Mister Latham, we do not have the time to debate which organisation I work for. Soon, those terrorists will realise you have escaped and they will be coming after us." Refocusing on the map, he elucidated, "just need to refresh my mind with the route I examined earlier. We need to head for the AH1 motorway."

"Where are you taking me?"

"To the British Consulate in Lahore. You're going to need some medical treatment."

"Can I at least ask the name of my saviour?"

"Ross Hunter."

"Well, Mister Hunter..." he began, catching his breath, "I am inexpressibly in your debt. If you hadn't rescued me, those terrorists were going to torture me to death."

Starting the car, Hunter then sedately headed along the dirt track without any car lights on, its undulating nature causing Latham to gyrate in the passenger seat, reigniting his afflictions. Eventually, they joined the main road connecting Nowshera Virkan to the AH1, Hunter switching on the headlights. Past midnight, the road abided quiet with only a few vehicles heading north to Nowshera Virkan, and even fewer travelling south. Watching his rearview mirror for fast advancing vehicles every ten seconds, it stayed clear, making Hunter surmise the takers were still blissfully unaware of Latham's escape.

30 minutes thereafter, they joined the motorway heading for Lahore. Totally exhausted, Latham had fallen asleep under the rocking motion of the car, Hunter glancing at him under the sparse illumination offered by the motorway's lighting.

During his career in the military and the security services, Hunter had seen many victims of torture, but judging by the congealed blood on Latham's face, he had received a thorough pounding. Cringing at the gruesome atrocity, he concentrated on driving. Mindful his task had only just began in the shape of preserving Latham's freedom and maybe even his life, he mentally worked out the vital steps to ensure the terrorists remained oblivious to Latham's whereabouts.

Chapter 15: Rescue

One of many pseudonyms adopted by Latham's rescuer, Ross Hunter indeed worked for HMG intelligence services. An ex-Special Boat Service RN officer, with a plethora of outstanding sorties to his name, he had been recruited by MI6 in 1985, primarily to counter Soviet insurgency into British protectorates in the Mediterranean, the Indian Ocean, and the Caribbean.

When the Berlin Wall came down in November 1989, signaling the end of the Soviet Empire and the rise of détente between the USSR and the West, Hunter was soon redirected to address various missions in the Middle East prior to the Gulf War kicking off August 1990. After Operation Desert Storm successfully expelled invading Iraqi forces from Kuwait in February 1991, he spent most of his time back in the UK and Europe, tracking down Muslim terrorist cells in concert with other UK and international intelligence agencies, embodying MI5 and the CIA.

When MoD alerted MI6 ex-RAF Wing Commander Dale Latham had run into a problem with the Pakistan police, and a breach of top-level security might prevail from the emergency, Hunter got the call to journey *tout de suite* to the Middle-East.

Shadowing Latham from the time he had undergone his bail hearing, he kept track of his movements, finally following the airport bound Rover 800 and its escort when they were intercepted by terrorist adductors on the Sherpao Bridge approach. Vastly outnumbered to counter their attack when the lightning snatch occurred, Hunter briskly stiffened his resolve to adopt a watching stance to see what subsequently developed.

Four cars behind the seizure, as the abductors bundled Latham into a waiting car, he turned his Fiat Tempra into the restricted gap between the east-going and west-going outside lanes of the bridge road. Forcing his way through the traffic jam, he spotted Fawbert being attended to by the consulate armed guards escort, before facing the narrow service road leading to the Mian Mir Bridge link road. Deliberately waiting to ensure they did not suspect being followed, he serenely set off after the escaping vehicles.

Temporarily losing them in central Lahore, he reacquired the getaway convoy on Circular Road, their leisurely pace and regular driving passage perplexing him. Usually, escaping hijackers made haste, police cars with wailing sirens not far behind. Seeming like they were unequivocal of their anonymity, he began to divine collusion between the Pakistani bureaus and the snatchers.

Over the Ravi River, the traffic thinned out in the outskirts of Lahore, Hunter still bridling his progress, so as not to alert his quarry. When they joined the AH1 motorway, he slipped further back, allowing other vehicles to overtake him, but always keeping them in sight. At Warn Chak, he saw them exit the motorway heading for Nowshera Virkan. Guessing they must have a hideout somewhere in the vicinity, again his pace slackened. Just past Baghanwala, they turned off the main road onto a dirt track, Hunter finishing short of it, and monitoring them with binoculars.

Sweeping all-round the vista, forward of the fleeing vehicles, he saw a farmhouse in the distance, at least a mile from his position. Switching back to mark the vehicles, he studied them turning left off the dirt track and along the farm driveway for at least 200 yards, before coming to a halt outside a bungalow-like farmhouse and bundling their captive inside.

Flat and unprotected, with no hiding spots in the foreground, Hunter knew if he made a frontal waylay on foot across the land between the main road and the farmhouse, he'd be easily spotted by watchers. Driving further up the main road, he located another dirt track running off to the left. Tentatively turning onto it, he braked almost immediately and explored his field of regard ahead through his binoculars. Rising slightly, the land blotted out most of the farmhouse from his vision. Further along, he noticed Arabic gum trees, known as kikers in the Punjab, lined the near side of the dirt track. On the basis the kikers provided some cover from potential watchers at the farmhouse, he decided to proceed on foot up the dirt track.

Closing in on the area adjacent to the farmhouse spread, some half mile away from the house, he began to get a feel for its scale and detail, but again supposed he'd become exposed if he went on across the fields. Carrying on along the dirt track, he picked up some camouflage behind the trees he had seen earlier, until he evaluated his position to be well north of the farmhouse. Taking in the land to his front, he fated it rendered a good disposition to reconnoiter the farmhouse at close quarters.

Dashing back to the Fiat, after exchanging his off-white suit and shoes for a black track suit and black trainers, again he walked up the dirt track to the same spot, then crouched down and proceeded across the field between his starting location and the farmhouse. Nearing the top of the field, he began to gauge the land must dip down beyond the field extremity, explaining why the building had been partially hidden from sight, but crucially, presenting an opportunity to scout the farmhouse at striking distance. Edging further, he rested just short of the field boundary, lay on his stomach and crawled over the terrain. As more of the target actualized, he noted at the ridge top that the rocky land sloped away on the other side of the field. Taking a stand behind a clump of overgrown grass, he parted it slightly with the binoculars and browsed the farmhouse, 150 yards away. All its windows were shuttered, not allowing him to see anyone inside. He thought about crossing the rocky terrain and holding up by the house back wall to listen for activity but negated the strategy on the assumption anyone peeking out from the shuttered windows might see him.

His cautiousness surged into validity when to the left of the farmhouse a Kalashnikov- carrying guard loomed into his aspect. Ducking down, Hunter gradually raised his head to traverse the guard with the binoculars. Moments expired before a second armed guard emerged, neither specifically focused on their duty, doubtless believing they had not been followed from Lahore. Persevering to mark them, the guards idly circled the farmhouse exterior, before reappearing again at its left-hand corner. *Could they be on duty at night?* he considered. If so, they needed to be dispatched before he went on to the farmhouse.

Stealthily backtracking across the field to his car, he resolved to return to the datum point under cover of darkness.

In the late afternoon, he drove up the dirt track to the Arabic gum tree line and reversed the car into an opening before facing it back down the track. Correlating his position on a map of Punjab, he roughly resolved the route back to the AH1 motorway, then settled down into observation mode.

When dusk evaporated into night, and after affixing a silencer to his Browning Hi-Power semi-automatic handgun, he made his move, replicating the path he made earlier in the day. Converging on the field ridge top, he saw electric light shafts darting from the window shutter gaps. Surveying the house exterior courtesy of the binoculars, he checked for patrolling guards over a 15-minute period. With no one coming into view, he figured all the miscreants were inside the farmhouse, giving him an advantage.

If possible, he planned to extricate Dale Latham from captivity without disturbing his abductors. Not taking on any odds before going on, he disengaged the Browning's safety catch, then stowed the binoculars in his tracksuit inside pocket.

Moving across the rocky land, he caught site of someone's shadow against a light source on the inside of one of the shuttered windows. Waiting until sure he could go on without being seen, moments later he pressed himself up against the left-hand end of the house back wall, again auditing for bustle. Hearing the slight drone of muffled voices coming from the house interior, he held his gun with both hands to his front, then silently edged his way forward to the left side of the building, ducking down under more shuttered windows to reach its front. Deducing sentries might have been posted along the house front to oversee the driveway leading to the farmhouse, its only plausible entry access vulnerable to motorised vehicles, he warily peered around the corner. No one actualised, confirming his hypothesis the entire gang were inside. Tiptoeing along the front, the drone he heard earlier increased. Crouching down by a shuttered window, he distinctly heard a discussion taking place in Urdu. During the Sherpao Bridge exploit, he had counted eight men abducting Latham. Spying into the gaps in the shuttered window, he counted eight debating participants, then sealed Latham must reside in another room, presumably tied and bound and maybe unconscious.

Creeping past the house front door, and another shuttered window room, Hunter turned down the opposite side of house scrutinizing for entry options, discovering all the shuttered windows down that side had been secured. Pushing on to the right-hand side of the house back, he turned the back-door handle, finding it to be locked. Whiffing the odour of recently cooked food, he noticed an adjacent shuttered window had been left slightly ajar. Used to making covert entries, he eased the shutter open and climbed through into what he identified to be the kitchen, his previous acclimatisation to the dark enabling him to avoid objects and gingerly explore his surroundings. Finding a door, he gently opened it to reveal a corridor leading to other rooms, the rascals conversational shrills and rasps markedly more evident. Planted on the factor, he metered his coordinates relative to the front room where their debate continued.

Edging along the corridor, his Browning again clasped in both hands and aiming forrad, he searched for Latham in the front room, adjacent to the room containing the perpetrators. Empty, apart from a wooden chair at one end, and a desk with two pairs of lamps and a hand-cranked, dc-generating, electrical bolt discharger at the other, he reasoned it to be the interrogation room. Concluding Latham must be in the room next to the kitchen, he began inversing along the corridor, still keeping the Browning elevated to his front, ready to fire, if need be.

Not bargaining for one of the band suddenly emerging into the corridor from the main front room and heading away from him in the direction of the kitchen, he instinctively slid into a small alcove, his gun at the ready should the thug see or sense him on his return. Shouts came from the front room to the man who had left to bring various food and drink. Replying in an aggravated brogue, his annoyance obvious, Hunter hoped having got the victuals it'd focus his absorption on further rebukes, leaving him undetected. Sure enough, pretty soon the man came back with a tray of sustenance, hurling abuse at his comrades and slamming the front room door shut behind him. Content the abductors were now unlikely to disturb his rescue, Hunter edged out of his refuge. Inspecting the kitchen again to make sure the shuttered window endured slightly ajar, inch by inch he then opened the door to the back room, where he came upon the kidnap victim.

~ * ~

Further along the AH1 motorway, Hunter peeped at the sleeping Latham, meditating for once the gods were on his side and the rescue had gone off without a hitch.

Undeniably not the norm, often his hush-hush sorties were characterised by gunfire and abductees not always coming out of the venture totally free of injury. Never an exact science, rescuing captives fell into a grey area, the intended exertion analysed in terms of the probabilities of success, nothing clear-cut or guaranteed. In spite of impeccable planning, the unforeseeable had a habit of wrecking carefully devised manoeuvres, necessitating invention on the spot to conclude the mission. A hit and miss quagmire, sometimes the *ad hoc* creation worked and the kidnapped person retained their life. On other occasions, it mushroomed, got out of control, the converse culminating in mayhem.

Settling his eyesight into the road distance, Hunter psychically recollected one such caper still plaguing him. It ensued soon after he joined MI6. Ordered with three other operatives to liberate a British man and woman abducted from a plush rented house on the shores of the Nile at Luxor by of a band of Somali warlord gangsters operating in Eastern Egypt, the team had been flown into the area aboard a RAF C-130 and parachuted into the locale under cover of darkness. A regular RAF flight from Nairobi to RAF Akrotiri in Cyprus, the C-130 attracted no response from Egyptian military air traffic control, or the watching warlord gangsters.

Deemed to be valuable assets, HMG were not inclined to let the Egyptian military mount a rescue. Though effective in eliminating terrorists and insurgents, invariably under Egyptian special forces action, hostages lost their lives. Whilst HMG participated in dialogue with the

Egyptian Government regarding a rescue mission, behind the scenes MI6 were assigned to liberate high-ranking British Government scientists, Anthony and Teresa Holmes. Both worked at the MoD's Atomic Weapons Establishment Aldermaston, and were cardinally important to the design, manufacture and maintenance of warheads for the UK's nuclear deterrent. Because the Somalis were randomly ransoming European captives at the time, MoD conceived it highly unlikely they knew the occupations of their latest plunder, the Holmes' selected indiscriminately on the basis they must be rich. Taking no chances, MI6 decided on a clandestine extraction mission.

Egyptian intelligence services knew the Somali warlord gangsters were operating in the popular tourist region between Qena and Aswan, and had set up a base camp in the mountainous Arabian Desert between the Nile and the Red Sea, their radio transmissions to their task masters in Mogadishu picked up by the Egyptian Army Signals Corps. Subsuming the Zircon signals intelligence satellite function in the late 1980s, the UK's Skynet 4 military communications satellite network sealed the gangster's precise position using Zircon's signals receiver and GPS facility, enabling the C-130 to drop the MI6 force close to their hideout.

Equipped with infrared, head-mounted, night vision goggles and standard issue Browning Hi-Power semi-automatic handguns with silencers, the four-man team landed within 2 miles of the warlord gang's camp. Reconnoitering the lodge from a hilltop, they saw two large tents and quantified 10 gangsters milling around the site, four more than were shown on the Skynet 4 video stream six hours earlier, plus an indeterminate number in the tents. As to which tent the captives were jailed in persisted as a matter of speculation. When six of the gangsters congregated together, then split into two groups of three entering the tents, the MI6 operatives formed two, two-man teams and made their way to the camp, their objective to enter both tents simultaneously, deal with the gangsters and rescue the captives.

Huddled around a fire, four of the gangsters were dispatched by the MI6 squad without any of them making the slightest sound. As a minimum, it left six in the two tents. Under armed guard, they had hypothesized the Holmes' had been congregated together in one of the tents. Wrong about the call, when Hunter and his companion burst into their designated tent, covering the guards with their weapons, they only unearthed Teresa Holmes' presence. One guard started to cry out before Hunter's companion shot him. Momentarily distracting the second MI6 team swarming into the other tent, in a flash, it allowed those guarding Anthony Holmes to fire their weapons, the MI6 team responding in kind, captive Holmes taking a slug in the chest during the barrage. Once the site had been secured, the MI6 team called in a Westland WS-61 Sea King from HMS Ark Royal, cruising off the Egyptian coast in the Red Sea.

Though Holmes underwent emergency surgery aboard the aircraft carrier, his left lung remained partially incapacitated by the gunshot wound, temporarily handicapping his mobility, the whole misadventure also leaving him highly traumatised. On return to England, AWE declared him unfit for work after he failed a medical, Holmes consigned to extended medical leave until he fully recovered. Similarly left disturbed and dismayed by the episode, when Teresa Holmes restarted at Aldermaston, she found work-incurred stress reignited her trauma, and like for her husband, AWE soon credited her to be unfit for work. Unable to cope, within three months she took her own life, the tragedy affecting Anthony Holmes to breaking point. Not only had the MoD been robbed of two major scientific players, their lives had also been destroyed, and in Teresa's case, forfeited.

Albeit the MI6 executive layer approved the endeavours of the operational team, exonerating them from any blame and disciplinary measures, Hunter agonised about the installment. Not in his untamed fancy could he have foreseen the trail of tragic events following the operation. Perhaps they should have waited until the Holmes' were taken out of their confinement for fresh air and picked off the kidnappers from concealed sites with sniper fire, he put forward to the command structure at the MI6 Century House HQ. Of course, the option did not guarantee the prisoners might not have been injured or shot. No matter which way he cut it, he assessed good or bad fortune played a significant role in determining a casualty-free sortie, or otherwise.

Most of his future forays had gone off like clockwork with no casualties, but for Hunter they never compensated for the Holmes' apocalypse.

~ * ~

When the Fiat reached the outskirts of Lahore, the rougher road surface jolted Latham awake. Instantaneously hit by pangs from his wounds, he winced.

"Not far to go," Hunter advised. "We'll soon be at the British Consulate."

"I'm exhausted." Sliding down in his seat, hollowness permeated his entire body, his face thick with painful swelling. "Only adrenalin fostered by your appearance got me out of that house, and across the field to your car." Wavering, he gibbered, "they'll be coming after me again, won't they?"

"Not necessarily," Hunter quashed. "We'll talk about it more when you've recovered your strength."

Not the time to cause his charge more torment, Hunter knew terrorists customarily tried to reacquire their quarry.

Chapter 16: Something in Common

After pulling up outside the British Consulate and perusing for conceivable watching terrorists, without seeing a soul on Mozang Road, Hunter rang the door intercom, a night guard answering him. Soon, Landon Fawbert and Doyle Blake were roused.

"*My god*," Fawbert uttered under his breath at the manifestation of a bedraggled and severely beaten Latham supported by his rescuer, the diplomat's mouth left wide open in revulsion. His burnt and bruised chest plus extensively blooded face had turned a well built, good-looking man into a slaughterhouse victim.

Following Hunter speaking a secret alpha-numeric code confirming him to be an MI6 agent, he and Latham were ushered inside the consulate foyer.

"I'm Landon Fawbert, First Secretary for Commercial and Diplomatic Affairs." Facing his colleague, he introduced, "and this is Doyle Blake, our chief security officer."

"Gentleman," Hunter acknowledged.

Under unforgiving lights, Hunter clocked Latham's horrendous injuries. Worse than he had appreciated during the journey, he arbitrated Latham must have undergone severe torture.

Gawking at Hunter as he talked to Fawbert, an amazed Blake took onboard he knew him, Hunter's corresponding eye movement confirming he had also made the correlation.

Whilst with the SAS, Blake had taken part in Operation Roundup, a combined MI5-SAS strike to neutralise, or preferably capture for cross examination, a band of Algerian Islamic terrorists known to be planning a series of bomb attacks in London. Along with other SAS section commanders, Blake attended a pre-operation briefing given by MI5 at their 140 Gower Street HQ. On secondment from MI6, Hunter acted as number two to the MI5 lead agent giving the briefing.

Enacted in the dead of night, Operation Roundup went off as prearranged, the terrorists apprehended or eliminated in their Tower Hamlets den, with minimal exchange of fire and no civilian casualties. After the ground floor had been secured, Hunter led Blake's section into the upper level of the terraced house hideaway. Gunshots rang out from the spooked terrorists, Blake in their line of fire until Hunter dispatched them with rapid fire from his Browning Hi-Power semi-automatic handgun. Without the intervention, Blake knew he'd not have survived the sortie, Hunter's face eternally etched in his mind. Right off after the operation, Hunter had left on instructions from his MI6 superiors to take care of another crisis, Blake not able to express his appreciation to the MI6 man for saving his life.

Still staring at Hunter, the Tower Hamlets escapade percolated the forefront of his mind. Though he could hear Fawbert making further rhetoric about Latham's disheveled state and querying the, as-yet, unnamed MI6 agent apropos his affiliation with Latham, he failed to absorb the dialogue, his mind set on axiomatic occurrences from the past. Only resuming an alert state when he heard Fawbert begin to segue into consulate security implications resultant from Latham's abduction, he snapped back into full mindfulness.

"You see, since we determined Mister Latham's safety to be at risk," Fawbert outlined, "the consulate has been in virtual lock down, the terrorist threat alert level heightened to severe. Alas, his kidnapping took us by complete surprise." Gaping thunderstruck at Latham again, he beseeched, "but more of that later. Right now, Mister Latham needs medical attention."

Summoning the consulate's Doctor Skelton, Fawbert requested him to take Latham to the medical centre for treatment.

Watching the pair depart, Fawbert declared, "once he has been cleaned up and examined, we'll get him over to the Combined Military Hospital."

"Mmmm, if I were you, I'd discount the hospital," Hunter icily advocated.

"Oh...why?"

"It'd be putting temptation in the way of those elements responsible for abducting Mister Latham and subjecting him to torture."

Initially cowering at the remark, thereupon Fawbert discerned its merits. "Yes, I see what you're driving at." Disseminating Latham's rescuer a jaundiced inspection, he quizzed, "by the way, just who are you?"

"My name is Ross Hunter and erm—" He frowned. "Just let's say for the time being, officially, I work for HMG. Broadcasting the presence of an MI6 officer in Pakistan is to be avoided for obvious reasons."

"Quite," he accepted. "Well, Mister Hunter, having rescued Mister Latham, evidently your work is not complete just yet."

"No—" His aspect descended into a solicitous display. "It isn't."

"Can you advise us as to your intentions?"

"I'm afraid not."

"I see." Ogling Blake, Fawcett affected a correct stance. "Right. We'd better continue this in the consulate's security room."

Whilst Latham underwent cleansing, checkup and repair, Hunter, Fawbert and Blake appraised outcomes to date.

"We weren't sure if you were real, or a figment of Latham's imagination," Fawbert revealed. "He claimed to have seen you several times, but I must confess you never came into my field of regard."

Still in a conservative scheme, Hunter economically explained, "London dispatched me to audit the situation, and if necessary, superintend action."

"Yes, brokered on Latham's top-secret security classification, howbeit over ten years obsolete, we argued something like that might happen." Trying again for clarification, a beseeching expression flooded his face. "Can you at least give us a hint about your brief?"

"You mean, what have I been instructed to do?"

"Forgive my probity and frankness," he begged, his tactful communication skills coming to the fore, "but are you here to ensure Dale Latham never enters a Pakistani State prison, or falls foul of terrorists?"

Dwelling, he sternly eyeballed the MI6 man. "Expressly, by one means or another."

"Aahh." Hunter smiled. "I can see you live up to your professional standing. You're quite the diplomat." Needfully vigilant, he then crustily chided, "do you mean, am I here to liquidate Latham under those circumstances?"

"Yes I do," Fawbert promptly replied.

"If it were so, Mister Fawbert, instead of rescuing him, I could have terminated him."

Straightaway, Fawbert's assertive manner faltered, the declaration clinical like Latham's shadow had been assigned to quell a minor mishap.

Hunter went on to outline how he had followed the abductors from the Sherpao Bridge area to the outskirts of Nowshera Virkan, and with care managed to extricate Latham from his captors.

Abruptly changing the topic after finishing his account, he asked, "what's your take on the incident at Lahore Basin Latham might have been involved in?"

"Oh..." Fawbert recoiled, taken aback by the unexpected inquiry. "You are aware of the entanglement?"

"We have our springs."

"Well er..." he tentatively began, "...it has been prolonged as the principle topic of contention for police scrutiny. Albeit releasing Latham from bail custody, Chief Inspector Aman, the man heading the enquiry, continues to search for witnesses and testimony proving he aided and abetted the escape of Chanda Govinda across the border."

"The so-called PRM terrorist."

"Phooey!" Fawbert quivered his brow dismissively. "That epithet has been blown out of all proportion. She's as likely to be an Indian terrorist, as Benazir Bhutto is to be a member of the Muslim Brotherhood. It's a trumped-up charge, nourished by political motives."

"I see, but did Latham get involved?"

Breathing out heavily, Fawbert replied, "I've not addressed him on the possibility, deeming an affirmative reply puts the Foreign Office in a very intricate position. However, it'd not come as a bombshell to me, if he did come to the aid of a distressed woman. He's a decent man."

Quitting briefly, envisaging he might have got too personal with Latham, he qualified, "it's not pertinent to the issue anyway. Whether he did or did not help her, our role in the Foreign Office is to ensure he ends up on a flight back to Blighty for aims I'm sure are all too crystal to you."

"Quite. Anyhow, it's academic but—" Pressing his lips together, his reticence obvious to Fawbert, he stipulated, "Latham must not be allowed to fall back into the hands of either the police or terrorists again. Though his understanding of MoD matters is largely out of date, some of what he knows is still extremely sensitive and material to the UK's current security."

"*What?*" Fawbert bawled, his customary cool momentarily sidelined. Exchanging a stunned mien with Blake, suddenly he comprehended the chief security officer had not said a word since Hunter arrived at the consulate with Latham in tow.

"I can't be specific," Hunter certified, "but as a Tornado IDS RAF Wing Commander, his expertise of our nuclear provisions and generic order of battle are key to an aggressor wanting to wage war on both the UK and NATO." Refining a discreet address, he stipulated, "you see, within the MoD and tri-services structure, only those commanders charged with the delivery of nuclear weapons are routinely briefed on defence blueprints, depending what's on the early warning threat board at Fylingdales Moor and intel picked up by the security services, including GCHQ. Though the nitty gritty in Latham's proficiency is out of date, the methodology remains the same. Hence the critical data could prove very useful to an attacking force."

"Yes, I see. So er—" Scratching his head, his face rippled into a mass of consternation. "Forgive my lack of nimble take-up, Mister Hunter, but what are you actually saying?"

"As I specified earlier, my brief is to ensure Dale Latham never becomes a prisoner of the Pakistani State or falls foul of terrorists. To wit…by one means or another."

~ * ~

Sequent to further discussion, Fawbert and Blake left the security room, leaving Hunter to contact MI6 to make his chronicle reflecting Latham's rescue at Nowshera Virkan.

Walking away, Fawbert voiced, "you've been remarkably quiet since Hunter returned Latham to us."

"Yes, er, you might find out anyway during the course of the next few days," Blake leaked, "so I may as well come clean."

"What?" He juddered in his tracks. "Don't tell me you have some revelatory intel to drop in my lap, just like friend Hunter did."

"I've met him before."

"Oh." Fawbert scrunched up his eyes. "Under what circumstances?"

Outlining the combined MI5-SAS Tower Hamlets sortie, and Hunter's role in saving his life, for the first time since Fawbert had known him, Blake neared diffidence, his usual no-nonsense, professional demeanour scuppered by the discomforting reunion.

"So you immediately recognised him?"

"Yes, and judging by the way he eyed me, the recognition was mutual."

"Well, Doyle, I can see you must feel gratitude towards him, but why were you two so sheepish about opening up in my presence?"

"I reckon it's down to my SAS training. You see, in general, intelligence officers should not divulge recognition of each other to third parties outside the domains of the SAS and MI6." Shrugging his shoulders, he admitted, "true, Hunter has set out his purpose, but until he says to me it's alright to formally acknowledge him, I'd prefer to prevail as a complete stranger to him."

"I see. Well, I'll let you two sort out the protocol by yourselves. In the meantime, I have to review Latham's shape and soundness with Doctor Skelton."

Reporting Latham's wounds were mainly superficial apart from a gash to his scalp above his left eye needing stitching, and some third degree burns to his chest, the consulate doctor assured Fawbert of the patient's swollen face deflation within days, the gels applied to his body soothing away his other hurts. With his chest and head bandaged, he had then been sedated, put to bed in the consulate medical centre, and watched over by a nurse.

"When do you think he will be fit enough to travel?" Fawbert queried.

"Oh, to be on the safe side, at least six to seven days, and er—" Skelton emitted an ominous cast at Fawbert. "Don't underestimate his state of mind after the beating he has taken. Sometimes victims of torture are mentally scarred for life. Others manage resultant from therapy counselling. None ever forget the encounter. How Latham reacts will be dependent on the robustness of his psyche."

"Mmmm. Let's hope his RAF drilling sufficiently hardened his willpower, enabling the experience not to present any legacy problems to him."

"Whatever you do, Landon," Skelton cautioned, "don't put him through the mill until he begins to feel a bit more human again. Even tough men can crack, and when they do, reconstruction is damn near to impossible. Though he might come across as being alright, the encounter will be hovering about somewhere in his mind, and the last thing he needs is to re-live whatever happened to him. If you have to probe him, be sensitive to his condition."

"I'll be careful," Fawbert promised, "nonetheless there is no way out of an official debrief for him with Soames in Karachi."

After Fawbert had left him for the medical centre, Blake retreated to the security room, wanting to test the temperature of the water with Hunter.

Instantly sensing reticence and the all too obvious on his mind, Hunter took the initiative. "Thank you for staying stum and persisting discreet."

"Hah, purely down to my SAS breeding."

"It's served you well."

"Do you remember—"

Hunter cut him off. "Do I remember the previous time we met?"

"Yes."

"The Tower Hamlets sortie."

"Mmmm. You saved my life. I never got a chance to thank you."

"There's no need for thanks."

"I suppose, you're going to say, you were just doing your job?"

"But it's true."

"Mmmm, yes," Blake indifferently endorsed. "You were going under a different moniker back then."

"Names are part of an identification credential for the purpose of forming attachments. Personal data facilitates binding an operational team together."

"But you didn't know my name."

"I did actually. MI6 always checks up on SAS teams prior to a sortie."

"My word." Grinning admiringly, he congratulated, "you seem to be ahead of me on every front."

"It goes with the territory. MI6 tend to be top of the heap when it comes to leading combined operations. We've studied everything in advance. We might not always have it altogether right, but we do try."

"Anyway," Blake insisted, "belatedly, thanks for what you did for me at Tower Hamlets."

"You're welcome. Maybe one day you can reciprocate the favour."

~ * ~

Seventy-two hours later, with his facial swelling vastly reduced and his injuries healing, though still exhibiting a ghostly pallor, Latham sat up in bed, well enough to talk to Fawbert and Hunter.

"Granted you've had a traumatic happenstance, Dale," Fawbert opened, "but erm…" Appreciating the patient's sorry state, he bred a concerned articulation of regret tempered by professional need. "…we need to establish what you told your kidnappers."

"Were they the Taliban?" Latham explored.

Fawbert glanced across at Hunter, nodding for him to reply.

"Going on their garb, MO, and the audacious way they apprehended you, it all bears the hallmarks of the Taliban, plausibly trained by the Mujahedeen."

"What did you tell them, Dale?" Fawbert cut it.

"Goodness, the answer to your question is what has got me beat." Jerking his head up to add substance to his reply, the exertion caused him to wince in agony attendant from the torture. "They—" Swiveling his neck to and fro, he attempted to reduce the spasm. "They wanted details on how to counter the Armstrong-Eliot battlefield target sensor systems, current MoD war strategies and the UK's intents for the Middle East." Lifting his hands in a show of disbelief, he then dropped them onto the bed. "Regarding sensor countermeasures, I told them they were barking up the wrong tree. They knew about ECM and postulated a similar counter inhibited light and audio-based sensors. But it's simply not the case. The only way to defeat passive sensor systems, is to destroy the platform they are installed on."

"What did you tell them about MoD?"

"Pointedly even more perplexing, they were sure I knew about MoD's current battlefield strategies." Shrugging his shoulders, the effort avoiding ache this time, he explained, "doubtless, they meant the order of battle, but I kept on telling them, I'd left the RAF in 1982 and as a contractor, I no longer had access to MoD battle plans, or more crucially, the UK's designs for the Middle East."

"They didn't believe you?" Hunter interjected.

"No…hence the state you found me in."

"Mmmm." Hunter caught Fawbert's eye. "I detect Mister Latham's snatchers were sold a pup by whoever told them about his journey from the consulate to the airport." Cogitating further, he concurrently turned to Latham. "If I hadn't gotten you out of there, eventually they'd have trusted your story…providing you continued to stand up against the torture. But in the end, they'd have cut their losses and killed you. Whoever set you up knew the score, and it's precisely why you were delivered into their hands." Dwelling to allow his valuation to sink in, he stringently stated, "someone wanted you dead."

"*Yes*, and I can nominate who," Fawbert attested. "Chief Inspector Aman."

"Probably," Hunter conceded. "With no further witnesses and corroborative proof coming to light *vis-a-vis* the Lahore Basin enmeshment, coupled with what you told me about his Muslim fundamentalism sympathies, after being ordered to release Mister Latham, as an ultimate resort, he might have informed those abductors about the journey to the airport."

"For goodness sake," Latham babbled. "Is Aman *really* so spiteful to such a diseased degree?"

"I did some further research on him with British High Commissioner Augustus Dawson in Islamabad," Fawbert aired. "Dawson has some contacts in the ruling Pakistani Peoples Party. It transpires Aman has champions in some government opposition circles, especially in the Jamiat-e-Ulema-e-Islam Party, an ultra-conservative, religious and theocratic sect, wanting to see Sharia Law subsume and eradicate democratic laws. Some parliamentary members of the Jamiat-e-Ulema-e-Islam Party sit on various government committees, embracing the judicial branch responsible for senior police appointments. He had a great deal of patronage from the party's judicial branch committee members, though many People's Party members opposed his engagement. Consequently, Aman has some latitude to pursue his anti-PRM campaigns and come down hard on foreigners thought to be aiding PRM members, like supposedly Chanda Govinda. Though outwardly Aman appears to be measured, he is a vindictive man, renowned for using instruments beyond the police to vent his wrath on those who the law fails to condemn." Pausing he warned, "incontestably, you have fallen into this category."

"So, he's still after me?"

"Regrettably, yes."

"Don't worry, Mister Latham," Hunter encouraged. "Now we're savvy as to what to expect, there is little scope for you to fall into the hands of the Taliban again."

~ * ~

As Doctor Skelton predicted, by early the following week, Latham's swollen face had receded to normal proportions, his chest pains reduced, and a rosy pigmentation infused his face with zest. Keen to be mobile again, he walked in the consulate's cordoned off garden, thankful to be tolerably well again and eagerly anticipating air passage to Blighty.

Under directives from Century House, Hunter had stayed on at the consulate, officially acting as a bodyguard to Latham, but still with the same brief appertaining to his liquidation should the Taliban or the Lahore Police reacquire him.

From the security room's window, Hunter noticed his charge sat on a bench in the garden and decided to join him.

"Mind if I sit down," he posed, as Latham saw him nearing.

"Not in the least. I owe you my life."

Casting a bolstering gleam at him, Hunter reassured, "all part of the service."

"Ross Hunter is not your real name, is it?"

"It's one of many *nom de plumes* I use."

"And presumably, it's no use asking for your real name?"

"Either way, I could tell you anything, but it'd be unprovable. Best just to keep to Ross Hunter."

"Why didn't you liquidate me back at the farmhouse near Nowshera Virkan?" His curiosity appetite ripening, he gave Hunter a sideways peek. "You had the opportunity. Why didn't you take it?"

"I had to find out what you had told them."

"I perceive there's more to it than my capacity to withstand torment."

Coasting into an amiable temperament, Hunter twinkled. He had grown to admire Latham for his undiminished resolve to hang onto himself when under the sustained glare of the Lahore Police, and more impressively, not relinquishing under harsh Taliban interrogation. "Let's just call it professional etiquette. I wanted to give you a chance."

"Why?"

Sliding his engrossment away from Latham, he murmured, "we er...we have something in common?"

"Oh yes. It's not old school tie, so what is it?"

"We have both lost our wives," Hunter coldly announced.

Astounded by the declaration, Latham momentarily froze before cognizance set in. "Of course, being ex-RAF, you chaps have a dossier on me."

"Quite. I reviewed your file prior to coming out to Pakistan and discovered your woe."

"And that's the real motivator behind your professed benevolence?"

"Notwithstanding the need to remain emotionally disconnected from marks, often field operatives can't help but form some sort of affinity, be it major or minor. Our common fatality stimulated the connection, affirmatively reinforced when I witnessed how you coped with your predicament."

"But surely you were issued an unambiguous instruction regarding how to deal with me?"

"Operatives are usually given some latitude when situations become indefinite. In your case, I wanted to take it."

"Just because we have lost wives in common?" Latham pushed.

"You'd have preferred me to shoot you?"

"Of course not. I have a lot to live for." Slipping into intimacy, he specified, "having inspected my record, you'll have gathered I have two daughters."

"Yes, it's another reason behind my apparent clemency."

Squinting at the remark, Latham ventured, "are children something else we have in common?"

"I have two boys, slightly younger than your girls. When their mother died, they were distraught and have needed at lot of succour ever since. I speculated your girls were the same way."

Taking a deep breath, Latham languidly exhaled relieving built-up tension. "When Fiona died, Nicol and Penny were inconsolable. My elder sister Amelia and her husband Clement helped me get them through the suffering, but it's arduous to say if they have ever completely gotten over their mother's death."

"Yes, I too often wonder how my boys are really feeling, and how they cope, particularly when I'm away on a field operation." Leaning forward, like he shifted a mega-load perpetually perched on his back to one side, he confided, "worse still, I censure myself I didn't do anything to prevent my wife's death. You see—" Uncharacteristically, his voice wobbled. "She was also an MI6 operative, and lost her life on active duty."

"Oh, for the love of god, I'm so sorry," Latham delicately bequeathed. "I assume you won't be able to tell me, so I shall refrain from asking about the circumstances."

"I can tell you, when MI6 took me off a behind-the-lines mission for another duty, she replaced me. It has been a gigantic thorn in my side ever since. You see, knowing the sortie to be highly dangerous, I should have seen to it the executive assigned someone else. She was an exceptional field agent, gifted with a keen eye and analytical powers, but I knew she was up against insurmountable odds, the shrewdness of her opposing number beyond her survival insights." Wrinkling his eyelids, his agony patently manifest to Latham, he added, "yet still I let it happen when I should have gone to the DG and insisted someone else took her place."

"Can you say, why you didn't?"

"When you join the security services, you are told in advance there is no scope for personal relationships to interfere with operations. Women operatives are treated no differently to men operatives. I suppose with this in mind, it superseded my want to protect her." Punching his left palm with his right fist he sunk further into remorse before rallying and asking, "how about you?"

Allowing his head to fall back, Latham gazed at the milky-tinted clouds above. "After Fiona's passing, secretly, I used to sob myself to sleep. Did it for months on end. Told myself I should have done more to make sure she didn't die, but in the end, I knew nobody could have done anything. Nevertheless, I figuratively applied the whip to my back in a vain attempt to chastise myself." A watershed flash, he faced Hunter revealing, "you are the only person I have ever disclosed my heartache to."

"And your sister and children never knew?"

"No. Principally in the company of the girls, I had to be steady. Amelia might have guessed, but she never burdened me with her propositions." Blanching at the remembrance, he catechized, "how did you confront it?"

"Much the same, and like you, I showed strength in front of the boys, and kept my grief to myself."

"You didn't marry again?"

"No. My loss happened fairly recently compared to yours. When I behold another woman's face, all I see is my wife, and if truth be told, I'm still in love with her."

"Yes, I can appreciate your sentiment. I too still find it difficult to form attachments with other women." Smiling at Hunter, a mighty association of union gushed about him. "Fancy promenading with me around the garden?"

"Huh, I'm getting far too close to you. How am I going to pull the trigger if the need ever arises?"

Chapter 17: Return to Karachi

Over the course of the next few days, Fawbert arranged for Bill Kimble to come up to Lahore. Along with Hunter, he'd escort Latham back to Karachi on a scheduled PIA flight. Though nowhere near 100 percent fit, Latham had elected to make the journey and onwards to Blighty, rather than wait until he fully recovered from his injuries. Telephoning Amelia, he relayed on his intentions, but refrained from mentioning his abduction by the Taliban.

"We've been expecting news about your homecoming for over two weeks," she reminded him.

"Yes, I apologise. Things—" Tempted to confide in his sister, he hesitated, finally deciding not to burden her. "Things got a little convoluted here. However, it looks like I will be on a Heathrow bound flight from Karachi within the next few days."

"Your voice sounds a little strange, Dale."

Still recovering from cuts inside his mouth, the damage had temporarily handicapped his ability to form words as he normally did.

"Oh, it's nothing, Amelia. I picked up a minor larynx infection, and it's affected my speech."

"Oh dear. You are in the wars, aren't you?"

Pulling the wool further, he forecast, "by the time you see me, it will have gone."

"What about this hang-up with the Lahore Police?"

"The British High Commission gauges nothing more will come of it."

"Thank god," she gurgled, her relief palpable to her brother. "I'd run out of excuses to Nicol and Penny, justifying your prolonged stay in Pakistan."

"Did either of them make the conjunction between those newspaper hearsays and me?"

"No, they didn't." She balked, as if not totally sure. "But if they did, they've kept it to themselves, and that's unprecedented. Usually, they tell me everything. Phone to give me your flight details, and Clem and I will take them to Heathrow to meet you."

Latham's face lit up. "Wonderful. I'd appreciate seeing them."

When the telecom ended, a rush of refreshment surged through him. With the objective of invigorating his nerve, he had disciplined himself not to think about his daughters whilst under the strong arm of the Taliban, and during his initial recovery period at the consulate. Conscious if he had begun to reminisce about them, he could have dissolved turning into a bag of nerves, he had perpetuated a resolute disposition, even in the presence of Fawcett, Hunter, and Doctor Skelton.

Whilst with the RAF, he had heard stories and talked to both British and NATO military servicemen captured by the enemy. Some had been badly affected by the stumble upon, others barely surviving. All of them said, engrossing their rumination with loved ones made their seizure worse, weakening their resolve to hold out under inquisition. When the Taliban abducted him in the Sherpao Bridge traffic queue, originally terror-stricken and disorientated, he had subsequently drifted into a kind of hibernation station, calculating a testing fate awaited him. Until he knew his torture-incurred injuries had healed, the leftovers of the psychological state would persist. After his enlightening talk with Hunter and the telephone call with Amelia, he now came over as near to normal again, keen to see his family, just as he did towards the end of any protracted business trip.

~ * ~

When Kimble arrived at the consulate, Fawbert and Hunter updated him on their deliberation germane to Latham's abduction, and the continuing threat posed by Chief Inspector Aman. Comprehensively in tune with products resultant from the incident at Lahore Basin, nothing they itemised shocked him. Instead, like Fawbert had done in securing Latham's bail, Kimble adopted a pragmatic M.O, his focus purely on assisting Latham back to Karachi and ensuring he boarded a flight to Blighty from Jinnah International.

Playing it safe, Fawbert sought red-alert security status from the consulate security personnel, Blake allowing no one access without prior appointment and identification. After Hunter's take on the likely parent behind Latham's abduction, he also set in place triple surety resources to escort the car taking Latham, Kimble and Hunter to Lahore Airport for the flight to Karachi.

On the departure day, Fawbert wished Latham the best of luck for the remainder of his stay in Pakistan, Hunter issuing Blake a cordial nod of approval for his discretion as to recognition of the MI6 man. During the journey, a burgeoning sense of *déjà vu* consumed Latham, notably as the three-vehicle cavalcade converged on the Sherpao Bridge. Half expecting masked men dressed in black thawbs and black headdresses and carrying Kalashnikovs to intercept them, his hands moistened and a curious pressure feeling rushed from his loins into his chest, but the journey went off without a twist, as did the flight to Karachi.

To comply with protocol, British Deputy High Commissioner John Soames needed to properly debrief Latham at the Deputy High Commission, Kimble and Hunter also set to attend. During the flight to Karachi, Latham began to ponder about the debrief. He had been subject to operational debriefing sessions on numerous junctures with the RAF, and generally after extended trade ventures abroad, get-togethers with Airborne Systems Group Managing Director Matthew Chapman at Armstrong-Eliot standard practice. Why then did meditations about the Soames debriefing conspire to make a pit in his stomach? All the British High Commission functionaries had given him the benefit of the doubt relating to his alleged assistance with Chanda Govinda's escape across the border, no one remotely censuring him for his friendship with her. Concluding his understandable fear came down to imagined consequences, he dismissed the reservation, deducing recovering his passport and climbing aboard a Heathrow bound BA flight, and thus avoiding a bullet from Hunter, to be far more daunting.

Despite his logic, he knew scratching beneath his very thin veneer of calm, a wealth of emotion awaited to erupt. Worse, he magnified reliving the upshots of the past few weeks for the benefit of John Soames necessary debriefing into a maelstrom of cataclysmic proportions, questioning how he'd stand up to the scrutiny.

When he entered the Deputy High Commissioner's office, the pit in his stomach sensation flared up again.

"I'm sorry to have to make you re-live this again, Dale," Soames apologised in his usual gentlemanly manner, "but the Foreign Office needs me to legitimately interview you about occurrences in Lahore."

"It's...quite alright...John," he replied, his wavering enunciation attracting disturbed pouts from Kimble and Hunter. "I expected it."

Soames noticed a cut on Latham's face slightly seeping blood and built-up water-based fluid. "Before I begin, do you need any medical attention? I er...I see your face is bleeding."

Instinctively, Latham touched the area he knew Soames referred to. A persistent legacy, unlike other afflicted parts of his face, nonstop swelling guaranteed it continued to seep after his bandages and plasters had been removed. Doctor Skelton had prescribed fresh air to heal and seal his wounds comprising the stubborn area on top of his upper left cheekbone, comforting Latham the seepage was temporary.

His defensive reaction prompted Kimble to make a terse observation. "That face wound has opened up again in the past few minutes."

"Yes..." Latham agreed, his voice even more brittle. "Must be...because of tension."

"I can postpone this, if you like, Dale," Soames offered. "Perhaps you'd like our doctor to take a gander at it?"

Though keen to complete formalities and exit Pakistan as swiftly as possible, Latham did not want to arrive at Heathrow resembling a disheveled war zone casualty, upsetting his family and prompting a plethora of queries he could not reply to due to security inhibitors. In his mindset he had predetermined to arrive in a near-to normal fettle, explaining his wounds away as a hangover from the helicopter crash at Lahore Pakistan AFB.

"Thanks for your concern," he edgily replied. "The shield measures enacted at both ends of the journey and the flight from Lahore have taken more out of me than I foresaw."

Soames summoned a deputy high commission nurse and Latham was led away to the medical centre for treatment.

After the door to his office shut, Soames turned to Kimble and Hunter. "I know Latham is a strong man, but abduction by the Taliban must have left a mark on his psyche, as well as his body."

"Undeniably," Hunter affirmed. "Nobody comes out of the other side of torture without incurring some psychic hang-ups. Doctor Skelton at the Lahore Consulate advised Fawbert not to put him through the mill until he felt a bit more human again. Accumulated from my line of work, I'd concur even hard men can crack, and when they do, repair is near to impossible."

"Hhmm," Soames gravely reacted. "We haven't any mental health practitioners within the realms of the Foreign Office, let alone the overseas embassy and high commission structure, but I'm anticipating when Latham goes home, MoD should offer him counselling. They have psychiatry resources versed in dealing with torture victims." Wincing at the notion, he queried, "tell me, Bill, did anyone at the Lahore British Consulate talk to him about his state of mind?"

"I don't think so." He cast an appealing mannerism at Hunter. "I'm right aren't I, Ross?"

"Landon Fawbert talked to Skelton about the issue. The doctor said Latham's wounds should be allowed to heal and he needs to be back home in the bosom of his family, before taking psychiatry steps."

"I see," Soames accepted. "It's not really my area of excellence, but I presume torture victims are plagued by memories of their confrontation?"

"It is often the case," Hunter validated. "I became tempted to ask Latham how he is coping after surviving his ordeal, but Skelton is right in his assertion."

"How do you mean?"

"It's tricky to tell if Latham is on the edge, and if he starts to open up, it could have everlasting adverse sequels." Raising his hands in a prescriptive manner, he counselled, "best to let a professional conduct the appraisal under the right controlled conditions."

"Mmmm, yes. I'm of the preconception the oozing on his left cheek could be a function of stress engendering high blood pressure."

"Very possibly, but if he doesn't volunteer his sentiments, if I were you, I'd not ignite them while he's still in Pakistan. As well as brave, he's very intelligent and perceptive. He will have worked out what's happening to him and put a lid on it."

"I see. I didn't fathom a ceremonial briefing could cause him such anxiety."

"Normally, it wouldn't. Having said that, we kept it all very informal at the consulate. He got used to the casual frame of reference. Proportionately speaking, participation in a stately meeting, is a big step for him, maybe even a chasm."

"For sure. I can see that now." Soames turned to Kimble. "Let's just keep a careful eye on him, Bill. Having survived a stretch in a Pakistani jail and the depraved work of the Taliban, it'd be a shame if he were to dissolve during the final hurdle."

"Absolutely," Kimble agreed, "but er—" His countenance sunk into weightiness. "His actual final hurdle is going to be getting past Chief Inspector Aman at Jinnah International and recovering his passport. Then, and only then, is he in the clear."

~ * ~

Anxious for his welfare, Soames visited the medical centre to check on Latham. After tending to his seeping wound, Head Physician Doctor Becker had administered a sedative sending him into a deep sleep.

"Whatever this chap has endured," he alerted, "it has hit him hard. Though he appears in control, beneath the shallow calmness, he is a whirlpool of conflicting sensibilities."

"Is he in pain?"

"Some," Becker replied, "but it is minor compared to the pent-up anxieties he is exhibiting. His nerves are not shot and he must have a very unbending constitution, but his blood pressure is higher than it should be, and he shows signs of chronic fatigue. The wound oozing on his left cheekbone is being brought on by tension. When he's reunited with his family in England, he's going to need to take it easy for a while, to allow all the stress and strain to drain from his being."

"Yes, I predicted you'd say something highly prescriptive."

Assuming a judicious posture Becker said, "I'm alert to the fact you must debrief Mister Latham, but I'd recommend you don't dwell too intensely on whatever demanding circumstances he's been subject to. Right now, the last thing he needs is re-living the origins behind his current physical and psychological state."

Defending the necessity of the debriefing, Soames detailed, "he *is* an ex-RAF Wing Commander and the record shows he has been in other testing situations."

"Well, believably, know-how and doggedness propped him throughout his latest ordeal." Stepping back, he gaped at Soames appealingly. "Although I admit its conjecture, John, please heed my warning."

Soames took onboard Becker's advice, relaying on his recommendation to Kimble and Hunter. Mutually deciding on a gently-gently fashion to debrief Latham the next day, Hunter most notably attuned himself not to drive the Armstrong-Eliot man too intensely. Instead of the formality of Soames's office, the Deputy High Commission state room was adopted for the convene, its relative vastness seen to be equitable with creating a non-constraining environment.

Having slept for 20 hours, Latham felt better than he had done for weeks. Before taking breakfast, he did ten lengths in the deputy high commission's pool, followed by a light massage from the nurse Doctor Becker had assigned to care for him. By the time set for the debrief, he had blended into his normal self, his jitters quelled, and his body though slightly sore, humming with zest, his wounded cheekbone no longer seeping. Becker notified Soames his patient had been blessed with agile recovery credentials, a very rare asset, albeit, Soames was left unsure of the claim.

Kimble collected him from his room, the pair exchanging small talk as they made their way to the state room, Soames and Hunter waiting inside.

"How are you today, Dale?" Soames wondered as a low-key start to proceedings.

"Better than I've been in quite some time." He glowed. "Please, there is no need to treat me with kid gloves. I'm now capable of retelling events without breaking down."

Astounded by the claim, principally after Doctor Becker's prognosis, Soames exchanged glances with Kimble and Hunter before fixing Latham. "Are you quite certain?"

"After surviving the Taliban interrogation, courtesy of Mister Hunter, everything is downhill."

"I see." As if to make a connecting bridge for the primary part of the meeting, he artificially cleared his throat. "Might we begin with the stimulus behind the embroilment, your hypothetical link with Miss Govinda, and what occurred at Lahore Basin? I'm not asking you to incriminate yourself, Dale, and even if you did, it'd go no further. It's more the case, the Foreign Office are keen to understand the circumstances behind her illegal crossing of the Pakistan-India border."

Detailing Chanda's potted family history, and her marginal affiliation to the PRM, he positioned her as small bait in terms of a Lahore Police target. Going on to explain, despite her peripheral status, she graduated into a Chief Inspector Aman mark, had been put under virtual house arrest and her passport confiscated, he finished by saying she had been fingered on the basis the PRM were responsible for downing the Pakistan Army Aviation Wing Puma helicopter.

"Aman wanted her to furnish him with the names and addresses of the PRM members she knew. He gave her 48 hours to comply, or steps were to be taken to detain her for further grilling."

"Mmmm." Soames turned to Kimble. "We know what that means."

"Abuse and conceivably, torture," Kimble replied.

"Quite," Latham notarized. "And after what eventuated to her family, encompassing her father and brother's murders, she couldn't live with herself if she betrayed fellow Indians, many of them Christian." Lingering, reflections of her common religious beliefs with Fiona's resurfaced. "By the way, she is a Christian."

"Christian," Soames echoed narrowing his eyes at Latham. "If I recollect correctly from your file, Dale, your wife was a devoted Christian."

"Yes...the same detail just filtered into my mind as well. Christianity bestowed guiding principles for Fiona to abide by."

"Did it have any bearing on your accord with Miss Govinda?"

"Demonstrably, it made me empathic to her plight."

"I see." Adopting a mindful proclivity, Soames particularized, "we are beginning to enter the contentious zone. Best to steer clear of it. By way of explicit cogency, it's irrelevant anyway." Dwelling, allowing his edict to sink in with the meeting members, he moved, "let's turn to aftermaths ensuing from the Lahore Basin incident. I am given to understand, most likely a white man aided Miss Govinda to cross the Pakistan-India border at Jattanwali. The man drove her Avenger, pursued by a Pakistani Army border patrol which lost the car in central Lahore. The identification of the white man is still to be substantiated by the Lahore Police."

"So I understand," Latham credited.

"Dale, you were suspected to be this man," Soames reminded him, "but lawful charges have not been brought against you."

"Correct."

"Again, I am given to understand when Chief Inspector Aman directly confronted you with the accusation, you denied any involvement."

"Yes, I did."

"I see." Resting momentarily, he formed a considerate mien. "Strictly off the record, whoever contributed white knight services to Miss Govinda, is to be applauded. The Foreign Office is well aware of how Hindus, Sikhs and Christians are treated in Pakistan, especially in the long-disputed Punjab region. Nevertheless, for a host of interrelated diplomatic and commercial grounds there is nothing HMG can do about it." Standing, he began listlessly pacing about the state room, hands clasped behind his back, his consideration plain. "Aiding minorities under the spotlight of the Pakistani police and intelligence services is not a unique occurrence. We've logged rumours of people being spirited over the border to India in the past, or through the fence line, as is the case for Miss Govinda. However, what is exclusive about this episode, is the abetting of the escape by a white man." Facing Latham, he delineated, "Europeans resident in Pakistan are exceedingly rare. Landon Fawbert tells me there are no British nationals registered with the Lahore Consulate at present. Granted there might be some other Europeans or Americans registered with their embassies, and of course there is a trickle of white tourists, but the likelihood of Miss Govinda nurturing a kinship from any of these groups is highly remote." Gawking plaintively at the Armstrong-Eliot man, he came across as almost embarrassed by the remark. "I'm telling you this, Dale, to impress upon you why the Lahore Police have concentrated their efforts on proving you are the man they are seeking."

Latham did not respond.

Resuming his seat, Soames glimpsed at Kimble and Hunter inquisitively. Both nodded back; a pre-arranged signal to desist the line of examination.

"Right," Soames positively began, "let's park that finicky strand for the time being." Peeking at his prompt sheet, made before the meeting, he then launched into his second item. "Now, after Aman tried to implicate the PRM in downing the Puma helicopter, an assertion thereafter proved to be incorrect derived from the preliminary air accident crash report, accommodated by Colonel Sharif of the Pakistani Army Corps Military Police, Aman upped the ante by arresting and detaining you."

"He did."

"And with pressure brought to bear from above in the Pakistani Ministry of Law & Justice, yielded at the bidding of British High Commissioner Augustus Dawson, you were subsequently released under bail conditions. When the time limit on the restraint expired, you were discharged from your bail bond, but Aman retained your passport."

"I understand it will be given to me at Jinnah International, before I travel back to England."

"Yes. To continue—" His articulation settled into a more pronounced timbre. "Upon your release, someone, most probably, Chief Inspector Aman, a mullah-run Islamic State sympathizer, made arrangements for the Taliban to abduct you."

"A very reasonable deduction."

"Hhmm, now we come onto the next strand of the envelopment I need to investigate." Ogling Latham sternly, he asked, "what did you tell the Taliban in respect of the equipment Armstrong-Eliot are set to supply, and, more importantly, UK national security?"

Latham mustered what he told Fawbert and Hunter at the Lahore Consulate, emphasising he thought the Taliban had been misled apropos his capacity to inform them about UK-MoD war strategies, and how to defeat the Armstrong-Eliot battlefield target sensor systems, and in Hunter's vision, he had been set up as a patsy to be killed.

"Yes, I am told by several well-informed fountainheads, behind Aman's cosmetic calmness, he is a vindictive man. Unarguably it can be deduced, once you had been relieved from bail conditions, and with no further witnesses or proof being presented by the police, as a supreme resort to inflict his brand of justice on you for a presupposed crime, he put you into the hands of the Taliban. My audit of the specifics is correct, isn't it, Mister Hunter?"

"Connected with previous proficiency, I submitted the same evaluation to Landon Fawbert."

"Yes, so I understand. Erm—" Shuffling in his chair, as if unsure of his next sentence, Soames conveyed in a measured vocalisation, "this is a good time for you to voice any concerns to Dale your organisation wants answered."

Anticipating the offer in advance of the meeting, Hunter had decided to wait and see what Soames tabled before quizzing Latham formally, one way or the other. Latham's reply to Soames cardinal enquiry pertaining to UK national security issues mirrored what he had said to Fawbert and himself back in Lahore.

"Thank you for allowing me the opportunity," Hunter imparted, "but you've covered all the salient issues of interest to MI6 and the MoD, and Mister Latham has made the same replies as he did at the Lahore Consulate." Pausing, he neutrally enunciated, "I see no point in putting him through the mill for a third time."

"Ohh, I'm so glad. Nonetheless—" Reactivating his agenda, Soames heralded, "the conundrum remains, is Aman going to pull an incriminating rabbit out of the hat at the eleventh hour and counting?"

"The same notion has crossed my mind," Hunter volunteered. "If he's going to, it will be at the airport in full public view. Instead of returning Mister Latham's passport, he will re-arrest him."

"So we need to make some kind of contingency. Any ideas, Bill?"

Frowning, Kimble tendered, "well, even if it's a put-up job, it might stand up in court. And of course, for security determinants, we don't want Dale to end up in jail."

"*What*?" Latham exclaimed. "What security determinants?"

"Fawbert didn't want to alarm you further whilst you were undergoing medical treatment at the Lahore Consulate," Kimble explained. "The Foreign Office has been informed some of the top-secret information you were privy to in the RAF is still current and highly classified. HMG does not want a foreign power gaining access to it by one means or another."

"You mean, *Jesus*—" Hit hard by a brand-new revelation, he flinched. "If imprisoned and out of the public eye, I might be put into the hands of Pakistani intelligence services?"

Kimble took a deep breath, his face awash with misgivings. "It is plausible."

"So," Soames persevered, "what we have to do is ensure it does not take place." Squinting at the MI6 man, he prompted, "Mister Hunter."

Assuming an incontrovertible air, Hunter accredited, "to be frank, you know my brief, and back in Lahore, Mister Latham worked out why I am here. As I see it, there are three options. One, we smuggle Mister Latham out of Pakistan using contracted resources. Two, we hire contractors to recover his passport, without alerting Chief Inspector Aman, thus allowing Mister Latham to leave unhindered. Three—" Dawdling, he produced a stoical visage. "We do nothing on the basis the Lahore Police do not table any incriminating verification or mount bogus witnesses in reference to Mister Latham's alleged complicity in Miss Govinda's escape, thereby preserving Aman's commitment to return Mister Latham's passport at Jinnah International."

"Mmmm." Soames pondered for a moment. "Regarding option one, it could well put the Foreign Office in the nasty stuff with the Pakistan Government. They will believe the British High Commission is responsible for the ploy, inexorably precluding Dale ever returning to Pakistan. But er…could you arrange such a subterfuge?"

"By all means. We'd have a helicopter fly in from a surface vessel in the Arabian Sea at night, pick up Mister Latham from a remote extraction location, and backtrack to the surface vessel."

"Good god," Soames trilled. "Apart from the SAS, I imagined sorties of this nature only happened in films." His dark humour giving way to practicalities, he challenged, "could such a scheme be fulfilled without incorporating MI6 resources directly?"

"Yes. Intrinsically involving nothing attributable and no recordable trial, the operation could be subcontracted to independent contractors by Century House."

"How?"

"Oh, it's very simple. *De facto* spy craft coupled with loose communication couplings. What you might call tricks of the trade."

"I see."

"Unequivocally, possibility two is even more breathtaking," Kimble reviewed. "It too could put the Foreign Office in hock, the Pakistani Government assuming British High Commission involvement." Musing further, he subconsciously rubbed his chin, before asking Hunter, "again, I guess Century House would hire contractors to perform the task?"

"Yes. They'd come into the country via an official port of entry, recover the passport, give it to me in Lahore, and I'd fly to Karachi with it, courtesy of PIA, enabling Mister Latham to depart from Jinnah

International. Even so—" Recoiling, he knew the mission to be fatally flawed. "The proposal pivots heavily on Aman not detecting the passport had been lifted for at least 10 hours."

"I'd surmise another selection," Soames began, "is to administer Dale a new passport and have him fly out at short notice, preventing Aman from making an interception."

"True," Kimble favoured. "We could have the Passport Office supervise a brand-new passport, and have it couriered out to Karachi in the diplomatic bag."

"How long does that take?" Hunter solicited.

"We'd make it a priority request, so no longer than two days for it to arrive here. Unfortunately, once again, the British High Commission and thereafter the Foreign Office are implicated, Aman checking the passport number with Jinnah's passport control and deducing it had been explicitly issued by the UK Passport Office, after Dale had flown the coup."

With no proposer or assessor totally sure which choice to take, they exchanged dubious gawps, their deliberations not providing a clear-cut way forward.

"Well, Dale," Soames itemised, "you're the man in the firing line. What's your take?"

Gyrating his head, the gesture signifying confirmation of his onerous position, he replied, "I have no wish to put the Foreign Office or the British High Commission into burdensome circumstances with the Pakistan Government and the Lahore Police. Though I appreciate Mister Hunter's contrivances for extricating me from this quagmire, there'd always be a spectre hanging over me, metaphorically, the executioner's axe waiting to fall. To sustain my career at Armstrong-Eliot, and hence have the means to take care of my daughters, I need to come out of this enigma clean. You see—" Licking his lips to find moisture, the realisation of his next words being axiomatic to his future caused anxiety, leading to his mouth drying. "The company will expect me to resume my sales campaign in Pakistan to finalise the transaction with Pakistan Armed Forces and take care of future military requirements. Therefore, I can't have a perpetual stain on my character, with people querying my integrity."

"So, are you saying," Soames speculated, "you are willing to take your chances at Jinnah International, on the basis Aman returns your passport and does not re-arrest you?"

"Yes."

He turned to Kimble. "What's your appraisement, Bill?"

"In principle, it is the soundest method of all the listed alternatives. We have established there is sponsorship from Pakistan Government conventional sectors plus pressure from Pakistan Armed Forces not to detain Dale. Q.E.D wise, it allows HMG to permit the required export licenses for the Armstrong-Eliot battlefield target sensor systems. Barring no other contributing or unpredicted dynamics, Dale taking the authorised way out of Pakistan is clean with no leftovers."

"Yes, I agree." Developing a statesman-like carriage, Soames declared, "before we categorically decide, I'm going to meet with Brigadier Cham and Vice Admiral Mahmood to confirm their support, and I'll ask Augustus Dawson to do the same with his contacts in the ruling Pakistani Peoples Party." Casting an optimistic eye to all quarters of the gathering, he dictated, "we'll reconvene in 24 hours."

~ * ~

Worried about his continuing freedom and longevity, in the afternoon Latham visited Hunter in the deputy high commission's security room, his mood ringing with foreboding, the MI6 man rapidly deciphering its syntax.

"You're going to ask me, if you take the official exit route, what will I do, if Chief Inspector Aman detains you at the airport."

"Yes."

"I've talked to my people back in London about your preferred option."

"And?"

"Dale—" Developing an anguished face, he pinpointed him full-on. "I'm not going to conceal from you what I have been instructed to do, should you be re-arrested. Despite the commonality we have akin to lost wives, the courtesy I showed you at Nowshera Virkan has not gone down well with MI6 at Century House. Should you go to trial, become convicted then imprisoned, be assured, Pakistani intelligence services will come for you. They will scrutinise your RAF background, and might even discover you once had access to top secret plans, some still current. Confidentially, in that eventuality, you could be subject to the same kind of interrogation you experienced with the Taliban. If such an occasion did occur, it negates HMG sending in an extraction force to rescue you."

"They'd think I'd talk?"

"If physical torture failed, truth serum would be applied." Wittingly raising his eyebrows, Hunter forewarned, "you'd spill everything, your brains becoming fried before they applied the terminal *coup de gras.*"

"I see. So—" Abjectly shaking his head, his meekness undeniable, his whole being sagged like a decaying flower. "If Aman does re-arrest me, you will carry out your kill order."

Hunter did not reply. Instead he lowered his head, Latham taking it as confirmation of his conjecture.

"Well," Latham began, breathing out heavily. "It seems I am completely in the hands of Soames and Dawson to deliver the guarantees needed from Pakistan Armed Forces and the Pakistani Peoples Party."

~ * ~

By the time Soames reconvened the players, Latham had resigned himself to a binary outcome to his predicament, either he'd be flying out of Jinnah International, or making his last will and testament.

"My meetings with Brigadier Cham and Vice Admiral Mahmood yielded some encouragement," Soames imparted. "Because it suits their agenda, both say Pakistan Armed Forces want Dale to be allowed to leave the country, untarnished by moments in Lahore. Augustus Dawson got the same reaction from the Pakistani Peoples Party, and unofficially, it is also the Pakistan Government's line. Apparently, behind the scenes, Aman's talons have been trimmed, and Dale should have no trouble at

Jinnah International. However—" Sniffily, he wrinkled his nose. "Jitender Shadid, Permanent Secretary to Minister Sardar Kanaan at the Ministry of Law & Justice, told Dawson that Aman intends to personally restore Dale's passport to him at Jinnah departures, immediately prior to him going through check-in and passport control."

"Are you implying Aman might play ducks and drakes *vis-a-vis* its return?" Latham posed.

"I suppose I am. Going on the notorious nature of the beast, we can't rule out he won't continue to prod and probe you about what transpired at Lahore Basin. And, though unlikely at this late stage in the game, he could present you with incriminating substantiation or a new witness."

"For sure, a streak of sadism runs in Aman's persona," Kimble put forward, "but it's problematic to comprehend he will play a master stroke at the eleventh hour and counting."

"Agreed," Hunter concurred. "Though I can see prolonging Dale's agony appealing to his base nature, bearing in mind he wants to nail him, if he did have anything new, he'd have played the clamping card before we left Lahore."

"Maybe," Soames allowed, "but Shadid told Dawson, Aman still has his resources searching for fresh testimony. If something does materialise, it'd suit his malicious itinerary to nab Dale just when he believed he was Blighty bound."

Chapter 18: Liberation

Departure day came around, with all interested parties resident at the Karachi British Deputy High Commission either buoyant or on tenterhooks. Though, in principle, Latham lingered confident he'd be climbing aboard a 747 and heading for Heathrow, a slither of dubiety continued to haunt him. Calling Amelia again the day after Soames's concluding round table conference, he relayed on his flight details. Trying to be as sanguine as possible during the telecom, he concealed his reservation relating to the possibility of never seeing his family again, Amelia only discerning a positive vibe in his voice.

At the appointed hour, Kimble and Hunter escorted him to Jinnah International in the same Daimler DS420 used to ferry Rendall Gilmour and Latham to the Deputy British High Commission, nearly seven weeks earlier. Back then, Latham could never have envisioned the series of interrelated developments culminating in his detainment by the Lahore Police and abduction by the Taliban. Aware of his reservations pertaining to his fate, Kimble and Hunter engaged Latham in light conversation, but still sensed apprehension in their charge, his monosyllabic replies to their banter confirming his wariness about sustaining his freedom, and thereby, his life.

Reliving the distasteful reception non-Pakistani inbound passengers had received in the customs hall, Latham wondered if the same intimating convention endured, outbound passengers also subjected to overly thorough hardships as an excuse to combat the war on drug traffickers. Mentally recapping the often barbaric and cruel instances of Sharia Law he had witnessed being applied to victims on the streets of Karachi, Rawalpindi and Lahore, Latham foresaw national fervour resulting in airport bureaucrats withstanding their obvious dislike of foreigners, specifically those of European ethnic origins.

Entering the departure terminal with his escort, Latham's trepidation heightened, a rush of negatives overwhelming him, generating visions of incarceration being forestalled by a silent bullet. Converging on the business class BA departures flight desk for London, ahead Latham clocked Chief Inspector Aman, flanked by two armed police officers. Tapping Kimble's arm and indicating at his incessant nemesis, Latham's mouth went dry.

Stopping just short of the police party, protocol required Kimble took charge.

"Chief Inspector Aman, you might recall I am Bill Kimble with the Deputy British High Commission Karachi."

"Mister Kimble," Aman acknowledged, his face blank of emotion, his eyes dull, his whole demeanour bereft of charity.

"Chief Inspector, do you have Mister Latham's passport?"

"Yes."

"Can you please return it?"

"First, I must ask him a few more questions about the incident at Lahore Basin."

Briefly maddened by the implausible insistence, Kimble regained his politic composure. "Chief Inspector, with the greatest of respect, the time has ended to conduct your detective work with regard to Mister Latham."

"There is no time limit to pursue police investigations," Aman contradicted. "The case persists open, and I am duty bound to carry on with my enquiries."

Seeking advocacy one way or the other, Kimble hit Hunter with a probing expression. Nodding back at him in response, the signal intended compliance with Aman's petition.

"Very well, but you need to be quick. Mister Latham does not have much time to complete his flight check-in."

Advancing with his usual menace, Aman stood in front of his suspect. "Mister Latham, do you still maintain you had nothing to do with

Chanda Govinda's illegal crossing of the Pakistan-India border in the Lahore Basin at Jattanwali?"

Overcoming his inhibited state, Latham emphatically avouched, "I do."

"Did you know on the night in question, you were the only foreign white man registered with the Pakistani authorities in Lahore, who both knew Miss Govinda, and cannot independently account for his whereabouts?"

"Chief Inspector Aman," Kimble assertively blurted, "you can't be sure of that."

"None we interviewed knew Miss Govinda," he inflexibly enumerated, "and all suspects have verifiable alibis with third parties. Mister Latham has no one to confirm his whereabouts during the hours under consideration."

"Chief inspector, you are going over old ground. Mister Latham resided in his bed at the Combined Military Hospital."

"Admittedly, the day staff endorsed his presence before the night shift came on at 9:30 pm. Notwithstanding, between the juncture and when the police entered his room at 5:15 a.m the following morning, the night shift did not disturb him, giving him the opportunity to aid in Miss Govinda's illegal border crossing."

"It still remains purely circumstantial," Kimble fervidly repudiated. "No evidence or witnesses have been presented by the police to buttress your accusation."

"Mister Kimble, after exhaustive investigations," Aman pushed, "what remains is a logical conclusion, and one we could have sent Mister Latham to trial on, albeit for intervention from his benefactors in the Pakistan Government administration."

Kimble did not argue the assertion.

Turning to Latham, Aman articulated, "you are very fortunate to have friends in high places, Mister Latham, however, we both know what really happened, don't we?"

Latham tarried tight-lipped.

"This case will be left open. If any evidence or witnesses come to light in the future verifying your collaboration in the criminality, the

Lahore Police will demand your extradition from England to stand trial in the Lahore High Court."

"Chief Inspector Aman," Kimble blathered in a trenchant voice, "I strongly object to your unwarranted badgering of Mister Latham. It is tantamount to a threat. I warn you, if you continue in this vain, the British High Commissioner will lodge a formal complaint against you with the Ministry of Law & Justice."

Indifferent to the danger, Aman scowled at his suspect. "If you ever journey to Pakistan again, Mister Latham, be very careful who you befriend." Whilst still eyeing him he spoke in Urdu, and one of his guards handed him Latham's passport.

Slapping the document in Latham's hand, he announced, "based on circumstantial evidence, I could re-arrest you."

"Oh, I don't think so, Chief Inspector," Hunter interposed. "After all, we don't want Mister Latham falling into the hands of the Taliban again, do we?"

Visibly fuming at the inference, Aman made no retort. Barking something in Urdu, he then turned, his guards escorting him out of the departures terminal.

Blowing out a sigh of relief, Kimble proclaimed, "well, we irrevocably have an end to the witch hunt. Congratulations, Dale, you're a free man."

"Yes," he unsteadily murmured, still not entirely believing his status, a small part of him imagining Aman had played another falsehood and he awaited at passport control, ready to reacquire his victim. "All I have to do now is deal with passport control and hand baggage inspection."

"Oh, you won't have any difficulty there," Kimble forecast, not in the slightest detecting his dread. "The officials might be uppity, but you are *au fait* with how to play their silly games without getting stung."

Latham eyeballed Hunter. Also transparent to his phobia, the MI6 man broke into an unexpected glint.

"Looks like you're not going to get me."

"For sure. This is one mission, I'm glad I didn't have to complete." Placing an encouraging hand on his shoulder, he wished, "good luck, Dale."

~ * ~

After Latham checked-in, made his final farewells to Kimble and Hunter, and successfully negotiated passport control and hand baggage check unbridled, he boarded the London-bound BA flight. For the first time since the police invaded his room in the early hours of the morning after he had helped Chanda Govinda escape to India, a mammoth flood of relaxation percolated his whole being, his misgivings regarding Chief Inspector Aman curtailing his departure without material foundation.

Pulling out a parched photograph of Nicol and Penny from his equally charred wallet, consequent from the Puma fatality, he stared into their beaming faces, tears forming not because of the aptness of paternal instinct, but relief. In less than nine hours, he'd be seeing them in the flesh at Heathrow. Kissing the photograph like it represented a cache of rare gems, he resolved to never put them at risk of becoming orphans again, no matter how much he perceived his late wife might applaud his deeds to help someone in a desperate fix. He had exercised his white knight in shining armour desire, surely the act metered out as sufficient to honour Fiona's memory.

Soon after the stewardess had served dinner, beginning to feel like a regular air traveler again, he nonchalantly nursed a large measure of Courvoisier Napoleon Cognac. Shortly thereafter, whilst only partially paying attention to in-flight movie *The Getaway*, Roger Donaldson's remake of the original 1972 film, most apt he thought, he relaxed into a deep sleep, free from demons, the forefront of his mind expunged from everything he had suffered after the Lahore Basin fracas, his psyche beginning to relieve itself from the aftermath of detainment in a filthy police cell, and torture at the hands of the Taliban.

Chapter 19: After the Psychiatrist's Couch

Sequent to a period of rest and counseling from an MoD psychiatrist, Dale Latham resumed work at Armstrong-Eliot. Whilst recuperating from his ordeal, HMG had issued export licenses, allowing the company's battlefield target sensor systems to be sold to Pakistan Armed Forces.

"They gave the go-ahead within hours of your inbound flight touching down at Heathrow," Rendall Gilmour told Latham after welcoming him back into the fold, and enquiring about his health.

"Any problems or issues with the supplied equipment?"

"Well—" Glad to see him back, he gently slapped his old sales partner on the shoulder. "After our meetings with Pakistan Armed Forces, they took up our references, finding them to be satisfactory, and placed preliminary orders for AF-486 and NF-486 systems. When we got export clearance, they were shipped out for testing on a Pakistan Army Aviation Wing Bell AH-1S attack helicopter and a navy Tariq class destroyer. Currently, we have Armstrong-Eliot technical resources in-country, supporting the Pakistan Armed Forces adjudication teams. They report no substantial issues."

"I take it our initial survey for production numbers still holds water?"

"Incontrovertibly it does. We have orders to cover 54 systems for the army, 46 for the air force, and 24 for the navy. It embodies the complete present inventory. Pakistan Armed Forces are also predicting the need for a further 120 systems for future tri-service requirements over the next decade. The total equated to £26.4m in equipment sales, plus a further £29m for in-service support over ten years, and £3.5m for a fully-integrated logistics support package." Twinkling with pride, he conveyed,

"Matthew Chapman and the group board of directors are cocker hoop about the deal."

"Yes, I spoke to Matthew before restarting with the company. He did come across as very upbeat, saying all systems were go with Pakistan Armed Forces, if you'll forgive the pun." Hesitating, he hit Gilmour with an oblique mannerism. "I guess, you had to grease the wheels with Brigadier Chan and Vice Admiral Mahmood?"

"Again, after you were confirmed to be back in Blighty, Chapman sanctioned a management consultancy package. I made a trip to Geneva a few days later, depositing thick wedges of readies in two numbered accounts provided by Cham and Mahmood."

"So it goes," Latham calmly upheld. "Although I know it's an integral part of the commercial model, I still don't feel good about that aspect of our work."

"No. The only cushioning thing about it is, we never make the foremost accost. It's always the buyer."

"Indeed," he supported. "And if we didn't comply, the company would be summarily black-listed."

Appreciating his heightened reservation about the unsavoury process, Gilmour smiled at Latham. "It's great to have you back, Dale. For a while, I feared I'd never see you in Blighty again."

"The same dismay crossed my mind many times whilst still in-country."

"What have you told your family?"

"As little as possible. Amelia and Clement know about the downed helicopter at Lahore AFB, and my hitch with the Lahore Police, but not about my abduction. Thankfully, Nicol and Penny know nothing, other than of my protracted undertaking dealing with business in Pakistan."

"How did you explain your period of rest to them at your homecoming?"

"I planned in advance to tell them, during the visit I had picked up a bug, and British High Commission medical staff prescribed a period of recovery on my return to England."

"Well—" He effervesced with pleasure. "I expect they were so pleased to see you again, they didn't table any exacting queries."

"Quite."

"What has Chapman said to you in the context of the future?"

"He's made me make a pledge to steer clear of non-business issues."

"Ohh!" Gilmour laughed. "So no more coming to the aid of damsels in distress?"

"No," he solemnly specified. "I've done my bit for humankind."

"By the way, have you been advised Pakistan intelligence services have apprehended the perpetrators of the Puma SAM attack? It was the Taliban."

"Yes, I received a message from Bill Kimble via the Foreign Office. *Huh*—" Shaking his head, he wilted into a reflective domain. "In a house-of-cards-like fallout, the tragedy led to Chief Inspector Aman mounting a concerted attack on Chanda Govinda and myself, in the artificial belief the PRM were responsible. The knock-on consequences of that fake ruse nearly finished me."

"I bet they did." Instinctively taking a step back to avoid crowding his clearly afflicted colleague, Gilmour sought, "have you put the whole episode into perspective yet?"

Latham's comportment spiraled into ambivalence. "I'm not sure, Rendall. Rationalising what happened has left a residual shadow across my whole being." Lifting his hands, he then let them flop by his sides, as if waiving any notion sequels resultant from the incident in the Lahore Basin could ever go away. "Oh, the MoD psychiatrist assured me it'd diminish with time, and necessarily, I've not burdened my family with the load, but like all significant memories, it will reemerge from time to time. I haven't woken up in a cold sweat from dreaming about it yet, but I've not dismissed the fancy it could occur downline."

"Maybe your RAF training has been a godsend, and it has empowered you to cope without breaking down?"

"Maybe, but I got damned close. I traversed right on the edge staring into the abyss, not in the hellhole of a police cell, or when the Taliban were torturing me, but afterwards." Making strained physiognomy, his rhetoric surged into incisiveness. "You see, during those ordeals, my mind became absorbed by other things, principally survival. The stress juggernaut really hit me when I flew to Karachi for a ceremonial debriefing with John Soames, and then had to face Aman for a final time at Jinnah International to retrieve my passport. Those latter trials were the straw nearly breaking the camel's back."

"Did you tell all this to the MoD psychiatrist?"

"Oh yes, and more besides. He wanted me to expunge any latent trauma by recounting every detail leaving a mark on me."

"And did you?"

"Do you know, I'm not sure." Latham grinned. "Part of me wanted to let the remnant gush out in the belief there'd be no recurrence downline. But it's not like pulling a tooth, the wound temporary and soon forgotten. The problem is in the mind, a magnificent organ having a law unto itself. Attempt to put it into neutral, and whatever has caused colossal upset rather than physical pain tends to resurface."

"So you didn't re-live the entire happening again on the psychiatrist's couch?"

"Some, feasibly most, just to get a sign off from him. But I didn't want to chance itemizing every detail. I worried it might drive me over the precipice, so I gave him a sanitized version."

"Did he believe it delineated the whole thing?"

"I'm not really sure, Supposedly not, but he never suggested I held back."

"A double bluff maybe?"

"How do you mean?"

"He could have been testing your psychic strength to cope with what you had been put through. If you had confessed everything, and as an upshot broken down, you might not have got a sign-off."

"Yes, it transpired as part of my delicate balancing act, on the basis Armstrong-Eliot wanted to verify if I truly met fit-for-work standards, without breaking down on the job."

Flabbergasted by the remark, Gilmour tabled, "so the company requested a copy of the psychiatrist's analysis on you commissioned by MoD?"

"Yes, I had to give my permission, but I wanted to demonstrate to Matthew Chapman, I qualified as being both physically and mentally fit for duty."

"Very bold, Dale."

"For sure, it was a calculated risk, but without sign-off, there'd have always been a shadow hanging over my sanity as far as Armstrong-Eliot were concerned."

Keen to lighten their conversation for fear of driving Latham too hard, Gilmour's challenges passed into domestic and professional territories, finishing with, "well, no doubt you plan to absorb yourself in your family and your work, as a means of pushing the misfortune to the back of your mind?"

"Yes I do, Rendall. From now on, there will be no tilts at playing Don Quixote. All I want to do is embroil myself in seeing Nicol and Penny grow up and win more deals for Armstrong-Eliot."

Chapter 20: Postscript

Not long after Latham returned to work, he received a letter marked private and care of Armstrong-Eliot, its envelope recipient details handwritten and with a Republic of India postmark. Immediately he knew the sender must be Chanda Govinda.

Dear Dale,

I hope this letter finds you in good health. After I evaporated from your view on the Indian side of the Pakistan-India border, and made my way to my cousin's house in Amritsar, I began to take stock of proceedings. Candidly, what you did for me, I evaluated as an act of altruistic heroism.

A week later, I telephoned a member of the Punjab Reunification Movement in Lahore. The organisation had picked up some intelligence concerning a white man arrested by the Lahore Police on conjecture of aiding an Indian woman to illegally cross the Pakistan-India border. I knew it must be you. It sent me into a whirlpool of regret and self-recriminations. Then friends in Lahore sent a message, saying you'd been freed and had flown to England. I have no idea what trials and tribulations you had to endure during your detainment, but my heart leapt for joy when I read the good news.

I must now confess to you; I was not quite truthful about my connection with the PRM. After my father and brothers were killed by persons unknown according to the Lahore Police, I knew Pakistani Muslims were responsible. I made a promise to myself to take revenge for their deaths by any means available to me. Chief Inspector Aman's suspicions appertaining to my attachment with the PRM were correct.

Through my confederation with the Combined Military Hospital, I obtained a lethal drug for a PRM splinter group, dedicated to assassinating Muslim zealots persecuting Hindu, Sikh and Christian minorities. These people were adjudged to have died under mysterious circumstances, the drug leaving no corporeal trace, unless a coroner knows what has been administered, and thereby what to check for. It evolved into a foolproof method for dispatching our oppressors, without resorting to guns and explosives.

On the basis natural causes were at work, often, no police investigation eventuated when a victim suddenly died. Then the frequency of Muslim zealots dying without warning alerted the police to a conceivable conspiracy plot. That's when Aman started to mark me for interrogation. You have doubtless found out by now, behind his official position, Aman is a Muslim zealot and advocates imposing an ultra-radical, mullah-run Islamic State. Many of the people assassinated were his fellow devotees of the selfsame cause. He knew some on a personal basis and dreaded he'd also be subject to an attack.

Of course, after he targeted me, the incidence of untimely deaths reduced. I could not risk obtaining more of the lethal drug, and the splinter group ran out of it. He had no proof but continued to cross-examine me. It registered as only a matter of time before he formally arrested me, then totally unforeseen, you came into my life, telling me about your deceased Christian wife. With me being Christian as well, I began to see a way to escape Aman's clutches by playing on the commonality and dragged you into my escape scheme. Something I now bear as a heavy burden.

There was always a chance you might be interviewed by the Lahore Police apropos my escape to India, but I put it to the back of my mind when we conceived the plan to get me across the border. I also made you think I was pure of mind and untainted by terrorist acts. Now you know it's not true.

I will never forget you, Dale, and I hope you can find it in your heart to forgive me for my deception and for using you.

Yours cordially,
Chanda Govinda

Shocked by what he had read, Latham put the letter down.

"Am I really so gullible and open to exploitation?" he asked himself.

There used to be a time when he could pick out a miscreant and smell a rat, but ostensibly it related to when the RAF regulated his world appreciation, his antennae on high-gain monitoring a plethora of people and data, searching for truth. Since Fiona's untimely death, the facility had lessened in effectiveness, leaving him open to distorted information and false contemplation.

Though he abided emotion-free in front of Nicol and Penny, and other family members, Fiona's going hit him very hard. As he had confessed to Hunter, in private he wept, agonising at length by testing could he have done anything more to sustain her life. It went on for a long time, until he put the loss of Fiona into perspective. During the sackcloth and ashes period, his defences were lowered, his ability to empathise with other people's losses and allegedly insoluble problems, amplified. True, outwardly he still came across as the same measured and resolute businessman to colleagues and clients, but beneath the surface, he had sunk into a benign state, ever ready to give the benefit of doubt to those delivered into stormy waters through their own inappropriate and stupid actions, or alternatively, innocent victims of grotesque forces.

Digesting the letter for a second time, it struck him those same unfortunates also possessed the capability for wrongdoing. Chanda Govinda was as guilty of evil as the nauseating labours she accused Chief Inspector Aman of perpetrating. It cast wariness on the perception that most people were inherently good and only a few were capable of sanctimonious duplicity. How many others had crossed his path appearing to be paragons of virtue, when beneath the covers they too were vipers, impure of thought and mind?

Holding no false illusions regarding what many adjudicated to be his warmonger associations with both the RAF and the defence industry, he absolutely knew if he had ever been ordered to open fire on the enemy or drop a tactical nuclear weapon into a battle zone from a Tornado GR-1 interdictor-strike aircraft, people would be killed. But he never covered up the reality, openingly admitting to those probing his role, it defended the realm and the British people against aggressors. Hypocrisy not lying within his temperament, he truthfully settled their reservations, without any sense of regret or malpractice.

When Chanda Govinda connected with him, he rested still in the throes of coming to terms with surviving the helicopter attack and crash. Vulnerable and susceptible to suggestion, brought on by a realisation he had been extremely fortunate, he had felt predisposed to help her, not just because, like Fiona, she displayed Christian beliefs, but also as a tribute to his own blessing. Shoved to the back of his mind in favour of good will and benevolence, his innate competency for rationality and qualifying tricky situations had been sidelined.

Whilst he had been in the limelight of the harrowing follow-on events sequent to the Lahore Basin rumpus, it never occurred to him Chanda might not be as virtuous as she claimed. Taking her veracity as seen, he had never quizzed himself as to the validity of her story or become skeptical about her rectitude. For sure, she had justified manipulating the absolute truth, on the basis he might not help her, and probably he considered her role in the poisoning of the PRM's enemies not to be legitimate.

Agonising about the deception, Latham reviewed Acts of Parliament sanctioned by the UN and NATO gave legitimacy to war and killing the enemy, those fighting men charged with executing the clarion call insulated from breaking the moral code by law. Terrorism of any kind lasted unlawful, and without general approval consensus. What the Taliban were doing definitely fell into the terrorist category, but some of the PRM's malodorous deeds were also without mandated legitimacy, poisoning Muslim zealots just as heinous as jihadists beheading Christians. If he had known about Chanda's entanglement in the assassination operation, despite her Christianity, he might not have come to her aid.

The more Latham dissected the unsavory revelation, the more he recognised the demarcation between virtue and evil did not neatly fit into groups understood to be good and bad, tolerant democracies and intolerant regimes, depended on from which side of the divide the assessment materialised. Not all Muslims were bad, and undeniably, not every Christian, Hindu and Sikh could be categorised as good. He had got caught up in an oppressive vortex in play since the partition of India in 1947, though its origins went back centuries.

Stung by the recognition, he cogitated further on the thorny dilemma. Were people like the affable and broad-minded Ghulam Bishara verily representative of most Pakistani Muslims, or beneath the covers of respectability, were they secret mullah-led Islamic State diehards? Though Indian Hindus and Sikhs were renowned for their gentle, non-aggressive doctrines, could it merely be a convenient facade to hide domination ambitions, as bad as those of the Taliban? And what of Christians? Were they really as universally moral as perceived? Inescapably, Chanda Govinda cast apprehension on the impression.

Whilst with the RAF, Latham never had the spare bandwidth to consider such lofty topics, dedication to marriage followed by bringing up two children accelerating the restriction of his capacity to engage in philosophical matters. His careers at Dandridge and Armstrong-Eliot had further consumed and focused his rumination along commercial lines, little scope existing to examine profound and abstract religious and cultural concepts. Fiona's Christian devotion had been one of convention and adherence to Church of England principles, her regular church going and participation in church activities never touching on a desire to make the whole world Christian. She represented the vast majority of C of E practitioners, benevolent in attitude, non-confrontational, and accommodating of secular society and other religions.

Howbeit, the untainted manner pictured a stable England, not the continuously shaky and erratic meltdown of the sub-continent, still in a state of flux caused by gigantic waves from partition, and a plethora of diametrically opposed religions and cultures. Could it be too much to expect sub-continent Christians to be as virtuous as their English counterparts?

The more Latham re-examined the letter, the more he authenticated he knew very little about the world. His professional and domestic life spotlight had caused him to skip over glaring contradictions and make unsubstantiated hunches about the nature of people, too often giving them the benefit of the doubt, and assuming goodness to be the central plank of their makeup. Traveling back, besides Chanda Govinda, others had deceived him, not to the extent and with the adverse ramifications she had, but nonetheless, he had discovered purity flaws, often retrospectively when the damage had been done.

Was he so bad a referee of people? Factored on his candid nature, were they able to pull the wool easily? Did the facet make him an easy mark for manipulation? These were enquiries raised against his post-RAF life, largely in the world of commerce and in foreign climes. Whereas in the main, service personnel adhered to a common set of moral principles, civvy street and civil government exhibited much more contentious traits, the surface gloss portraying trustworthiness and probity, hiding the tools of deceit and falsehood beneath its thin veneer. Certainly, it existed off-shore, and in his experience, a venomous strain in the Middle-East and the sub-continent. Even the most noble were imperfect. Though Ghulam Bishara showed him infinite consideration, like so many Pakistani officers, Latham knew he had a dark side, capable of using his rank to browbeat subordinates. Forasmuch, it equated to a court martial offence in the RAF and the other British military forces, but not so in the austere and ruthless environment of Muslim countries. There, it seemed to be an expectation, the M.O apparently necessary to keep rulers well above the ruled, with no recourse for those under the cosh.

The more he agonised, the more he realised the RAF code had not distilled elsewhere. Indeed, it barely existed beyond the white cliffs of Dover. Though many admired British traits and sensibilities, particularly those associated with untarnished truth and rigid integrity, in reality, few practiced the discipline, often seeing it as weakness to be exploited.

~ * ~

When Latham left his office in the early evening, his heart heavy with a combination of disappointment and sorrow, he resolved himself to adopt a far more robust approach to the professedly maltreated. But for some good fortune, his involvement in the Lahore Basin affair could have ultimately terminated in his death from an assassin's bullet. Imprudently, he had risked never seeing his loved ones again. From now on, it'd not take place under any heart-rendering circumstances, whether true or false.

With the cold English winter starting to close in, a welcome antithesis to the blistering summer heat in Pakistan, he had dinner with Nicol and Penny at Amelia and Clement's house, marveling at both their physical and character development. Should the worst have happened, and they had been orphaned, he knew if Fiona gazed down from heaven above, she'd never have forgiven him. In observer and listening mode, he delighted in seeing and hearing their joyful frolics and girly conversations and looked forward to being a part of their future lives.

Chanda Govinda, the incident at Lahore Basin, and its knock-on consequences would not be entering the forefront of his mind again.

About the Author

Clive Radford began writing at school, then university but mainly through subsequent life experience.

His poetry has been published in numerous poetry magazines such as *The Journal, The Cannon's Mouth, Poetry Monthly, Poetry Now, Storming Heaven, Poetry Nottingham, Scripsi and Modern Review*, plus in many compilations by United Press.

A series of his short stories and poems have been published by Ether Books. The Arts Council has sponsored publication of his novels *One Night in Tunisia* and *The Sounds of Silence*. His contemporary satire *Doghouse Blues* was number one in Harper Collins Authonomy chart and has been awarded gold medal status. It has been published by Black Rose. His spy thriller *Zavrazin* has been published by Triplicity Publishing. Its companion sequel 'Nexus Bullet' is published by Ex-L-Ence Publishing. His three-book series *Disclosures of a Femme Fatale Addict* is published by Wild Dreams Publishing.

His science fiction novel *Maggie's Farm* and suspense-thriller *Incident at Lahore Basin* are published by Rogue Phoenix Press.

One Night in Tunisia, Zavrazin and *Bullet* have all been converted into three-act screenplays.

The *Zavrazin* screenplay is under contract with Story Merchant/Atchity Productions for film production.

Wild Dreams Publishing re-published *Disclosures of a Femme Fatale Addict* as a deluxe edition, May 2020.

Rogue Phoenix Press will be publishing his satire *Doghouse Blues 2* in March 2021.

Melange Books will be publishing his mystery thriller *Monsoon in the Making* in April 2021.

Currently, he is working on a number of works, including *Doghouse Blues 3, Alpha Centauri,* a futuristic dystopian thriller, *Oklahoma City Looks Oh So Pretty,* a rite of passage sojourn along Route 66, and *The Spiral Staircase and other Novellas*, a mix of psychological, modern satire and rite of passage sagas.

His work has a distinctive voice setting it apart and appealing to those fascinated by intrigue and who question status quo accepted views.

Maggie's Farm

Cody and Carolyn Redford enjoy a carefree lifestyle in Kent County, with friends Gavin and Melanie Maynard. In Cornwall, the Redfords encounter a soothsayer predicting a bleak future for mankind. The foursome then notes some unexplained changes in the behaviour of wild animals and migrating birds, giving credence to the prediction. When a terrorist outrage in South Africa leads to further major atrocities in Israel and India, détente finally fails. Global nuclear war is sparked off by an unforeseen source, resulting in the superpowers exchanging H-bomb punches like drunken boxers. In the midst of survival, Cody Redford becomes aware of the artificial insemination and incubation (AI2) programme, an initiative hatched in the Cold War years to store the sperm of prominent scientists with the objective of using surrogate hosts to factory farm children in a post-holocaust world. Though appalled, nonetheless, he resigns himself to supporting the programme, unaware of the significant down the road consequences to the nature of human life.

Chapter 1: Desolation

Cody Redford stared blankly at the remnants of his house, scarred by battle wounds, and defaced with pockmarks. Tears welled up as he took in the unbending gravity of the wretched sight; the fragile impermanence of life brought into sharp focus under a brooding sky with distant thunder echoing over a barren landscape.

Akin to sleepwalking into cinematic fancy, the world had shrunk into the void, bereft of sane, mortal cognition, the realisation creeping into him as if through osmosis. A once great nation, now devoid of tangible credit, left a sentiment of ambiguity and introspection nestled on his shoulder.

Cursing the structural failure brought on by self-aggrandising, Teflon skinned, anointed demigods, he knew he'd done nothing to stop them abusing the high church of humanity. Instituting feral barbarism and spouting jaw breaking edicts, they had used the ballot box as their duped factotum, their citizens brainwashed and set in a line of their choosing, their worship of the hydrogen bomb without any forbearance of its worldwide catastrophic effect. Savagely insulting and delivered in such an ignoble way, the resultant wild party tore through flesh and bone, beggared of all moral restraint.

Like running alongside a driverless express train, the cabal of devils could not stop the juggernaut they had started. All came crashing down, the cradle of civilisation destroyed, three thousand years of human upward mobility thrown onto the funeral pyre, bi-products of narrow and parochial views, higher ideals sacrificed on the altar of dark spiritualism. Comparable to blind bombardiers indiscriminately dropping bombs on the innocent, in the shadow of the event hinterland, it equated to fiendishness at its finest.

Monumental and without precedence, the epic outcome left horizons lost forever, and took few prisoners. In the aftermath, there'd be no phoenix rising rejuvenescent from its immolating ashes, no chance of reportage, only galvanised resolve to commune with yesteryear's ghosts and angels of repose.

Blacker than black, shorn and bleached of all cellulose and fibre, with every spore and amoeba obliterated and consigned to desolation, the juxtaposition represented a far cry from the fun-filled, good times Redford once knew.